Dead House
Gabriella Creighton

Gabriella Creighton

ISBN Information

eBook: 979-8-9939808-0-5
Print: 979-8-9939808-1-2

Find more books by the author at:

GabriellaCreighton.com

To My Hearts
I bounce through life without a seeming dedication to you,
you make my life better, my will stronger,
thank you, even if I don't always show it,
you are loved.

PREFACE

This book was written for NaNoWriMo (National November Writing Month) 2025. It was started on November 1st, 2025 and completed within my self set goal of 75,000 words on November 21st, 2025. The challenge is traditionally to write a 50,000 words (or greater) novel in November.

A majority of my novels and works are NaNoWriMo novels that I did not complete in time, it was not until later in my life when I learned to self discipline to declare an hour or so every night to writing that now makes my work possible, rapid and spread out so amazingly. With this completion I am confident that my writing will only get better as I finish completing all these discarded manuscripts and have to think up a new idea. Like Riley, I just needed a big shake up to get my life in order.

About the Author

Gabriella Creighton is a life long lover of the Fantasy and Science Fiction Genres. She has been fascinated by Dragons and other mythical creatures from a young age and grew up dreaming of being a writer. Inspired by great authors like Jane Yolen, Anne McCaffrey, JRR Tolkien and Phillip Pullman, she loves to take an alternative view of myth and weave her own versions. After a long life of working, gaming and enjoying the works of others, she has finally decided to put her nigh on useless Masters Degree in English Literature to work to tell stories of her own.

Growing up in Rural New York, as well as having been thrown all over the United States, Gabriella has learned she has only three desires. To write until the nail her coffin shut, to never answer the phone and for a cool glass of Salted Caramel Crowne Royal mixed with Cream Soda and Dr Pepper, which she calls a magic elixir.

It helps get the writing done.

You can find more of her works at:
GabriellaCreighton.com

CONTENTS

PROLOGUE

THE RAIN STARTS TEN minutes out, not a storm, just enough to turn the asphalt into a skin you should not trust. Wipers squeak on their tired cycle. My playlists will not decide between an old pop song and the news, so I turn them both off and let the heater chew at the fog on the windshield. My brother rides shotgun with his feet on the floor because I told him the dash is not a footrest. He answers with the smile that always made me forgive him, then drops it because he thinks I need the look of responsibility tonight. We are twenty minutes from home along a two-lane that runs past a feed store, a closed antique mall, and a church sign that says God is always hiring.

He is telling me something about a kid from his class who cut his own hair and came to school shaped like a bowl. He makes scissors with his fingers and snips the air. I laugh because I am not dead yet and neither is he. He fiddles with the vents and points one at me like I am going to melt if I do not cool my face. I tell him to stop trying to mother me. He says I would not survive without him. The joke lands, then goes quiet like all good jokes do when the road decides to ask for attention.

The light up ahead turns yellow and I ease off because I have always been a person who would rather wait than argue with metal. The intersection is one of those four-ways that make bad decisions for people. A gas station sits on the right with two pumps and a clerk who never looks up from his phone. To the left is a grocery that closes early, big dark windows reflecting the lanes like a river in winter. The rain thickens enough to smear the headlights behind us. I check the rearview, watch the glow lose focus, and see my own eyes look older

1

than they should at twenty-one. The light goes red. I roll to a clean stop behind the line. The engine hums its small honest song. My brother drums once on his knees and then flips through stations because he cannot stand the sound of waiting.

The drunk does not blow through the light fast. He comes like a mistake that believes in itself. His pickup rolls out of the grocery lot without braking and takes the turn across our noses as if my lane were an idea he does not agree with. There is no squeal, no warning, only the wrong angle of his headlights in my side window and the two seconds where I try to make my foot go through the brake pedal and into the street. I manage one word that is not worth printing. My brother turns in time to see it.

Impact is not a bang so much as a folding. The truck hits us at the front quarter on the passenger side, right at the wheel, and the world tightens, then lets go. The sound is a dropped piano, strings snapping while the case comes apart. The hood folds into my brother's door. The windshield spiders out from a point that does not make sense. The seatbelt seizes across my chest and yanks me hard enough to pull a bruise through the skin. I feel the steering wheel jump and turn under my hands. The airbag detonates and slaps my face with a hot powder that tastes like old pennies. My brother's name is in my mouth but my lungs have decided to take a second to figure out if they are still in the club.

We spin on wet asphalt, a flat, tight carousel that puts the pumps on my left, then the black windows on my right, then the wrong red of a taillight above me. Glass grinds under the body like sugar. Something heavy claps from the trunk and then stays down. The car stops with one back wheel on gravel and the nose in the gutter. The heater fan keeps going because it never got the message. The wipers drag a full squeak that belongs in a comedy. The smell is coolant, hot metal, and that airbag powder, a scent I will know in my sleep for years.

At first there is no sound except the arrival of tinnitus, a smooth tone that fills the car and makes me think of television snow. I taste blood. My face is a hot mask. My seatbelt has to be pried up off my ribs and it fights me, then gives with a click that lands like a final exam. My hands are shaking hard enough that everything they touch seems to tremble. I turn toward my brother and the world narrows to his side of the car.

His door has pushed in around him until the window frame sits where his shoulder should be. The glass is a bright confetti on his hoodie. The airbag on his side did not deploy, which is a fact I will look up later and learn too late to be useful. His face is turned toward me but his eyes are halfway open and not seeing anything. His mouth works once with no sound. There is blood in a line at his hairline and another along his collarbone, the neat kind that lies and says everything is manageable. The dashboard has shifted. The glove box is a new shape. The front quarter panel is inside the car and it should not be.

"Hey," I say, and my voice sounds like it belongs to someone who drank whiskey for breakfast. "Hey, stay with me. Hey."

He does not answer. A thin wet sound comes from somewhere under the dashboard. I do not know if it is him or the car. I put my palm against his cheek and it is warm. I tell myself warm means something. I reach for his hand and cannot find it at first because the seat has moved and the belt is wrapped strange, but then my fingers close around his and the grip is there, weak but real. He squeezes once and then stops. I keep talking because that is what you do when the world turns dumb. I say his name. I say mine. I tell him we are fine. I tell him I am here. I tell him help is coming, and even as I say it I am already pulling the phone out of my pocket with my free hand.

I dial 911 and the operator answers in a voice that tries to be the whole town. I give the intersection, the car model, the license plate, the direction the truck came from. I say there is a teenager unconscious and probably pinned. I say I can smell coolant. I say please three times without meaning to. The operator keeps her voice level and keeps me counting. She tells me to keep him warm. She tells me to keep him talking if I can. She tells me the ambulance is on the way, that I am not alone, which is technically true and not at all what I feel.

People appear in the rain like the town remembered how to care. The gas station clerk wakes up and runs out with a jacket he shrugs off without noticing. A woman pulls over and brings a blanket that smells like a dog. A man kneels by my window and tells me to hold still because my neck might be hurt. I tell him I am fine to keep him where he is, which is wrong and right in the same breath. He wriggles his arms through the broken window to cover my brother's chest with the jacket. He says, "Hey buddy," in a tone you reserve for your own and it breaks something soft in me. The drunk stands by his idling pickup thirty yards away and stares. He has the look of a man who thought he would make it and did not. A woman on her phone points at him and shouts words that do not carry through the rain.

The sirens build from flat hum to something sharp. Red and blue show up on the black grocery windows and turn them into a kind of lake. The paramedics are already moving before the ambulance rocks to a stop. One comes to my side and shines a light in my eyes. One goes to my brother with the calm of a person who refuses to move faster for fear. The police do their job in a neat, ugly choreography. The drunk's breath is a cloud no one can ignore. He says something about the light, about how it was yellow, about how it was nothing, and the words sound like broken plastic. The officer clips a breathalyzer to his mouth and the display tells a story I will hear again in a courtroom.

They put a collar on my neck and slide a board under me because the body is a liar in shock. I keep my hand on my brother's fingers as long as they let me. The paramedic at his side calls numbers, blood pressure, O2, and a phrase that includes the word trauma center. They work around the crushed frame with the practiced violence that saves lives. The jaws of life bite the door and chew. The sound is monstrous and holy at the same time. They free him from the shape the truck made for him and load him into a world that still has a chance. I watch them close the doors and all that hope goes away on wheels.

In the hospital the hall light is a long, dull smear. Someone cuts my shirt away because my ribs are planned to be purple by tomorrow and a bruise under the collarbone is a necklace I will wear for months. They clean my face and tell me I am lucky. The words sit on my chest like a cat that does not care if you can breathe. A doctor with tired eyes says they are working on my brother. He says it the way people say a prayer without the name of God.

They do not let me in. They let my mother in, later, and my father, later than that, after someone has said a sentence that breaks timelines.

When they come to my curtain I know before they open it that the story has picked a shape that I cannot change. My mother looks like we borrowed someone else's mother and forgot to take care of her. My father is a man my age would recognize only at a funeral. He stands behind her and holds his hands in front of his belt like school. My mother says my name and it is the first time my name has sounded like an accusation. I start to tell her about the light and the turn and the truck and the smell of pennies and the way his hand squeezed mine, and she says the word you in a sentence that does not have room for facts.

The police say the other driver was over the limit. The report says failure to yield. The tow yard gives back what is left of my car for a price. None of that fixes what my mother sees when she looks at me. None of it helps me when I close my eyes and the moment of impact stretches into a loop that will play for years. I was driving. He died. These are the bones of the story everyone can lift. The skin is all the small times I could have taken the other route, left five minutes before, asked him to sit in the back, pulled into the gas station and made a joke about snacks. The brain knows blame is a crooked instrument and uses it anyway because it is something to hold when the ground will not hold you.

At the funeral the church smells like lilies and starch. People talk about God's plan in a way that makes God sound like a man who cannot read a map. My parents sit together and do not touch. I sit three rows back with my hands in my lap and work on memorizing the ceiling so I do not have to remember the casket. After the service my mother tells me to go home and not to follow them to the cemetery. The words are clean and small. She says them as if she is saving me from a weather report. I nod because there is nothing else to do. I watch the line of cars go out under a sky that refuses to be dramatic. I stand in the parking lot until no one is left and then I put my hand on the cool brick because it is something solid in a day that refuses to be.

I move out within the month. I fail a class and then all of them. I sleep on a friend's couch and learn the hours of the diner because grief wants coffee at three in the morning. People tell me time will help and I want to ask them where they bought their time because mine only makes more of what I already have. The calls home get shorter and then stop. The apartment in another town does not have room for family photos and that is its own mercy. I work and sleep and go through days that do not leave fingerprints.

Years later, when a pantry door in a bad house learns the shape of my palm, none of this will be news to my body. It already knows how a moment can decide to live with you. It already knows how a simple thing can open and let the worst in.

Chapter 1
112 Weaver Street

"It really used to be such a beautiful property, but sadly the owner let it go before they passed. Pity. Pity." Her voice was high enough to pinch the eardrum. Massive glasses caught the window light and hid her eyes as the portly woman turned toward me, the kindest, warmest, most sellable smile arranged on her face. Shiela was every real estate agent trope in one body, right down to the overly nice clothes for such a routine passing of keys. I was only renting from the bank after all.

"It's fine. I chose it for the cheap rent, not the molding," I said, setting down my bags. All three of them, pretty much everything I owned. The house came furnished with whatever the old bat had not ruined or given away. I pulled my dirty red hair, mottled with blonde, into a ponytail and accepted the keys Shiela jingled in front of me.

A five-dollar smile and a nod. When the keys passed into my hand she seemed to let go of a great weight. I had the feeling she was not happy to be here. Still she puffed up and recited it. "If that's all you'll be needing, rent is due at the end of the month. Your deposit and first month cleared or we would not be here. Do not mind the pantry in the kitchen, it is sealed from an old issue. The bank will send someone. Welcome to Bakersville, Riley."

I nodded and saw her out. The front door was a creaking old thing, heavy and good wood, paint peeling from decades of use and more years of none. For the amount I was paying, I half expected the place to collapse. I was not a fool though. The house had that neighborhood stain you get when an old woman dies in her bed and kids whisper that a witch used to live here. The yard made it easy to believe. Grass a foot too high. Bushes gone wild. The bank had promised to send a crew to tame it. I did not count on that. I did not really care.

She made her way up the nearly invisible walk to her car, a nice '87 Beemer parked just ahead of my more modern but very mortal Toyota. When she pulled away, I closed the door and turned to face my new home. Sheets still covered most of the furniture. Even under dust I could tell it was antique, decent once, smothered now. I grabbed my backpack, the sack of clothes, and my computer bag and carried them to the room I had already claimed. Not the master. The old coot died in there, and I was not using it until I was sure it had been scrubbed twice. Times being what they were, I could always rent it and the other two bedrooms. A four-bedroom colonial in the middle of nowhere could pay for itself if you did not mind strangers breathing nearby.

112 Weaver Street sat in a quiet grid of streets in a town big enough to boast a strip mall and a small metroplex. Like any small American town within commuting distance of a city, it offered safety to those who could afford it and an address to those who worked the local factory. Here it was a factory. Whatever they made came with the roar of trucks hauling out every dawn and dusk. For me the town was a job posting for a librarian and a shortage of people who cared enough about books to need someone better than an incomplete English degree. The pay was local government, which is to say almost a joke. It was also a living, which is to say enough.

I set my bags on the old bed in the second-biggest bedroom. It had probably belonged to a son or daughter once, then later to a nurse who sat vigil. Furniture was barren and practical. I pulled out my e-reader, my small stack of real books, and my laptop. I found a plug for my phone and made sure it took a charge. My clothing bag went into an old wardrobe that smelled like cedar and dust. The backpack stayed by the bed where I could grab it without thinking. When I finally peeled off my shoes and the road grit of the day, I aimed myself at the bathroom and the first shower I had had in days.

On the way I brushed an old shoebox off a shelf and sent its contents spilling across the floor. I grumbled, considered cleaning it, then let the mess be. A scatter of Polaroids and a few notebooks waited to be discovered. It could be tonight's entertainment. It could be tomorrow's problem.

Showers are a kind of time machine. The static hiss of water, the soft cave of steam, the heat that fools your body into believing it is held. My mind wandered and climbed out of the pit where I keep the facts about me. Woman approaching thirty. No real career. A history I do not tell on first dates. The heat let the thoughts drift just long enough to feel like a person and not a file.

"You have been in there long enough," said a voice.

I nearly slipped in the porcelain tub. My laugh came out too loud, a bark in the echo of tile. A trick of the mind. For a moment I had heard my mother telling me to save the hot water, which she did in every rental we ever lived in. I took the hint, adulted for once, and turned off the tap. I toweled off and went back to my room, set up the laptop, and let nineties punk fill the air. The noise helped. Pajamas and a T-shirt with a dragon hoarding books helped more. I sat cross-legged on the floor and faced the mess I had made.

Polaroids first. Paper squares from a time I barely knew outside of movies. All the pictures seemed to be parts of the house. Maybe a previous tenant or the nurse took them for an inspector. I recognized most of the rooms in the top pile. The living room with bay windows that looked like heavy eyelids. The formal dining room I would never use and planned to convert into a computer space. The kitchen with its slightly out-of-date appliances that I had been assured met basic standards of living.

One picture caught my eye. The pantry door was open. Inside looked normal enough. Shelves. Canned goods. A narrow crack where someone had sealed an old shaft, maybe for a dumbwaiter. I made a note to check if anything was still there. Vermin found every path in old houses. Maybe that was why the pantry was sealed now.

The notebooks were black-and-white composition books, the kind you grab from a drugstore bin. Each label simply said "Mara." I opened one and skimmed. Notes about the house. Lines about rooms. An architectural diary, or just the hobby of a person who cared too much about where they slept. Midway through the first volume I read:

> *...could find the other end of the basement. I swear it feels like going in circles down here. Hate this part of the house. Soon as I located the breaker I reset and went back upstairs. Note to self, send an electrician next time, pay them extra so long as I do not have to go down there.*

I snorted. Courageous in print, sensible in practice. The notebooks and photos felt a little too intimate to rifle, like picking through a stranger's purse, but I did not stop. A guide to the bones of my new place was a kindness, whether Mara meant it or not. When I was done skimming I stacked the books, slid the Polaroids into the shoebox, and put it back on the shelf with my own paperbacks and small trinkets. A photo of my family. Another of me and my little brother. I smiled at both and felt the familiar ache of a home you cannot go back to.

I flopped on the bed and let the playlist run. Kindle in hand, I found my place in a paperback about pretty girls and the monsters they let into their rooms. I had a type. Sue me.

The weekend became a ritual of dust and progress. I pulled the sheets off the furniture and let the wood breathe. When the furniture breathed too much, I hit it with bug spray and let the windows stand open. I swept the floors, ordered a rug or two, and measured the living room for an eventual television. That would be a later paycheck problem. If I stayed. If the job stayed.

Groceries came from Grocery Mart in the strip mall. Dinner came from the Chinese place across the lot. I brought home chicken lo mein and fried rice and watched a movie on my laptop like a teenager with a first apartment. When I slid the leftovers into a refrigerator that had survived the 1950s by stubbornness alone, my eyes pulled toward the pantry. It sat wrong in the kitchen, offset from the basement door and the fridge. It did not belong to the room so much as loom into it. It looked like a wall someone decided to turn into a door after the house was finished.

I went to it and ran my fingers along the paint. At first it felt like a door painted on a wall. Grainwood skinned in acrylic. Then my hand found the latch. Real. Just a sliver, but real. I took a breath and pulled. A stuck mechanism complained. Nothing gave. I let my breath out and shrugged, curiosity dented, not broken. I poured a glass of water, took it back to my room, and told myself the pantry would be someone else's problem soon enough.

Time slid past and turned itself into Monday. I woke before my alarm, nervous energy doing the work. First days have a taste, like pennies under the tongue. I dressed for a job that would not care what I wore, tied my hair back, and checked that the phone had charged. In the kitchen, the morning light made the paint look more tired than haunted. I filled a travel mug, glanced once at the pantry door that had not moved, and set my hand on the front knob.

The house made a small settling sound somewhere above me, the kind of tick that belongs to radiators and old boards. Outside, Bakersville breathed diesel and wet leaves. I locked up and started down the nearly invisible walk. The grass brushed my ankles. Trucks on the hill changed gears. It felt like a place where people woke and went to work and came home again and slept. It felt almost normal. I put the key in my pocket and told myself that was enough.

Chapter 2
OLD DIARIES

IT WAS WORK. IT happened. I will not bore you. Home was what mattered. Home had begun to creep into my thoughts when I was not there, a slow tide that reached my ankles in the quiet moments between patrons that did not come. By four I was back with my bag and a key that worked on a building that only opened when I felt like being its librarian. I had not even unlocked the doors on day one. I told myself I was planning signage and a schedule. I told myself a lot of things. What mattered was Weaver Street.

I sat on the bed and flipped through Mara's journals. Most of it read like nonsense at first pass, notes on time periods that predated the house, odd sketches, lists of doors that did not exist. A mess. Then every few pages the voice sharpened and the entries bent toward something that felt like the house I lived in now. Those were the ones that kept my pulse a little high while I turned pages.

> *I could not tell where the house began and ended some nights. I am beginning to think I am losing it. This house only has four bedrooms, a living room, dining room, kitchen, and the sunroom. There is a basement and an attic, but nothing worth finding in either. I cannot even remember anything interesting I saw there. So where did this door come from. I will find out tonight.*

The line sat there like a hook in my lip. Was Mara mad, or was I missing something obvious in daylight. I had been scouring the place for days. No secret doors. No tricks. Only the pantry that felt like a painted joke and clicked like a real latch under my hand.

I stacked the notebooks, slid a ribbon into the one I was reading, and stood. The house gave me the quiet kind of welcome only old lumber can. Floors answered with a soft talk when I crossed them, not complaining, not quite inviting, but always talkative. In the hall the shoebox of Polaroids still waited on the shelf where I had set it back. I lifted the lid and took out the kitchen pictures. The pantry was open in one. Shelves. Canned goods. A faint vertical seam where plaster could hide a shaft or a regret. Nothing supernatural. Nothing worth feeling watched over.

I carried the photo to the kitchen anyway. Late afternoon light came in flat through the window above the sink and laid a pale strip on the floorboards, the kind of light that remembers school cafeterias and dentist waiting rooms. I set the Polaroid on the counter and stood facing the pantry. Paint looked paint. Grain looked like grain under paint. My hand found the latch again, that thin interruption where the surface pretended to be seamless.

I pulled. The mechanism stuck, then gave a fraction, then stuck again. The sound that came out was small and dry, like a book page turning in a quiet room.

"Fine," I said to the door. "Later."

I heated soup and ate it at the counter while the refrigerator hummed its patient hum. When the light outside slid from flat to blue and the first truck on the hill downshifted for the night, I washed the bowl and left it to dry. I turned off the kitchen light, then turned it on again because the dark in that room felt more complete than the dark in other rooms. I told myself I was being dramatic. I told myself I was tired. I went back to the bedroom and read until the words would not hold.

The house settled in small clicks. Somewhere in the walls air moved like someone deciding what to say. The sounds that for generations people would say was a the home "settling", from what upset I could not quite imagine. I got up, because sitting with the thought was worse than walking with it, and carried my phone like a candle back to the kitchen.

The pantry waited. It had no reason not to. I put my ear to the paint. The wood felt cool and slightly damp, as if it had been breathing through the evening. The smell there was lemon cleaner over old smoke, the same polite scent you get in houses shown for sale by people who know the leak is in the next room.

I turned the knob.

The latch moved with a neat little cluck. The door opened a finger's width and stopped against itself, a habit more than a block. A thin draft slid across my wrist like a cat that wanted attention and not touch. The air inside was a few degrees colder. No shelves showed in the narrow slice, only dimness and the impression of distance where there should have been wood a hand away.

I widened the gap until the edge caught, then set my palm flat on the paint and felt the grain through it, as if that should mean anything. Behind me the refrigerator motor clicked off. The room went very still.

"Tonight," I said, because Mara had written it, because I had read it, because now the line belonged to me. I took a breath that felt too loud and leaned in.

I put my shoulder to the door and it gave with a weary sigh, the kind old wood makes when it remembers how to move. The smell of lemon cleaner slid around me, then thinned until something colder took over. The kitchen light fell a few feet and then seemed to be swallowed by the dim, as if the dark inside did not allow other rooms to borrow space.

Inside was not shelves. Inside was a corridor that had no business connecting to my house. The ceiling ran low, lined with small bulbs that did not quite agree about being on. The floorboards were narrow and dull with age. The baseboards hummed at a pitch just below hearing, the kind of tone that makes your tongue feel wrong against your teeth.

I said my name out loud without thinking. Riley. The hum did not change. A draft touched my wrist and followed the bones up to my elbow. The chill was not deep, more like the inside of a church or a gym in winter. I stepped over the threshold and counted under my breath because silence did not feel like a good idea.

One. Two. Three. The air tasted like pennies. Four. Five. The bulbs warmed and cooled, not in rhythm with each other, but in a slow wave that moved forward as if to lead. Six. Seven. A small scuff whisper came from somewhere ahead, the sound of paper dragged across plaster. Eight. Nine. Ten.

At ten paces a square of white waited on the left wall, taped crooked. A Polaroid. My hand reached before I told it to. The tape peeled cleanly. In the photo, the kitchen I had just left looked slightly brighter and newer. The pantry door stood open and I stood half inside, caught in the act of stepping in. My head was turned to listen to something behind me that did not exist in the picture. The sight made my stomach funk with that small sickness you get on a boat. I put the photo against my chest and felt the paper warm through the cotton of my shirt.

Farther down the corridor the wall showed a rectangle the size of a book cover where dust had collected around the absence of a frame. I could see the shadow of old nail holes in pairs, as if something had hung there for years and then been taken down in a hurry. The feeling of a space made ready for me to fill it was very strong. I told myself not to think in sentences like that.

A whisper of air pressed my cheek, gentle and coaxing. I took one more step and saw the corner of a note tucked behind a loose piece of baseboard trim. It was receipt paper. Torn, yellowed, the ink smudged enough to soften the numbers. Someone had written on the back in pencil and then gone over it a second time as if the first pass had not been dark enough to keep.

> *Count with the pipes. In four. Hold four. Out six. Do not let it set the pace. You set it.*

I read it again with my thumb along the bottom edge, the way you pin a thought to your skull. Somewhere behind the walls something clicked, a slow metronome, not quite even. I matched my breath for a few cycles and felt the pressure in my chest loosen by a hair. Not better. Not worse. Just different.

"Thank you," I said without meaning to. The corridor did not answer. It did not have to. The note felt like a handoff in a relay.

I put the paper in my pocket and looked ahead. The bulbs seemed dimmer past where I stood, or maybe the air just thickened. The ceiling lowered a finger's width, then another. I could go. I could see whatever made me think of boats and receipts. Or I could do the simplest thing first.

I turned around to the pantry door to be sure it was still there. It was. The kitchen light made a warm square on the floor where the threshold cut it. That square looked very kind. The corridor behind me made a tiny sound like a swallowed laugh. The kind of noise old ductwork can make when metal cools and shifts. I did not like how much it sounded like a person deciding not to speak.

"Tomorrow," I said to the dark. It felt ridiculous, the way talking to yourself feels when you are both alone and very sure you are not. I kept my hand against the wall as I walked the ten paces back. The plaster under the paint felt cool and faintly damp. When I stepped into the kitchen the smell changed again, from pennies and lemon to the quiet odor of old varnish and dish soap.

I closed the pantry door with a gentle push. The latch met home with a neat little cluck. I stood with my palm on the paint and waited to see if anything pressed back. It did not. The refrigerator clicked on. Somewhere upstairs a board settled with a sound that might have been a footstep in another life. I stayed with the door until my breathing went back to normal, then I took my hand away and looked at the Polaroid.

In this copy, the kitchen looked as it did now. The pantry door was painted shut. No me in the frame. No open dark. The corner of the photo bent when I touched it and then did not stay bent. When I turned it over I saw a list in a neat, square hand.

> *Open all the doors. Do not answer when it is still deciding what voice to use. If it offers you anything, do not take it in your hands.*

The last line was darker than the others, pressed hard enough to ghost through the paper into my fingertips. I wanted very much to set the picture down and not look at it again. Instead I carried it to the refrigerator and pinned it under the lighthouse magnet. The magnet clicked. The photo behaved.

The kitchen clock read just after ten. Too late to pretend I had any business in a corridor that did not belong to me. I turned out the light and carried the note back to the bedroom, slid it under the ribbon in

Mara's notebook, and circled the sentence about finding the door in the night. The pencil dug into the paper and made a groove that would feel angry in a calmer morning.

I lay on the bed with the lamp off and let the laptop cycle through a playlist that had once lived in a car. When the quiet came all the way in, I heard the house do what old houses do. Pipes pinged as water cooled. Heat found corners and left them. There was nothing to be afraid of. There was also something to be afraid of. Both things sat side by side on my sternum like small birds.

I slept in short, shallow dips. In one of those dips I stood in the corridor again, except the bulbs were out and the dark had a weight you could carry. A voice that made me think of a receptionist said my name the way a stranger says it after reading it from a clipboard. The sound came from a vent. I woke with my mouth open and one hand pressed to my throat.

Morning arrived as if it had been waiting on the porch. I went to the kitchen and made coffee. The pantry looked exactly like a sealed door and a paint job done by a person who did not care. The Polaroid on the refrigerator showed a clean kitchen, a clean door, a clean girl who had chosen a safe rental and a quiet job and meant to keep both until they expired on their own. I sipped coffee and felt that picture watch me the way empty rooms do.

On my way to the bathroom I paused at the shelf in the hall. The shoebox sat where I had left it. The notebooks sat where I had stacked them. I lifted the lid and took out the top book. The first page I opened held a fresh sentence I would have sworn was not there.

It gets bigger for you and smaller for others. Do not make it comfortable.

I closed the book and put it back. The words followed me anyway. I dressed for work, picked at my hair until it looked like a decision instead of a guess, and put on the face I keep for first weeks. The house did not say anything when I left. The grass brushed my ankles. A truck on the hill worked its way into a higher gear.

Work could pretend to matter for a few hours. A library is good at that. I unlocked doors no one tried. I printed a sign with hours I knew

I would ignore. I put a stack of paperback thrillers on a table near the entrance and pretended the choice would meet anyone's needs. I ate a sandwich at a computer meant for public use and read policy pages that were out of date. Each time I stood and looked at the clock, the time was a little wrong, not in a way numbers could prove, but in the body sense where you feel the afternoon in your shoulders. I turned the sign to closed because the sign needed turning.

At four I was back in the kitchen. The clock read the right numbers. The Polaroid on the refrigerator had not changed. The only new thing was me. I could either stand here and let the house make the first move, or I could set the terms while I still felt like a person who owned one good habit.

I took the note from my pocket and read it again. Count with the pipes. In four. Hold four. Out six. Do not let it set the pace. You set it. My mouth said the words without my permission. The sound steadied me. I set a glass of water on the counter where I could reach it, turned on the kitchen light, and placed my hand on the pantry paint. Cool. Slightly damp. Like breath held near skin.

"Tonight," I said, as if making a promise to myself. "We find the other end."

The latch clucked. The door gave. The hum greeted me. I stepped once, then twice, then counted to ten with the pipes. The bulbs warmed in a slow wave, and the corridor lifted its head like a cat who has just remembered your voice. I felt the small fear and kept it. I felt the small curiosity and let it lead. I went on.

Chapter 3
CORRIDOR OF TEN

THE PANTRY DOOR GAVE under my hand like it had learned how to open from someone who once cared about it. Cold air rolled out, cooler than the kitchen, sweet in a way that had nothing to do with sugar. Lemon cleaner over old smoke. I stepped inside with my fingers sliding along the wall and matched my breathing to the pipes in the house. In for four, hold for four, out for six, just like the note on the receipt had told me.

The bulbs in the corridor woke up in a lazy wave. One brightened a little. The next one dimmed. The third seemed to think about it before joining in. The floor under my shoes shifted as I walked. Narrow boards gave way to wider planks. The shiny finish dulled until it looked like wood that had been handled for a hundred years.

By the time I had taken ten steps, the wallpaper was gone. White plaster took its place, brushed with a thin, chalky coat of lime. Tiny holes showed where nails had been pulled out a long time ago. Pegs lined one wall at about shoulder height. Someone had left a mourning brooch hanging there, a small oval with braided hair set behind glass. The hair had started as light brown and faded toward honey with age. The metal frame was black now, but underneath the tarnish it had probably been gold in some better room.

I lifted it. It had more weight than it should have. Not metal weight, memory weight. Clean hair. Someone patient, standing behind someone shorter. Fingers twisting a braid with quiet care around a loss they could not fix. It all settled into my hands like a story I did not live through but could still feel.

19

On the opposite wall, an old sampler hung crooked on the plaster. The linen was rough and uneven. Threads had risen from the surface here and there, like the cloth had been breathing through someone's worry for too long. The stitched verse jumped when I tried to read it straight on. The letters leaned sideways, then snapped back.

Forgive. Then E N. Then a weird tail of thread that could have belonged to a capital J or the start of a blessing.

I pressed my thumb under my tongue to keep from licking my lips and tried again. Slower this time. I let each exhale settle all the tiny movements in the cloth. On the long breath, the letters finally held still. Together they pulled themselves into a name, like they had been trying to decide if I deserved to see it.

Elenor.

The first e looked like the person sewing had been shaking. A date followed, from a century when women died too young and children died in small groups instead of one at a time.

The room on my left had been a pantry once. Shelves ran along the walls, deep and low, the kind of shelves meant for jars and sacks and extra flour. The door frame was plain, the wood hand-planed, the edges worn soft by a lifetime of sleeves brushing past on the way to stir something, measure something, feed someone.

A woman stood in the doorway. She was not really looking at me. She was looking past me or through me, the way nurses do when they have already figured out the next ten steps and none of them are good. Her dress was simple and colorless in the way old fabric gets. Her hands were red up to the wrists, like lye had stripped them raw and never given them back.

She did not jump. She did not speak. When she finally moved, it was only to shift her weight and take the pressure off one hip, like she had been standing too long. Her face turned toward the hearth on the far wall. The fireplace yawned black, iron grate still in place. It did not smell like fire. It smelled like tallow, vinegar, and the iron taste of well water.

"Elenor," I said, because the sampler had given me her name and I figured that counted as permission.

The woman's head turned, just a fraction. Not toward me. Toward the brooch in my hand.

The hearth was too clean. No ash in the throat, just a few crumbs of char clinging to the grate like freckles a damp rag had missed. I knelt and opened the brooch. The hair did what hair always does when you undo whatever held it together. It tried to breathe.

I laid it gently on the grate like a braid set down for a moment and said her name again.

Elenor.

The air in the hearth shivered, then loosened. A faint heat pushed against my hands, thin and stringy, just enough to touch the bones of my fingers and no more. Behind me, the woman exhaled.

That was all. Not a word. Not a sigh of relief. Just that heavy, empty sound that rooms make when someone who has been holding still for too long finally decides to move.

The hum in the floorboards under my knees dropped half a note. It felt like taking off a shoe that had been too tight all day. My heart stuttered, then settled. I kept my breathing steady with the pipes. In. Hold. Out.

The hair on the grate darkened, though no flame touched it. The smell that rose was old but clean, like opening a trunk that has been packed carefully, not abandoned. I did not turn to check if the woman was still there. I did not want her absence or her presence to be the proof.

I wanted the room itself to decide it had been heard.

Behind me, the sampler shifted its mind. One crooked leg of a letter pulled back through the fabric, thread whispering across linen in a sound so soft I would have missed it if I had been speaking. The name did not disappear. It stayed there, sitting on the cloth the way someone sits when they have finally been offered a chair after standing too long.

There was a nursery beyond the old pantry. I did not need anyone to say it out loud. The doorway had that shape.

I wiped my fingers off along the side of my shirt and stepped through. The air changed as soon as I crossed the threshold. It got closer and thicker, not warmer exactly, just more crowded. Peg rails circled the walls, holding tiny gowns no bigger than my hands.

A small wooden chair waited where a rocking chair should have been. Someone had polished it until the seat shone like still water. The window did not show a yard or trees or the street. It only showed a dim outline of another wall and the ghost of beams beyond that. No sky. No outside. The House was not interested in outside when it wanted you to stay put.

The cradle rocked.

It had not been rocking when I came in. I knew that. That mattered. It rocked now, and the rhythm was painfully familiar. The exact pace my heartbeat picked up when I let a day run away with me and only noticed once I was already exhausted.

The cradle was patient at first. Slow, steady, like someone tired but stubborn. Then the motion wanted a little more. The slats blurred at the edges. The top rail warmed, the way wood does when a child's hands have been gripping it tight.

A soft hiss crawled up the back of my hearing, the first warning edge of tinnitus. My fingertips went faint and glassy, the way they do right before a wave of panic hits.

A lullaby drifted down out of the vent in the ceiling. The voice was mine, except it sounded older by at least a year I did not remember living through. Every line hit the same note almost right, then fell flat on the exact same syllable, every single time.

The wrongness of it dried my throat. Songs you sing to children should land where they mean to land. This one dropped short and slid sideways.

I put my hand on the foot of the cradle. The rhythm grabbed hold of me at once, asking my arm to help keep it going. That was the worst part. It did not try to scare me. It tried to get me to cooperate.

I let go.

I dug in my pocket and pulled out the wooden spoon I had taken from my own kitchen earlier without really thinking about it. I wedged the spoon under one of the cradle runners until the motion had to fight for every inch. Wood squeaked against the floor in small, honest complaints.

22

The cradle slowed. My pulse tried to speed up to keep the rocking alive, like my body thought motion was required. I sat in the little chair and started counting with the pipes again. In. Hold. Out.

The lullaby did not stop. The bad note wobbled, then steadied and kept right on missing its mark. My fingers tingled harder, then less. My jaw tightened in that small, specific way that says, This is where the headache starts, if you invite it in.

The woman from the pantry sat in the corner now. Same dress. Same raw red hands. Her shoulders had been leaning forward for a lifetime and were now pulling back, just the tiniest bit, like a string slowly loosening.

She watched the vent as if it might finally say something worth hearing.

When the cradle finally gave up and settled, still as a photograph, the wrong note in the lullaby died out. The sound became only air moving through the metal grid. No melody. Just breath.

The woman's chin dipped once. That was all. A nod, maybe. A thank you, maybe. Or just that tiny bow people give to moments that have taken too much from them and are finally over.

Something like stiff paper slid out from under the cradle runner where the spoon pressed. I leaned down and pinched it free, careful not to let the cradle move. More receipt paper. Pencil writing over older pencil writing.

> Break rhythms. Do not let it take your pulse.

The initials at the bottom had been written twice, once lightly and once so hard the pencil had almost torn through. M. E. Or maybe W. E. The lines overlapped in places. Time and damp had smudged the strokes until the letters leaned into each other like they were trying to blur into one person.

I folded the note and tucked it with the first one in my pocket. The motion had already started to feel like part of a ritual. I had no idea when that happened. I only knew that if I left these notes behind, the House would swallow them. They would become part of it again.

I did not think that was wrong.

I just wanted something small I could carry with me.

On the peg rail, one of the tiny gowns had a dark oval right at the chest, a patch of darker cloth that would not let the air through. It looked more like damp than stain. It looked like something, or someone, had pressed a mouth there and kept it there too long.

I did not touch it.

The woman's eyes were on my hands now. Not my face. Not my body. Just my hands, as if what I chose to do with them mattered more than who I was.

"Break the motion," I whispered, just loud enough for me to hear. "Keep your breath."

Saying it out loud made it more solid.

I stood and slid the spoon out from under the cradle. The wood scraped softly, like a chair being pushed back from a table. The cradle stayed still. It could have moved. It did not.

The hum in the room dropped again, a faint sigh rolling through the bones of the house.

I stepped backward out of the nursery and into the hall with the pegs and the sampler. The sampler had given up on letters completely. The last of the stitched word had been picked apart and replaced with a row of small flowers the color of weak tea.

The peg where the brooch had hung was empty. The hearth smell had faded into something dry and old, more iron than vinegar now.

I kept one hand on the cool limewashed wall and walked, syncing my breath to the steady knocks inside the pipes so I would not rush. When I stopped paying attention, the distance stretched. When I focused, it shortened. I did not get the feeling the House was trying to trick me. It felt more like walking past someone you knew well, watching them straighten up or slump, depending on who had walked into the room.

I tried not to think of it that way.

A cradle block sat by the pantry threshold, a wedge of wood worn smooth by years of doing one small job in the dark. It did not belong to my century, but I picked it up anyway, turned it over in my hand, then set it down on the floor where the corridor turned another corner.

I did not want to carry every object that knew how to make a meaningful sound. Some things needed to stay in their own place.

THE PARLOR AROUND THE next angle tried very hard to be polite. A rough-woven carpet covered most of the floor, a simple border pattern holding the room together. Two interior doors faced each other like cousins stuck at the same reunion, smiling thinly at different parts of the same story.

The door on the left stood slightly open, spilling a soft, welcoming light into the hall, the kind you get from a lamp someone left on on purpose. The door on the right was closed with the kind of seriousness that did not invite questions.

A small side table between them held a pocket Bible open to a verse about keeping watch. Beside it, three keys hung on a ring. None of them matched any lock in my actual house. A portrait hung above the table, face turned toward the wall.

I am not a superstitious person.

I turned it toward the room anyway.

The eyes in the painting were too careful, like the painter had tried to flatter someone who had not asked to be flattered and maybe did not deserve it. The gaze made my shoulders crawl. I turned the picture back to the wall and felt my chest tighten, like someone had pressed a thumb into soft skin.

The room brightened when I looked at the cracked, inviting door. The light dimmed when I turned my attention to the formal, closed one. The push was not subtle. The house might as well have put up a sign that said This Way.

I did not like being steered.

The rule I had already decided on sat solid in my head: open every door.

So I did.

I slid the cradle block under the friendly door on the left to keep it from swinging shut. I wedged the right-hand door open with the Bible without bothering to read the verse.

Air folded and reshaped itself around me. The room took a long, thin breath and let it out. Dust along the baseboards lifted in a pale, moving line and drifted toward both open doorways at once. Somewhere in the woodwork, the hum changed key.

In the window glass, I saw him.

He was not standing in the room and he was not outside the house. He was in the glass the way a reflection holds a different time of day. A clerk, tidy shirt, tie just a little too tight. His name tag could not settle on what it said. Letters crawled, second-guessed themselves, blurred, tried again.

He held out a driver's license with my face on it, my features smeared into charcoal at the edges. The county printed on it was a place I had never lived. His mouth shaped words I already knew by heart.

You dropped something.

I forced myself to look at the floorboards instead. Only the boards. Long grain, worn but steady.

If I had learned anything from the journals, it was this: do not accept returns.

The license that had never actually been in my hand slid under the window frame a fraction of an inch, then crumbled into grit. It turned into the same dusty crumbs that make old window tracks stick and grind.

On the wall, the shadow of clapboard went by like a slow wave of cloud. The light in the room shifted to a green I knew before I could explain it.

The inviting door on the left threw that color across the plaster and the back of the turned portrait. Somewhere beyond the right-hand doorway, a crosswalk chirped. Two sharp notes, then silence. Two more. A bird trying very hard to sound like a machine.

That sound did not belong to this house or this century.

My breath shortened in the very specific way it does when your body remembers an intersection and a quiet, ordinary voice in the passenger seat asking if you think you should stop for gas.

I reached out and found the edge of the closed door with my fingertips. Open every door, yes. Walk through all of them, not yet.

"Not tonight," I said.

The words fit my mouth better than I wanted to admit.

I stepped back, both doors still propped so the room could breathe on its own without me inside it.

The corridor accepted me like it had been expecting this choice. Patient, almost kind. I counted with the pipes again, feeling the green light at my back like algae spread on lake water. Bulbs warmed in their usual, slow turn. A single plank complained softly under my heel, then settled.

When the pantry door opened into my kitchen again, it felt like taking off a mask I had been wearing too long. The refrigerator hummed its normal hum. The clock disagreed with my sense of time but had not actually moved.

I closed the pantry door with a careful little push and waited until I heard the latch catch. The faint cluck of it made something in my shoulders relax. The paint felt cooler under my palm. I stood there until my pulse stopped trying to race on purpose.

I poured a glass of water and drank all of it in three long pulls without really tasting it. Then I went to the hall and slid the new receipt note into Mara's notebook. I pressed the fold down with my thumb like flattening the paper could press the rule deeper into reality.

Break rhythms. Do not let it take your pulse.

The words lived there now, pencil layered over pencil, my hand stacking itself on top of her hand across time.

Back in the kitchen, the room looked like a regular kitchen. The Polaroid on the fridge showed the safe version. The pantry door sat there behaving. The only green in sight belonged to the little plant in the window that forgave me every time I forgot to water it.

My shoulders dropped the rest of the way. The weight slid down through my ribs, out through the soles of my feet, into floorboards that had already carried other people's lives before mine. No lullaby leaked down through the vent. Just air.

I put the wooden spoon back in its drawer and closed it quietly, the way you do when someone is sleeping in the next room and you actually care if they stay asleep.

My thoughts went to the journals. Mara had put together a map of this place, more detailed than anything I could have made alone. A guidebook to living with a house that moved. That led to the question I had been trying not to look at straight on.

Where had she gone?

Why were her notebooks in my hands instead of hers?

I had work to do. I had to find her if I wanted any real chance of understanding what I was standing inside.

For now, though, the house was quiet. It waited for me. It did not call my name. It did not push.

For now, when that door was shut, I was safe.

I told myself the smart thing would be to leave it alone for the night.

I even went through the motions. I rinsed the glass and set it upside down on a towel to dry. Little chores make good anchors. They tell your body, See, we are normal, everything is normal, nothing is wrong.

I turned off the kitchen light and let the dark fold down in layers. The refrigerator motor wound to a stop. Pipes clicked somewhere inside the walls, like someone clearing their throat politely in another room.

I stood there long enough that a sensible person would have called it done.

Then I turned the light back on.

The pantry paint felt cool and a little damp under my palm, as if it had been breathing while I tried to be responsible. The latch gave with the same neat little cluck. The lemon-and-smoke smell slid around my wrist and into my sleeve, like it knew the way by now.

I stepped inside and picked up the breathing pattern again. In for four. Hold for four. Out for six. The corridor bulbs brightened in their usual lazy wave, agreeing with one another one by one. The floorboards tested out grains and widths like the house could not choose a favorite decade.

I walked past the sampler and did not check whether it held a name or only flowers. The hearth room felt lighter somehow, as if some small weight had stepped off the floor. The nursery stayed solid and still. The cradle did not move. The spoon rested on the chair where I had left it, a worn little piece of wood waiting for whatever job came next.

The woman was either gone or sitting so quietly that the air had folded over her. I did not go looking. Gratitude does not require an audience.

The corridor bent again and brought me back to the parlor that wanted very badly to be polite. The same rough rug. The same two doors facing each other across it. The same side table with the pocket Bible and the three old keys. The same portrait with its face turned toward the plaster. Dust clung in the corners, stubborn and familiar.

I did not wait this time.

Cradle block under the left door. Bible wedged under the right. Open every door.

It felt like setting a bone that had been knocked out of place. The room took a thin, shaky breath and let it go. Dust peeled up from the baseboards and drifted toward both openings in a torn, moving line. The hum in the walls lowered another notch, from nervous to thoughtful.

The window held a night that did not match the one outside on Weaver Street. It looked like the kind of dark you get in office buildings that never actually shut off all their lights.

In that glass, the clerk waited. Same neat shirt. Same stubborn, shifting name tag.

He held up a driver's license. My face stared back, younger, edges smudged like charcoal someone had tried to erase and then stopped. The county line belonged to a place from my file, not my life.

He did not tap the glass. He did not smile. He shaped the same words again.

You dropped something.

I watched the floor instead of him. The boards there had been sanded by somebody who knew this room would be their last view of the world. Long even strokes. No shortcuts.

The reflection hung there for a beat, waiting me out. Then it thinned, like he leaned away from the frame. The license nosed just under the sill and crumbled into gray grit. Plastic dust.

The keys on the side table chimed once against the wood. A small, bright note, like a memory trying to get my attention.

Air moved through both open doors, each stream with its own personality. From the left came the house's indoor breath, warm and stale, scented with wax and old flowers, the kind of air that lives in curtains. From the right came something colder and thinner, with a metallic edge that found my tongue. City taste.

Streetlights. Car exhaust. The inside of a crosswalk button under your thumb.

The light went green, but not on any lamp I could see. It washed across the ceiling and over the turned portrait, climbed down onto my hands where they rested against the door frames.

It was not plant green or paint green. It was screen green. Pixel glow. The light of a machine waiting for input.

I knew that color the way you know your own handwriting.

From beyond the formal door, the crosswalk chirp started up again. Two sharp beats, a gap, two more, patient and precise. Tires hissed through a wet intersection. A brake sighed. An engine idled. Somewhere in the mix, a radio voice read off a traffic update, bored and careful, listing delays on streets that meant nothing to the house and everything to some old part of me.

The report gave the wrong interchange. It named a street I did not know. None of it mattered. My chest pulled tight around a memory anyway, clean and sharp.

I forced myself to count. In for four. Hold for four. Out for six.

My body wanted to rush every number.

The cradle block stayed put. The Bible edge dug into the floor and held. Its pages fluttered once like a vent sighing. The cool air along my wrists felt like a hand settling there, light and polite, testing how much it could get away with.

Behind me, the portrait shifted its opinion. The top edge tipped forward, just a little. Not enough to fall, just enough to show. Paintings lean in storms, during fights, during births and funerals. This one leaned for the sound of a crosswalk.

I reached up and set it gently back against the wall, because it was something I could fix while my heart remembered every wrong lesson at once.

In the glass, the clerk slid back into the center. He had no right to me. I had decided that. I clung to that tiny, stubborn rule. Whatever he was, he would not step fully into this room unless I opened a specific door.

He lifted another license and pressed it up where I could see.

This one was from the year before I dropped out of college. The hair. The angle. The forced smile. All of it baked into the plastic like something pressed in amber.

You dropped something, his lips said again. Then his mouth shifted without his eyes changing and formed the shape of my name.

I looked past him, into the not-night he lived in. The green climbed the crown molding. The crosswalk sound cut out, then snapped back in slightly out of time, like a system rebooting. Somewhere in that space, a walk signal flashed from a red hand to a white figure I could not see but could feel.

Heat pushed up behind my eyes, cold and tight, the way crying sometimes starts without tears.

I could step through. I knew it in the way you know the next note of a song without hearing it. I could cross the threshold into a parlor that stopped being a parlor as soon as my foot landed, and find an intersection hung in the air like a memory trapped in glass.

"Not tonight," I said again, softer, like I was telling a kid that bedtime really did mean bedtime.

The rug under my heel lifted a fraction, like a dog leaning against your leg to see if you will stay. I took one slow step back.

The air tugged lightly at my shirt. Another step. The room did not snap shut behind me. It did not slam. It did not punish. It just kept offering, patient as a bad habit.

The keys chimed once more. A smaller note now, like a little question.

I left them where they were. I left the Bible in its crooked wedge and the cradle block holding its door. Both rooms stayed open. The currents could argue with each other without me standing in the middle.

At the edge of the corridor, I paused and let myself take one last look at the window.

The clerk had not moved closer. He had set the license down where I could not see it and folded his hands in front of him in that customer service pose everyone recognizes. His name tag flickered through a few different arrangements of letters, then went still out of pure embarrassment.

He tilted his chin toward the formal doorway in a way that was not quite a nod and not quite a dare. Green light climbed the wall behind him like pond water in sun.

My throat worked around air. That was the real horror of it. No demon. No monster. No chase. Just systems doing exactly what they were designed to do, and my own history standing in the perfect place to meet them.

I took the corridor back one measured step at a time. The bulbs rolled their light ahead of me the way a line of people in a hallway might pass along news too quietly to hear the words. My palm brushed the cool chalky lime on the wall.

The sampler had fully committed to its floral phase again, no letters left, only little stitched flowers the color of tea. The hearth room smelled less like vinegar and more like iron that had finally decided to rest.

At the pantry, the warm kitchen light spilled in a square across the boards. I stepped into it and let it claim me for a full breath. The house behind me kept breathing in its slow, complicated way. The green did not follow. The clerk did not knock. The crosswalk chirp flattened into the background hum and became just one sound among many.

I closed the door on the corridor and felt the latch catch. The paint was still a little damp, but my hand came away clean. I listened until I heard the refrigerator kick back on. When it did, my shoulders dropped the last inch they had been holding.

The glass I had washed earlier sat on the towel inside a small circle of light, a single drop of water bulging on the rim.

I went to the fridge and grabbed a blank index card from the little stack I kept there with the magnets. I pinned it up with the lighthouse magnet and picked up a dull pencil.

I wrote two lines, pressing hard enough that I knew the words would ghost onto the card beneath it.

> Open every door.
> Do not accept returns.

I hesitated for half a second, then added a third line before I could talk myself out of it.

> Green is not an instruction. It is only a color.

The pencil bit deeper on the last word. I left the card where it was, right at my eye line, where I would see it while I made coffee in the morning.

Then I turned off the kitchen light and waited until my eyes got used to the soft, honest dark of my own rooms.

From somewhere that belonged to another building entirely, a brake released with a tired sigh. A radio voice named a street again, the wrong one, relaxed and bored.

I waited to see if my heart would chase after it.

It did not.

It really wanted to. It chose not to. That tiny choice felt like a win so small it might have been imaginary. I decided to believe it anyway.

In the hall, the shoebox with the old Polaroids and the stack of notebooks sat in their usual places. The receipt notes in Mara's journal rested together, their pencil lines pressing little rules into each other through the paper. I let my hand drift over the shelf without touching anything and felt the cool lift of air houses keep in their quiet moments.

"Tomorrow," I said, to myself and to the green that did not need words to keep existing. "Tomorrow we see what you call a street."

Chapter 4

WRONG ROOMS

THE PARLOR HAD FINISHED deciding what it wanted to be. The wool rug lay flatter than anything that old had any right to. The two interior doors I had propped open last night were still holding, one caught with the cradle block, the other wedged with the pocket Bible.

Now there was a velvet rope stretched between waist-high brass posts, a tiny theater flourish, like the House wanted me to feel like a special guest. Past the rope, a big inner window ran from floor to ceiling, glass so clear it disappeared unless the light caught the edge just right.

Green slid across the far wall in a slow wash. Not paint. Not reflection. A machine's idea of color trying to pretend it was natural. A crosswalk chirp clicked out beats in the background. Two notes, pause. Two notes, pause. A city boiled down to a mechanical bird that never got tired.

I came prepared this time.

Index card in my pocket, rules written in blunt pencil. Green is only a color. Radio off. Car in park. Do not wait. Walk.

I read them again before I stepped fully into the room. I put both palms flat on the doorjambs and felt the wood grain under the paint. Just one small, physical proof that I was touching something real.

Behind me, the corridor seemed to hold its breath, the way halls do in a theater right before the lights go down.

I propped both doors open again, more habit than superstition at this point. Air moved through each doorway with its own attitude, streams colliding in the middle of the parlor. The room accepted me with the quiet weight of a museum after closing.

A small brass sign sat on a stanchion next to the rope. Please Remain Seated, it said in a rounded, friendly font, the same fake-comfort style dentists use on their appointment cards.

The chairs were upholstered in fabric that tried very hard to look expensive and mostly succeeded if you did not actually touch it. Rows of four, one narrow aisle down the middle.

I did not sit.

The room had already drawn the shape of my body into the nearest cushion, a little invisible hollow that waited patiently for me to give in and let something else hold my weight.

Through the glass, the street existed without weather. Someone had built an indoor intersection with weirdly perfect care. Tape marked the crosswalk lines. A fire hydrant sat exactly where hydrants sit. A newsbox sulked on the opposite curb with yesterday's paper trapped inside forever.

The signal head washed its machine green over brick and a blank storefront window that displayed absolutely nothing anyone would want to buy. At the near curb, my old sedan idled without making any sound. Dash lights glowed with the soft, familiar color I had seen a thousand times.

The radio inside the car murmured to itself. A calm voice read a traffic report I almost recognized. Then it swapped one street name for a slightly wrong version and rolled on like nothing had changed. The report clicked, reset, and started again.

I did not put my hand on the glass. The impulse flared and faded. Skin passes heat into glass and leaves prints behind. I wanted proof. I also did not want to gift the House the outline of my hand. So I stood my ground and let the cold from the pane touch my face and stop there.

In the black metal frame of the window, a reflection shifted.

The clerk in the neat shirt stood just behind my shoulder in the strip of metal, not in the room, not outside either. His name tag still refused to pick a set of letters. They crawled, jittered, settled, then pretended nothing had happened.

He held a driver's license and an old insurance card fanned neatly in one hand. His mouth formed the line he had been built to say.

You dropped something.

"I did not," I said to the frame, keeping my eyes on the street.

His reflection thinned, then stayed, like he had just shifted his weight to one hip to take the pressure off a long shift.

The nearest chair gave a tiny sigh when I did not sit down. The sound was so soft it could have just been fabric cooling, but my chest picked it up anyway and started that pre-tightness, the one that says, Here comes the test.

I reached for the index card in my pocket and read the rules out loud in a low voice, like I was reminding a kid how to cross a street. "Green is only a color. Radio off. Car in park. Do not wait. Walk."

To my right, a clipboard slid smoothly into a metal slot on the wall, as clean and showy as a magician's trick. The top sheet had lines for describing the sound and a box for the time it happened. A pen clipped at the top waited, unused and ready.

I glanced up at the clock in the corner, hanging above the window. I did not look because I planned to write anything down. I looked because the room had placed a clock in my line of sight and my brain followed the prompt. The hands said a quarter to two.

In my kitchen, that time meant nothing. In this room, it meant whatever the House wanted it to mean.

I took the pen, then paused. It was heavier than it needed to be, cool against my fingers, as if extra weight could pretend to be importance. The form asked me to tell it what I heard. There was no box for what I did not hear.

The words rose to my mouth anyway. They had been worn smooth over years of being thought through and swallowed.

I slid the clipboard back into the slot.

The pen was still in my hand when I noticed I had not let it go. I slid it into my pocket instead. The slot made the soft sound of paper shifting and produced a fresh clipboard with another identical form, just in case I had not meant to keep the first pen.

On the other side of the glass, the sedan ticked invisible ticks. The dash glowed. In my peripheral vision, a smear of chrome dragged itself across the scene too slowly, the way a drunk driver's car takes forever to resolve into something real.

The signal light held that deep camera-confusing green. The crosswalk chirp kept up its two-beat, pause, two-beat pattern. Start. Wait. Start. Wait.

I wrapped my hand around the brass post of the rope. It was warm with no human reason to be, heated by a system instead of skin. It did not really steady anything, but my body took it like it was help. Bodies do that. They accept whatever grounding they can get.

I let my eyes go soft. With the whole room blurred, the green stopped trying to talk to me and went back to just being a color. I read the card again under my breath. "Green is only a color. Radio off. Car in park. Do not wait. Walk."

In the metal frame, the clerk's reflection carefully formed my name. He did not use his voice. The shape of the syllables was enough. He lifted the insurance card a little higher, still absurdly polite. His hands were spotless. I refused to look closely at them.

The chair sighed again, a tiny puff of disappointment. Panic tested paths through my body. My arm buzzed. A thin, high ring started at the edge of my hearing. I let it happen and did not feed it.

The crosswalk chirp slipped once, like a program glitching, then restarted on beat. The traffic report jumped back in halfway through a sentence, naming the wrong interchange with complete confidence. My throat tightened. I answered with the only tools I had.

I read the card calmly, naming each rule as if I were counting objects on a table.

Then I lifted the rope off its hook and stepped past it. The brass post felt lighter than it looked. I set the rope back between the posts with deliberate care. The House liked order. I could honor that without obeying the rest.

The Please Remain Seated sign glared in its soft, polite way. I stared back.

I still did not sit. I still did not take a clipboard.

Instead, I walked over to the inner door to the right of the window and set my hand on the push bar. The metal under my palm had the same feel as a car hood in winter. For one second, my body believed I was outside already, standing in real air, under real sky.

I let myself look at the sedan and feel the ache straight on, just for a breath. The ache could exist at the same time as action. That was the point. Not erasing it. Carrying it.

I pushed the bar. The door opened with the easy swing of hinges that had been taken care of.

Green light rippled along the far wall like wind brushing pond water. Behind me, the nearest chair tried to adjust itself for a body that was not coming, then gave up and settled.

The indoor street waited. I kept one foot in the parlor a moment longer, because it made me feel like I owned the threshold as much as the House did.

In the black metal of the window frame, the clerk held his license and insurance card at the edge of the view like a waiter hovering just offstage. He stayed where he was. He never crossed over unless I invited him. I had decided that, and I chose to keep that decision as law.

"Green is only a color," I said quietly, like reassuring a scared kid.

The crosswalk chirp kept counting. The radio voice tried the wrong street again.

I lifted the index card one more time and touched each line with my thumb.

Radio off. Car in park. Do not wait. Walk.

Then I stepped through the inner door, onto the street that was not a street, and let it close behind me with a soft click.

The velvet rope upstairs sagged gently in an empty room. The chairs kept their perfect shapes around the space where a person might have sat down and handed over their memory for replay.

I did not give it that. I gave it motion instead.

Two shallow steps led down to the painted crosswalk. The white bars glowed too bright under the signal's green, like the color had bled into them by mistake. Cold metal smell lived in the air. Coins. Batteries. Winter tires.

The machine green washed over my hands and sleeves.

My sedan waited with the driver's door unlocked and the passenger seat warm.

Across the street, a frosted glass door sat shut. Faded lettering I could not quite read layered against the glow behind it. I knew, without having to test it, that somewhere past that door a kind voice had already queued up its script.

I tucked the index card into my back pocket so it would press against bone.

The door behind me made a small, pleased sound as it latched.

I set my palm on the roof of the car and let that touch say everything my mouth would not. The metal was real. My hand was real. The rest was up for debate.

I did not look at the passenger seat. I did not look at the smear of chrome thinking about becoming a speeding car. I looked at the shifter. I looked at the radio. I looked at the light.

"Okay," I said, to the room, my hands, the card, and the House. "We are going to do this in order."

I leaned in and touched the key.

THE KEY SAT IN the ignition at exactly the angle I remembered, small and silver against the black plastic. I did not climb in. Both my feet stayed firmly on the painted crosswalk.

I leaned across the driver's seat and turned the key one notch, just enough to bring the dash to life without waking the engine. The radio clicked on. The same calm, local voice flowed out of the speakers, giving the same wrong interchange in the same careful tone, like repetition could eventually make it accurate.

I pressed the power button.

The voice cut off mid-syllable. The silence that followed was not empty. It was thick, like the air in a room where a judge has just finished speaking.

I rested my fingers on the shifter. The leather wrap was worn in all the spots my hand had smoothed years ago. The car was not mine anymore. The habit still was.

I pulled the shifter gently into Park. It settled with a soft, satisfying click. On the dash, a little green square lit up. Green again. The House really wanted me to treat that color like a sentence instead of a fact.

"Green is a color, not a command," I said. My voice stayed steady, which felt like a small miracle.

The room pushed back immediately.

The signal lamps flared brighter, until the whole fake corner glowed that unreal machine green. The crosswalk bars went white-blue where the light hit them.

The chirp doubled its speed and held it, as if someone had hit a fast-forward button they did not intend to let go. The air felt thinner, not because there was less oxygen, but because my nervous system decided to lie about it.

My fingers tingled. My jaw edged toward an ache. I flattened my palm on the car roof, cool metal grounding my skin, and pulled in the breathing pattern that had saved me in other rooms.

In for four. Hold for four. Out for six.

The count did not erase what my body was doing. It gave me one more thing to hold alongside it.

Something moved in the glass to my right.

Not in the street. In the reflection of a storefront window where a dressmaker's dummy stood wrapped in a gown that had never left the hanger.

A reflected car glided forward in the glass, not quite taking full shape. A driver sat behind the wheel. When I turned my head just enough to admit I could see him, I caught the blank white film of cataracts where his eyes should have been. Little reflector flecks glittered there, like his pupils had become road studs.

His mouth moved slowly, forming words that never reached the air.

Thank you, he said. Simple. Polite. Exactly the tone you never want to hear from a stranger in that context.

I shifted my focus back inside my own car.

The passenger seat waited with a shallow dip in the fabric, the exact shape of a head after a long ride. Warmth rose from the cushion, not hot, just the kind of residual heat that says someone has just stood up.

I did not look at the door. I did not want to see who would be sitting there if I opened it.

The keys felt solid and cold when I wrapped my hand around them. I pulled them out of the ignition and shoved them into my pocket.

The engine could not idle on its own anymore.

A small, petty part of me liked that. The House could fake a lot of things, but turning actual metal in a real ignition cylinder still belonged to me.

The crosswalk chirp pushed harder at my ribs.

My body wanted to stand and wait the way it had that night, locked into the rhythm of a terrible moment, feeding it with fresh oxygen and attention.

I let that want exist and did not serve it.

I closed the driver's door to a soft, familiar latch. The sound was so exact it made my throat jump.

From the passenger side, a voice rode the air the House had created. Not a full ghost. Not a clear image. Just the sound of nineteen years old condensed into one casual question.

"Do we have gas?" Evan's voice asked, the rising note on gas landing in the same place it always had when he was half joking and half actually worried.

I set my hand on the passenger door and shut it without letting myself look through the window.

The latch caught. The voice cut off clean. My chest squeezed like it had been punished and then released when nothing else followed.

In for four. Hold for four. Out for six.

The breath pattern gave me a lane to walk in.

I stepped into the crosswalk and moved at a normal pace. Not daring myself. Not dragging my feet. Just walking like a person who had groceries and a schedule.

The painted bars glowed strangely where the green light hit them. My shoes made a soft scraping sound on the surface, like paper being pulled across a tabletop. The air tasted like pennies and old batteries.

The chirp clung to its too-fast tempo, trying to hurry my steps. Then it skipped one beat, scrambled, and fell back into place. I stayed with the pipes in my head, not the machine at my side.

At the center of the intersection, the smear of chrome finally tried to become a full car, pulling itself into recognizable lines and then losing them again, like gum stretching between teeth.

Heat climbed behind my eyes, the exact pressure of a brain trying to hold two versions of one event at the same time.

I let the heat be there and did not describe the sound that wanted to come with it. That was the point. Do not give the House new vocabulary.

Do not describe the noise.

On the far curb, the hydrant's cap was scratched the way real tools scratch real metal. The newsbox behind it displayed yesterday's headlines and would never be updated. The frosted door in the brick wall bore letters I could almost read. I did not slow.

The signal stayed green. It did not have any other gear.

Across the street, a radio voice floated from somewhere it did not belong, soothing and useless. Wrong interchange. Wrong street. Right tone for comforting strangers about disasters that were not theirs.

Three white bars left. Two. One.

The last step tried to glue my foot down.

The clerk stood half in the crosswalk, hands held out, driver's license balanced on his palms like a gift. His name tag hung there, letters hunting and failing. He did not reach for me. He just stood exactly where a human body becomes an obstacle.

"Not mine," I said, as calmly as I could. Calm felt like an actual spell, quiet and practical.

I did not walk into him. I set my foot down a single inch shy of the curb and held my balance there for a beat.

He did not offer again.

The plastic of the license softened at the edges. The letters on the tag abandoned their hunt and dissolved into blank silver. His shape folded inward at the corners like a grocery bag left in the rain. He disappeared without a sound.

I took the last step up onto the curb.

My heel made a normal, solid sound on concrete. I wanted to keep that sound in a jar forever.

The crosswalk chirp slowed, pretending it had never changed tempo at all. The machine green faded to a dull, ordinary lens color. The smear of chrome in the window reverted to nothing more than bent glass and interior fixtures.

The white-eyed driver in the reflection turned back into a dressmaker's dummy, wearing a dress that had never fit anyone.

The baseball game on the radio did not restart. The radio was off. My car did not idle. The keys were in my pocket, not the column. I turned to look back only once.

The driver's seat was empty. The headrest still held a darker oval where a head had lived for years. Slowly, from the outside inward, the fabric lightened, drying the way cloth does after rain.

I stayed long enough to see the darkest part fade. I did not stay to watch it finish.

A narrow side door to my left unlatched with a tiny internal click. Frosted glass above the handle spelled out letters that threw shadows down the hallway beyond.

The sound that drifted from behind the glass was the packaged kind of kindness offices use, poured out in measured doses.

"Claims," the door said without sound, the word so clear in my brain it might as well have been printed there.

I checked my pocket. The index card was still tucked against my hip. The pen I had pocketed earlier rested beside it.

I put my palm on the door and felt the cool paint.

Behind me, the intersection held its position, frozen in a permanent almost. Green light washing. Glass reflecting. Nothing moving unless I said so.

"Car in park," I reminded myself. "Radio off. Green is only a color."

The Claims door waited.

The kindness waited.

The hallway behind it smelled like lemon cleaner mixed with copier toner and long nights in small offices where people fill out forms to survive the worst day of their lives.

I was not going to sit. I was not going to sign. I was going to look, listen, and keep my pulse.

I wrapped my hand around the handle and pulled.

THE FROSTED GLASS HUMMED the way old televisions used to hum when they were on with no picture. A clean serif font hovered in the blur. Claims.

The handle was brushed metal, smooth and cool, taking my hand-print like it had been waiting. When I pushed, the door gave easily. Someone, or something, took care of these hinges.

Inside, the space was small.

A short hallway, carpeted in the kind of low-pile stuff that eats sound and hides stains. A metal chair was bolted to the wall, seat tilted just enough to make sitting still look responsible.

The air smelled like toner and lemon wiped over old smoke, the House's favorite perfume for "We are trying to be gentle."

"Good evening."

The voice came from behind a second panel of frosted glass at the far end. It sounded like an aunt who had run this office for decades and honestly believed she was helping.

"If you would like to amend your statement, the form is simple," she said. "We can begin with the sound."

A slot at waist height lit up with a tiny bulb. Paper slid out in one smooth, practiced motion.

The form was covered in boxes and lines, space for my name that I was not about to fill in. Across the top, in neat letters: Please describe the noise as you remember it.

A pen followed, identical to the others, resting exactly in reach.

I ran my thumb along the edge of the paper. It was thicker stock than normal, heavy in a way that felt intentional. The boxes were inviting, all that blank space waiting to be controlled.

The polite part of me, the one trained to behave in offices, wanted to write something. Anything.

Instead, I set the pen on the floor and pushed the form back into the slot.

The slot accepted it with a small intake of air. Then it fed another page out toward me. This one had checkboxes for emotions. Shock. Sadness. Anger. Guilt.

There was a line for Other with extra space, like they were proud to be open-minded.

"Not tonight," I said. My voice stayed low, but it did not shake. I kept my hands where I could see them, fingers loose, because I did not trust them not to reach for the pen on their own.

"We can ease your burden," the voice said. Warmer now, like we were sharing a secret. "There are several versions of the event. You do not need to carry all of them. Choose one you can live with, and we will keep the rest."

A shadow passed behind the frosted glass. Tall, narrow, holding a ledger along one forearm. Paper edges glowed faintly, lined in dates and numbers, like veins inside a translucent skin.

The figure paused near the edge of the window, then moved on without turning its head. The carpet did not show any footprints after it passed.

The room clearly wanted me to read that as proof nobody was really there.

I looked down instead, along the line where the carpet met the baseboard. A small corner of receipt paper stuck out from under the metal leg of the chair.

I crouched. The chair did not shift. I pinched the paper free. Pencil over pencil, multiple passes to darken the words until they would never fade.

Do not describe the noise. If you name it, it will keep it for you.

The initials beneath were J. L., written small and a little tilted, the way people sign things they hope no one ever looks at closely. The last stroke trailed away, like the writer had stood up quickly or been pulled away mid-letter.

I folded the note and slid it into my pocket with the others. My heart tried to speed up, then tripped over itself, then settled into something in-between. Behind the glass, the kind voice listened for the scratch of a pen. When it never came, she shifted tactics.

"Many people find it helps to write just a little," she said, still calm, still kind. "We can start with one word. Or we can make choices for you. We are here to help."

The slot pushed the pen back toward me, nudging it against the carpet, almost petulant. The light above it flickered and came back brighter. I left the pen where it lay. I did not crush it. I did not pick it up. The chair beside me kept offering its tilted seat with the same quiet eagerness as the movie chairs upstairs.

I stayed standing.

My palms remembered the feel of the car roof, cool metal and real edges. I breathed with the pipes I could not see. In for four. Hold for four. Out for six. The rhythm opened a pocket of space in my chest where none of this paper could reach.

"Would you like to amend your prior statement?" the voice asked. Still patient. Maybe a little proud of the phrase. "It will ease your burden. We can ease your burden."

"I did not make one," I said. "I have nothing to amend."

A long shadow drifted behind the glass again. This time, when the ledger passed close to the thinner part of the frosting, I could just make out the bottom lines. A neat row of dates. Two months I had already lived.

A third month I had not reached yet.

The pencil line under that one was empty and waiting. I took a slow step backward without turning away. The carpet tried to catch my heel for half a second and failed. The slot accepted my silence like it was a kind of payment. A third form slid out, this one with blank spaces for license numbers, policy details, witness names. A whole section waited for me to list what I wished I had done differently.

"Not tonight," I said again, softer, like I was closing a door on a pushy neighbor. "Not ever would be better."

"As you wish," the voice answered. I hated that phrase. It sounded so gentle while it rearranged things behind the scenes. "We are here when you are ready. We will keep your place."

The ledger-shadow pivoted and walked away. The edge of the paper flashed once like fish in a murky tank.

I did not want to know how many parts of me the book had already copied. I only needed to hang on to the parts it wanted most: the words for the sound, the comfort of chairs, the permission to let green light push me forward.

I backed up until my hand found the door bar. A thin layer of cool had collected there, the residue of people who had told themselves the weight was lighter once it lived on a form. The smell of toner followed me as I stepped back into the little entry and out into the fake street. The frosted glass hummed in the background, quiet as a TV on mute in an empty room. The voice did not say my name. It did not need to. I had already handed that over in other places.

At the pantry threshold, my real kitchen light laid its familiar square across the wood floor. I stepped into it and let my body remember what warm light feels like on skin. The refrigerator motor kicked on, humming in its normal off-key way. I closed the pantry door. The latch caught with that tidy little cluck I trusted more than anything that talked from behind frosted glass. The index card on the refrigerator was still where I had left it.

I took it down and picked up the blunt pencil that had somehow migrated into my pocket along with the others. I added a new line and pressed hard enough that I could feel the impression on the card behind it.

Car in park.
Radio off.
Green is only a color.
Do not describe the noise.

I pinned the card back up with the lighthouse magnet. It clicked and held, like it approved.

The kitchen smelled faintly like leftover coffee. Morning already felt older than it had any right to. I stood there long enough to be sure my hands were not shaking. The hallway beyond looked ordinary. The shoebox and the stack of notebooks sat where I had left them. Paper does not move itself. Rooms do. Something ticked inside Mara's journal, a tiny shift of graphite against paper that traveled like a sound through my teeth.

I did not open it to see if a new line had appeared in her handwriting where there was no one left to write. I just rested my palm on the cardboard lid of the shoebox. The only thing under my hand was the cool of a house that had started to learn my body temperature. The rest of the evening happened in the slow way evenings do when you have drawn a line around what you will not give up.

I washed a plate. I put on music and let it fill the kitchen, then stop neatly at the doorway. I checked the lock twice, then one more time, in case the House decided it had a sense of humor I could not tolerate. In bed, the dark belonged to my room. The other kind of dark stayed behind paint and wood and whatever passed for rules in the House's favorite corridors. My pillow held its normal shape. When I closed my eyes, I saw a traffic light that was quiet as a regular bulb and a curb I had reached with my own steps.

I fell asleep without the taste of coins in my mouth. Sometime in the night, a vent paused like it was listening and then went back to breathing. The building rotated one old joint a fraction of an inch to settle deeper into its foundations.

I did not wake all the way. A dream about forms waited at a counter, offering me pens I refused to take. The dream, amazingly, let me go.

In the morning, the card on the refrigerator gave me my own rules in my own handwriting.

I read them and felt that small, practical lift you get when you have picked your doors on purpose.

Chapter 5
NIGHT AND DAY

I MADE COFFEE BEFORE I made a decision, because some promises are easier to keep if your hands have something to do. The index card on the refrigerator sat under the lighthouse magnet with its blunt little list of rules. I picked up the pencil and added one more line at the bottom in smaller letters so it would not crowd the rest.

One day. No rooms.

Steam fogged the window over the sink. The yard on Weaver Street held its wet leaves like a heavy quilt nobody had bothered to shake out. A truck on the hill shifted gears and let its engine brake carry a long breath down into town.

I drank half my mug standing by the stove and the other half by the kitchen doorway, because I could not stop glancing at the pantry every time I crossed the room. The chair I had wedged under the knob last night still leaned against it, steady and solid, like a friend braced against the door without making a big deal out of it.

I brushed my fingers along the chair back the way you touch someone's shoulder in passing and told the room, quietly, that I planned to be kind to myself and cruel to the door. That felt fair.

I pocketed the index card and the two receipt notes with their precise little messages that had kept me company. The pencil lines on the thermal paper had smudged a bit from handling, but they still read like instructions from someone who actually wanted me to keep my heartbeat.

> Count with the pipes.
> Break rhythms.
> Do not describe the noise.

I slid the notes into the small inside pocket of my jacket where they would sit right over my ribs.

Outside, the morning air had that iron taste you get in small towns near water and truck routes. Engine brakes on the ridge let out long, tired sighs. The grass along the barely visible front walk kept its wild height like everyone had politely agreed to ignore it.

When I pulled the front door shut, the hinges gave a long creak that sounded like someone turning over in an old bed. I told myself to hear wood and not breath. That is a trick I am learning. Like all tricks, it is easier in daylight.

Bakersville looked like a town that minded its own business until it suddenly did not. On my first Monday here, I had noticed how porch flags matched by coincidence, how the same plastic pumpkins reappeared on three houses in a row, how doors opened just wide enough to take mail and closed with the same careful motion.

Today those details felt sharper, like the town had decided to do a welfare check with its eyes. A motion sensor on a porch two houses up clicked its floodlight on in full sunlight when I walked past, then realized how dumb that looked and switched back off. On the beige ranch across the street, a blind lifted a finger's width and froze there, the exact breath of someone trying to decide if they knew me from somewhere important.

At the corner, three kids coasted their scooters slower. They had that shared-bravery look all small-town kids get in groups, one spine stretched out across three different jackets.

The oldest boy, the one in the sticker-covered helmet, made that warding gesture I had only ever seen in movies. First and ring finger tucked in, middle and index pointing down like little horns. He tried to hide it by dragging his hand down the leg of his jeans like he was just scratching.

The girl next to him pretended to check her phone and snapped a picture of me without raising the screen high enough to be obvious. The smallest one just stared.

I thought about giving them a friendly wave and decided to let it go. You do not wave at birds you want to see again.

"You live there," the little one said, not even trying to whisper.

"For now," I said. Accuracy felt safer than yes.

"That place eats cats," the helmet boy announced, full of home-town authority.

"It does not," the girl said. "That was the old woman. Before she died."

"Cats eat mice," I said. "Everybody picks a job."

They all stared at me like I had confirmed some rumor they had not finished writing yet, then pushed off and rolled on. The rubber clack of their wheels hitting the same crack in the sidewalk followed me all the way to the end of the block.

At the next corner, the pedestrian light flipped to green for a cross-walk nobody had walked up to. The little chirp started, two beats and a pause, bright and patient. I kept moving with my head turned slightly away from it and counted my breathing on a rhythm that belonged to pipes, not birds.

The strip mall's parking lot held its early cars like pieces at the start of a chess game. Grocery Mart anchored one end, a nail salon sat in the middle, and the two-chair barbershop at the far side had the same two men in the front window I saw every time I passed by.

The post office door was propped with a wooden wedge. Inside, a clerk I had not met yet sorted mail with the kind of fast, precise motions that say a person measures their worth in how big the outgoing pile gets before lunch. He looked up just long enough to say,

"Morning, Ellison place. Crew keeps saying they cannot find the right hedge trimmer for that yard. Funny, right."

"Very," I said. There are places where accuracy has to step aside for polite.

At the library, I was the one who decided if the lights meant open. A hand-lettered sign leaned against the glass. I flipped it. OPEN faced the quiet street like a dare.

The lobby smelled like copier paper and the soft plastic of old book covers. The public computers along the far wall blinked their empty login screens at no one. When the heat kicked on, the vent in the ceiling breathed in a way that belonged to metal ductwork, not to a House, and I felt something in my chest loosen without needing to name it.

I unlocked the small staff door, dropped my bag behind the circulation desk, and lined up the jar of stubby pencils in the center of the counter like a tiny altar to simple tools. Two teens came in, walked the fiction aisle like the shelves could absolve them of something, grabbed paperbacks, and left with a whispered agreement to bring them back late. I did not mention late fees. The only debt I cared about today lived on Weaver Street.

The public terminals had access to county records if you clicked in the right order. Property cards hide in weird corners of websites designed by people who want to seem important.

112 Weaver had a record that started with the bank and rolled backward like a slow tide. Ellison, Mara L., last listed owner before the line jumped to Heirs to Bank.

Further up the chain, past her, the names ran neatly for a few screens. Then the dates stopped behaving. Two different years had been typed in, then scratched out. Their replacements were not dates at all. One field said Parlor. The other said Pantry.

Someone, at some point, had realized the system would accept letters where it wanted numbers and left a private joke for the next unlucky person.

Even further back, a couple of entries carried a red rubber stamp: Inspection Deferred. The ink color changed, but the phrase did not. It showed up again twenty years later in blue, then again in black, each in a slightly different handwriting. Pantry sealed pending remediation, someone had written in the margin three separate times, as if they all needed to make sure it stayed on the record.

The local history shelf leaned under the weight of binders the way old houses lean under snow.

A Sanborn fire map from about a hundred years ago spread Bakersville out in little squares of pink and yellow. A lane used to run behind the lot where my kitchen sits now. A narrow pen line led from that lane to a small square drawn inside the footprint of my house. Too straight and too deliberate to be plumbing.

The index called it a service shaft.

In the margin, someone had added a note in fountain pen: dumb-waiter?

The curl on the M in dumbwaiter matched the M on Mara's note-book sitting on my hallway shelf at home. My thumb traced the loop the way you follow a faint path through long grass and tell yourself you just happened to walk there.

Bound newspaper volumes sat in canvas slings on a cart that always looked like it might collapse and somehow never did.

The Bakersville Gazette from 1891 had obituaries pressed near the back, like death should always come after the ads. A midwife's name sat in one column, praised for her strong hands and her long walks. Survived by no children, it said. The address put her near Weaver.

The sentence tried very hard not to say what everyone probably knew.

I made a copy of the page. The paper came out warm and thin. It smelled like old cloth and dust and ink, and something about that combination always feels like truth, even when it is not.

Next, the 1956 volume. One tiny article about a household ac-cident on Weaver Street. No names. No picture. Just a line about community meals left on a doorstep. Underneath, a photo of smiling teenagers at a school car wash. That is how towns like this tell stories. We will tell you something bad happened, then distract you with soap and sunshine.

I copied that too.

Then 1979. A missing person notice tucked near the classifieds. J. L., last seen near Weaver Street. No foul play suspected. The phrase sits wrong by design. The photo was a grainy stamp, face turned slightly away like the camera had take two and someone printed take one.

I ran a copy and wrote J. L. at the bottom in my own writing to see how the letters felt coming off my pencil. They felt like a pebble caught in my shoe. The bell over the front door chimed and pulled me back to the present. An older woman with careful blue eyes and hair set into a style that could survive a windstorm walked up to the desk with a large print paperback. She slid it over and said,

"Large print is a blessing these days." Her smile arrived a second after her words, like it had to travel farther.

She glanced at the folder I had started and read the penciled label without asking. Weaver, 112.

"You fixing the pantry?" she asked, too bright, like a joke that showed up wearing its own laugh track. Then her face flinched, as if her mouth had jumped ahead of her brain.

"Just trying to keep the raccoons honest," I said.

"Oh, honey," she said, hitching her purse strap higher on her shoulder like it might save her. "Raccoons know more about honesty than most folks."

She walked away without taking the checkout slip, made it halfway to the door, then turned just enough to add,

"My mother said that house had a larder for the dead. People say things. People say a lot."

The bell over the door made a short, sharp sound I did not like, and she was gone. Three faces smooshed up against the front windows a minute later, forming circles in their breath on the glass. My scooter kids had followed me this far for the entertainment value of watching me act normal. The smallest one mouthed witch with the kind of delighted meanness kids try on before they understand how heavy real meanness is. The girl traced DOOR in the fog and drew a rectangle around it. I raised my sleeve and wiped the letters away from my side of the glass.

We stared at each other through the clear patch, both sides pretending this was not a conversation. They held for one more breath, then shoved off, clack, clack, clack over the crack in the sidewalk.

Back at the staff desk, I made a neat little stack. Property card printout. Sanborn map slice. Three clippings. One Historical Society flyer with the absurd title Bakersville Mysteries and a bullet point about The Weaver Widow's Larder for the Dead in spooky Halloween font.

I slid everything into a manila folder and wrote Weaver, 112 on the tab in pencil, clean and square, the way I write when I want something to feel official but not sacred.

I tucked the folder into my bag and locked the drawer by habit, even though the folder was coming home with me. It felt good to label the thing that kept trying to label me.

By midafternoon, I had helped one man find a book on outboard motors, shown two teens where the horror shelf really was, and replaced a toner cartridge with the quiet, sharp movements that make a person feel like maybe everything could be fixed with the right clicks and a firm push.

The bulletin board by the entrance still held last spring's flyer for that Historical Society talk, the same Bakersville Mysteries headline, the same paragraph about a widow and a pantry and unnamed dead. No dates. No sources. Just story.

When I locked up, the sky had turned that flat pewter of a November four thirty, when the day decides it is too tired to keep trying. I flipped the sign to CLOSED and watched my reflection smudge around the letters in the glass. The walk back down the hill to Weaver felt both shorter and longer, the way routes do when you know exactly what waits at both ends.

At the corner near my street, the pedestrian signal went green again with no one there to use it. The chirp kicked in, chipper and expectant. I kept my eyes on the ghost of a hopscotch grid chalked into the sidewalk, the colored squares faded but still holding enough of their shape to count.

My house had not made any decisions while I was gone. The curtains kept their blank faces. The motion light next door flickered on and off twice like it could not make up its mind and then gave up. On the porch, the key turned in the front door with that right note that sounds like something fitting back where it belongs. Inside, the air smelled like lemon cleaner over old smoke. I had decided that smell could belong to dinners and cigarettes and everyday human mess, not just hauntings.

I put my bag on the dining table and did not open the folder inside. Instead, I swept the floor. Old houses like it when you take care of their surfaces. I filled a pot with water, chopped carrots into coins, dumped noodles into broth, and told myself that soup counts as a plan.

While it simmered, I wrote another rule on a fresh index card, small and neat like talking to a stubborn kid.

> Do not let other people name it for you.

I slid that card into my jacket pocket with the receipt notes.

The kitchen chair was nothing special. Plain straight back, wooden seat with one shallow burn mark where someone had set down a hot pan years ago. I carried it to the pantry, jammed the top rail under the knob, and leaned into it until the front legs scraped an inch across the tile and then settled.

I tapped the top of the chair twice. Not superstition. Physics.

"Not today," I told the paint. "You will keep until I choose you."

The house settled into its evening soundtrack. Pipes cooling. A low thrum in the baseboards that tried to sync with my breathing and slipped when I stretched the exhale. I ate my soup standing at the counter because stools invite more thinking than I wanted.

When I washed the bowl, I left the kitchen light on and checked the chair again without touching it. It threw a long, regular shadow across the tile and up the pantry door, the kind of shadow a person could step over without noticing.

In bed, I read two pages of a book and could not tell you what either one said. The street outside held the kind of quiet that belongs to towns that know their own bedtime. Far off, a train laid down a thin, straight line of sound I could have slept inside like a hallway. I let my body do the work of sleeping. That is a skill like anything else. You practice it. The dream came late, the kind that slides in after the deep part of sleep and floats on top so it feels like waking.

In the dream, my hallway had a new door at the very end. I knew without being told that it was a door I had not earned yet. The velvet rope from the viewing parlor lay coiled in the middle of the floor like a sleeping animal waiting for someone to walk close enough. The pantry door opened itself a finger's width and stopped, like it was embarrassed I caught it moving.

A draft crept along the floor, reached my wrist without missing, and rested there, accurate as a cat that knows which hand has the treats. A lullaby leaked from a vent. It was my voice, wrong by one note, and it got quieter every time I leaned in to hear it better, like someone on the other side was matching my distance for sport.

I said, *Not tonight*, to the dream and to the House that loves pretending it is a dream, and I woke up to the refrigerator motor kicking on. Pre-dawn blue pressed against the kitchen window. The chair was still where I had put it, shoulder against the pantry knob like a friend who had fallen asleep guarding the door. The card I had taped to the paint had a tiny crease curling up in one corner. I did not remember that happening. I did not touch it.

I stood and listened. The hum under the floor hesitated, shifted, then fell back into regular house noise. The vent breathed only what the kitchen air gave it.

One day, I told the room. One day, no rooms. Then we will see.

BY LATE MORNING, THE library had settled into that special quiet it saves for people who need to think while pretending they are just pretending to think.

The heat ran at a steady hum that belonged to the building and not to anything else. Every time I caught myself listening for a lullaby or a crosswalk chirp, I forced myself to count ceiling tiles instead.

The front door chime behaved. Once when someone came in, once when they left. Predictable sounds can feel like medicine. Local history lived in a narrow side room off the main stacks. The light in there was terrible and the information was excellent. I hit the switch near the doorway. The fluorescent tubes flickered, argued, then came fully on.

Dust floated in the air, visible in the bright bars like tiny, honest planets. Along one wall, binders in cracked vinyl held tax rolls and assessor records, most of them typed and then corrected in ink by clerks who had stayed in the same job for too many winters.

I went back to where property turns into story.

> Parcel card, 112 Weaver Street. Owner of record: Ellison, Mara L. Then Heirs to Bank.

The older entries looked normal until they did not.

Two years had been typed, then scratched out in thin fountain-pen lines. Their replacements were not years, just words. One box read Parlor. The other read Pantry. In the margin, someone had written Inspection deferred. It appeared three times, three different pens, three different handwritings, three different decades. Same phrase.

I copied the card on the library copier. The machine and I had reached an understanding this morning, so it worked on the first try. The warm sheet rolled out. I set it on the table and flattened the edges with my hand.

The Sanborn map came back down. Bakersville sprawled out again in pastel blocks. In the margin of my copy, I circled the tiny service lane behind my house and the little square that might be a dumbwaiter shaft, or something less willing to be named. I traced the fountain-pen question mark with my pencil. The bound papers sat waiting in their canvas slings. I pulled the 1891 volume again and let my eye find the midwife's obituary on its own. My thumb hovered over the address on Weaver and then moved on. The 1956 accident note read the same as this morning. A house on Weaver. An unnamed mishap. Community meals on steps. Small towns love that sentence almost as much as no foul play suspected.

The 1979 missing person notice with J. L. was still as thin and unsatisfying as ever. No follow-up story. No resolution. Just a photo that refused to sharpen no matter how long I looked. I made sure each copy had the date clear at the top. I did not trust my own memory to keep the years from blurring. On the community board, the Historical Society flyer still offered Bakersville Mysteries in festive lettering. The Weaver Widow line about a larder for the dead made my teeth itch.

I pulled down one copy of the flyer just to have it in the folder with everything else the town thought the house was. Back at the circulation desk, a shadow fell across the counter. The mail carrier, in his reflective vest, set a stack of envelopes in front of me. His smile had the ease of someone who always knows where the next stop is.

"Morning, Librarian," he said. "Got some notices for you and one for the Ellison place. Want me to toss it in your box or leave it here."

"Here is good," I said.

He slid a window envelope toward me with a finger. The return address was the lawn service the bank had sworn would show up.

"Crew keeps missing that address," he said, using the same joke as the post office clerk, like the town was rotating one shared line between them. "Sensor lights on that block think they are in charge. Fun when we are still out after dark."

"Lights confuse everyone," I said.

He grinned like I had agreed to something bigger and left. The bell over the door chimed, clean and mechanical. The silence after felt like a room closing its eyes. The lawn service notice said Service postponed, stamped in friendly red ink. The reason box was checked Other, with no explanation. I slipped the paper into the back of my Weaver folder and wrote another line on a fresh index card, small enough that I had to lean close to read it.

> Do not create a docket number.

It felt like a rule I would need for the House's favorite kind of bureaucracy.

The older woman from earlier drifted through again with a second book, no chitchat this time. I checked it out without asking for her card. Our fingers brushed for a second. She opened her mouth like she had something rehearsed, then closed it again and walked out.

The bell chimed once. I watched the glass settle back into stillness. After lunch, I opened twenty years of town meeting minutes on the public computer and regretted it almost immediately. The search bar was not my friend, so I had to read the pages. Three hours and one focused headache later, I had a short list of scribbles in my notebook.

> 112 Weaver: lawn abatement tabled.
> 112 Weaver: inspection deferred pending legal.

112 Weaver: erosion grant denied on technical grounds.

The items always sat near the bottom of the agenda, always pushed forward, never resolved. You could build a whole life out of things that get carried to the next meeting. People do.

At the bottom of one scanned page, a clerk's name made me say it out loud.

Ellison, M.

The town hall signature was smaller than you would expect from someone old enough to own a house and argue with a council. The loop on the M had the same little hook as Mara's handwriting at home. The date on the minutes matched the stamp on the property card that had turned a year into the word Parlor.

I printed that page and slid it under the others without letting my fingers brush the names too long. The afternoon moved forward in small chunks. Teens swapped paperbacks and giggled down by the horror section. A man walked in and asked about outboard motors again, thanked me like I had personally invented gasoline. The copier tried to throw a tantrum about toner. I replaced the cartridge and shut the tray twice, firm. It accepted the change and went back to pretending it had never complained.

In the window, my reflection floated behind the OPEN sign. For a second I looked like a face printed right onto the glass.

Outside, the scooter kids pressed their breath circles onto the window again, testing the boundary. The smallest one drew a heart on the fog and capped it around the word DOOR like a joke or a spell. The girl swatted his arm, not really mad, and turned her phone camera on herself instead.

I wiped away the letters from my side of the window. Their expressions went wide, then broke into that half-scared, half-thrilled laugh that means the world has spoken back to them. They rolled away, wheels clacking over the same crack, again and again. I locked up twenty minutes late because it felt better to say I had been working than to say I had been avoiding going home.

The sign flipped to CLOSED with a little plastic protest. I turned the key in the door until the lock caught. Inside, the building shifted its weight like it was relieved it would not have to pretend to be public again until tomorrow.

In the local history room, one low drawer waited under the bottom shelf. The label said Internals. When I had started this job, I had opened it once, seen the word, and decided it was not my problem.

Today I pulled the drawer all the way out. A metal card tray inside held handwritten reference cards. Each card carried a name, a date, and a subject. The handwriting changed, but one card made something tighten in my chest.

> Ellison, Mara.

Map requests. Plat surveys. Utility easements. Pantry sealed for health.

The last line ran off the card like the writer had stood up too fast. I held the card between two fingers until the paper warmed. Then I copied it onto a fresh index card in my own hand. I put the original back and closed the drawer. Standing up, I let the quiet of the room flow back into the space I had disturbed.

On my way out of the local history room, I flicked off the light and waited. The fluorescents said their soft buzzing goodbye and died. Dust drifted in the dark for a second, then disappeared. No voice came from the vent. I liked that. That was a kind of boundary I wanted to keep.

I locked the library door and checked it twice. Checking locks and counting breaths live in the same part of the brain. Outside, the air had cooled into that metal taste four thirty always brings in November. I tucked the folder against my ribs so the manila edge pressed into my bones and reminded me that paper weighs something when you choose to carry it.

When I turned toward Weaver, the sun hung in that indecisive place where it cannot decide whether to set. Porch lights began to blink on one by one. Houses settled into themselves. I slid one hand into my pocket and felt the soft edges of the receipt notes and the index card with the line I had written this morning.

> Do not let other people name it for you.

I said it once under my breath, for me more than for the House. Words land differently when you hear them in your own voice.

Then I walked.

EVENING DROPPED A FLAT coin of light in the kitchen window and stepped back.

I set the manila folder on the dining table and deliberately did not open it. Soup steamed and cooled. I rinsed the bowl, dried it, and waited until the refrigerator slid into its familiar hum. Small tasks make a fence between you and everything else. I dragged the plain kitchen chair over to the pantry and wedged the back under the knob again until the front legs scraped and settled.

On a new index card, I wrote three lines and taped it right above the chair back.

> Not tonight.
> No returns.
> No descriptions.

I smoothed the tape with my thumb. The chair looked as boring as ever, which made me feel better. The thing guarding the door should not look like a hero. It should look like furniture.

The house did its night practice. Pipes cooled and creaked. Baseboards murmured. Somewhere behind the walls a low vibration tried to match my breathing. I stretched my exhale until the rhythm slipped and the sound wandered off. I left the kitchen light on. Checked the chair one more time without touching it. Still braced. Still ordinary.

Then I went to bed.

Sleep came in short, separate rooms. In one, the hallway grew an extra door and the velvet rope lay coiled in the center like a pet that only wakes up for certain people. In another, the pantry eased open one finger's width and stopped, and cool air slipped out, feeling for my wrist with the confidence of something that already knew my pulse.

A lullaby leaked through a vent in my own bent version of my voice and shrank away every time I tried to listen closer. It was like someone else was pacing their distance to stay just out of reach.

When I turned away in the dream, green light crawled along a wall that does not exist in my real house and held there, steady as glass. A kind office voice started listing accident types in the tone of a relative who has done this speech for a lot of families.

If you would like to amend, it began, over and over, and each time I opened my mouth to answer, the sentence stitched itself closed before the words reached my teeth.

I woke up when the refrigerator motor clicked on again. Pre-dawn light pressed against the window above the sink, washed blue and thin. The kitchen light I had left on made a square of bright on the tile. The chair still leaned into the pantry knob like it had been there all its life. The taped card had a new little curl on one corner, lifting up like a paper hangnail. I did not remember that being there. I did not smooth it down.

I listened.

The baseboards held their silence like someone standing very straight on purpose. The vent over the stove only moved the air it was given. For a second I believed that the boundary would hold if I just kept choosing it.

Then I heard it.

Not loud. Not dramatic. Just the small, neat cluck of a latch, shifting on its own on the other side of the door, the way people test a lock they already know is locked.

"Not tonight," I told the card, the chair, and the part of me that wanted to put my ear to the door.

I said it again, quieter. Saying it quietly felt ruder. It also felt right. The sound did not repeat. The feeling of being watched did not go anywhere. In the hall, Mara's notebook lay where I had left it on the shelf. A pencil ticked once inside the closed cover, faint as someone holding their breath too long.

I stood in the doorway and let the house see me not walking toward it. The chair did not shift. The corner of the card lifted a little more, curling toward the room, the way paper learns whatever space it lives in. I made coffee because that is what mornings are for. Steam fogged the glass. I kept my eyes on the mug and not on the pantry.

The first swallow went down like a promise I knew I was going to have to keep. One day, I had written. No rooms. The House had heard the second part.

It had already started to test the first.

Chapter 6
LULLABY TRIAL

I TOLD THE KITCHEN what I was doing before I did it. The light over the sink made a clean square on the counter, bright and honest in a way the rest of the house never was. Steam lifted from a mug I already knew I was not going to finish. The index card on the refrigerator held my rules in blunt pencil, and I read them out loud so the room could not pretend I had only thought them. Break rhythms. Keep your breath. Do not describe the noise. Green is only a color. Do not accept returns. Do not let other people name it for you. Saying the rules out loud made them feel like more than scribbles. It made them feel like a contract.

I slid the card into my pocket and felt the edge settle against the receipt slips from M. E. and J. L. The thermal paper had gone soft from being handled, but their writing still pressed through the years. Do not ring the bell. Do not describe the noise. If it asks you to carry, make it carry air. I pressed the notes against my ribs, like they could reinforce my bones. Then I set my hand on the back of the chair that had spent the night braced under the pantry knob. The chair had done its work. It deserved a break. I eased it back an inch, then another, just far enough that the latch would be free without letting the door throw itself open and pretend this was its idea.

"I am choosing the door," I said, so the House could not claim it had pulled me in. Who speaks first matters. Who sets the story matters.

The latch gave its neat little cluck. Lemon cleaner over old smoke slid around my wrist, cool and polite, like the house was breathing right against my skin. The corridor on the other side woke up in the slow, showy way it liked, bulbs brightening one by one in a lazy wave that made a straight hallway look like it bent if you watched it long enough. The floor under my feet thickened; the narrow kitchen strips spread into wide old planks with dull varnish that looked like skin that had been touched too many times. Limewash crawled up the walls and caught the light in a flat, chalky way. Peg rails ran at my shoulder height, each peg worn smooth from sleeves and shawls and aprons. Sooty handprints marked the plaster, fingers and palms where someone had pushed themselves upright a thousand times and the wall had remembered.

The lullaby started as one wrong note in the vent, thin as weak tea and just as persistent. It found my ear the way water finds a crack. Every time I inhaled, it held. Every time I exhaled, it tried to slide into my rhythm and ride it. My throat wanted to hum along out of pure reflex. I kept my mouth closed and counted instead. In for four. Hold for four. Out for six. The hum in the baseboards shifted toward my chest, like the whole corridor was trying to sync up with me and carry my breathing for me. I lengthened the exhale until the house's rhythm missed my step and had to chase to catch up. It was petty, but it felt like a win.

I passed the sampler I had already seen once and deliberately did not look straight at it. Letters behave better when they know you are not desperate to read them. The hearth room kept its cool iron smell, still sour with old vinegar and tallow, but without the heavy ache that had hit me the first time. The cradle block I had left leaned where I had propped that parlor door open. Little drafts in the air tugged toward the nursery, subtle and honest, like the house had finally given up pretending the direction was an accident.

The nursery threshold felt like a line my body recognized whether the house marked it or not. Peg rail hung with tiny gowns the size of my hands. A rocker shone with polish worn in by backs and fingers. The window showed only another wall and its beams, no hint of sky or trees, because apparently this room did not rate an outside. The cradle sat in the middle of the floor like a solution nobody had actually asked for. The vent perched high above the rocker, grille too clean for its age, like a mouth that has never had to do anything but breathe in.

The midwife waited where she always did, built of the same strength and the same exhaustion. She sat in the plain chair with her raw hands folded on nothing, skin red to the wrists like she had washed them in lye for forty years and never quite gotten them dry. Her eyes stayed on the vent the way nurses stare at monitors when all the real decisions have already been made. Her dress was simple, the color of old bone that has been scrubbed too often. From the peg behind her, a narrow ribbon hung, a little metal tag pinned to it. The letters on the tag slipped and blurred when I tried to look at them straight on, sliding sideways like minnows in a bucket. In the corner of my vision they held steady for a breath, then slid again.

The cradle rocked with my pulse and then a little past it, like it wanted to drag my heart rate uphill. The rocker creaked in a practiced, soothing rhythm, like a metronome set by someone who believed "calm" meant "never changing." Across the room, the sampler stitched and unstitched itself in time with my breathing. On the exhale, thread lined up into letters. On the inhale, it pulled back to bare linen. Names go home, Mara had written in her journal, and I could still remember the warmth that had leaked out of the cold grate when I put hair back where it was supposed to be.

I did not sit. I did not touch the cradle. I walked the edges of the room like it belonged to me first and the House second, and put my hand on the window frame. Wood is honest even when everything built around it lies. The frame was cool, solid. The wall beyond the glass felt too close and too flat, like scenery in a school play. My lungs wanted to sync with the lullaby so badly it hurt. I kept counting anyway. In for four. Hold for four. Out for six. Once or twice, the vent landed right on my exhale and rode it. Then it slid off again. The song sounded like my voice, but it was not mine. I decided that mattered.

The wooden spoon in my pocket still felt like a stupid little magic trick, but so far it worked better than anything else I had. I slid it out and wedged it under the cradle runner until the wood squeaked on the floor. The cradle rocked harder for a few passes, like a machine pushing against a new gear. Then it hit the wedge, remembered what "no" felt like, and had to decide. It chose to stop. My pulse tried to jump in and keep the momentum. I told it no, too. The rocker creaked louder, like it was offended and volunteering itself. The air at the vent warmed until the tune felt like breath at my ear instead of sound in the room.

"Not that," I said, to the chair, the cradle, the vent, and the house that thought this counted as comfort. I stood behind the rocker and set two fingers on the back rail, close enough to claim it, not enough to let it claim me. I rocked it myself, off beat, a little too fast, two swings, three, and then stopped it cold mid-swing with my palm on the arm. Wood hit wood with a clean, hard sound. The room's breathing flinched and tried again.

The sampler fussed for my attention next. Thread whipped into shapes fast enough to make the letters blur. I did not lean toward it. I turned my head toward the midwife instead. She had not moved much, but some part of her posture had softened, like a knot in her back finally let go. Her chin lifted the smallest bit toward the section of wall where a hearth would be in a sane house. It felt like a hint: look there, not at me.

I read the sampler the way you read a sign while you are driving, quick and at the edge of vision, only at the ends of breaths. It took four full exhales for the letters to lock into place. Elenor, spelled in rowed stitches that tried hard to be steady. The last name pulled itself together, clear and heavy, and I let it sit there without saying it. I did not mouth it. I did not roll it around in my head like a charm. Names go home. I was not going to turn this one into a token I carried.

I took the ribbon and tag down from its peg. The point where the thread had stuck to the wood snagged for a second before it gave. Up close, the tag's letters jittered even harder, sliding away from my focus as fast as I tried to pin them. From the side they behaved, briefly, then melted back into nonsense. I did not force it. I carried the ribbon in both hands like it might break and walked to the empty patch of floor where a real house would have put a hearth. I laid the ribbon down there instead of placing it anywhere fancy. No frame. No bowl. Just bare wood, open space on all sides, the way you set down something alive and step back so it can choose a direction.

"You can rest," I said. No names. No dates. No deals.

Heat moved along the boards underneath my fingers, faint and steady, like sun stored in stone. The vent's note wobbled and dipped, thinner than it had been. The cradle shoved once at the spoon, then settled because the wedge refused to move. The rocker creaked one last time, like an old man grumbling, and then quieted. The air in the room stopped feeling like someone else's hands on my ribs.

The midwife shifted. It was not dramatic. The tightness in her shoulders eased. Her chin tipped toward the ceiling in that exhausted way people have when the worst of a shift is over. Her eyes went to my hands, then to the sampler, then to the blank hearth spot. It was a whole conversation without words. Keep using your hands. Watch what you say.

One of the little gowns on the peg rail still showed that damp oval on the chest, the not-quite-mouth mark that refused to act like a regular stain. While I stared at it, it looked wet. When I deliberately turned my head, following the lullaby back toward the vent, the edges of the oval lightened, like something drying in slow motion. When I glanced back, it darkened again, as if someone had breathed on the fabric. I decided to let it do whatever it was going to do without my help. Not everything needed my eyes on it to heal.

The House tried another angle. The window stopped pretending to open onto blank wall and, for a second, turned into a screen. A thin man in a clerk's shirt stood inside the glass, not outside the house, not in the room with me, but hanging in the pane like a reflection from the wrong world. He held a folded paper with a seal in one corner, edges sharp like legal stock. His mouth formed the words I had already heard him try. You dropped something. On the line where a mother's name should go, my name sat in somebody else's handwriting. The month listed underneath was not one I had lived through yet. I kept my gaze on the floorboards and watched the grain instead. In the corner of my eye, the clerk thinned and drifted, and the paper at the sill browned, flaked, and turned into nothing but grit.

The lullaby made a real push then. It came from the vent, from the window, from the rocker's joints, all slightly out of sync, like listening to the same song on two different radios in different rooms. My body wanted to find the middle and line up. I kept my count. In for four. Hold for four. Out for six. The tune hunted for my breath and kept landing just short. The baseboards knocked now and then, the boiler's rhythm reaching up through the walls, but it stayed background noise for the moment. I logged it under "future problems" and kept my lungs on my side.

That was the turning point. That was the moment where everything that could try to move me had already tried.

I stepped up on the rocker seat and braced one hand lightly on the plaster beside the vent grille, careful not to touch the metal itself. Warm air brushed over my knuckles, carrying the faint smells of vinegar and cold grease, like a kitchen after a long day with the windows shut. I exhaled right at the vent, long and steady, and then did it again. And again. After a few rounds, the vent's note wobbled, tried to blend with me, and kept ending up flat. Eventually it sagged into nothing more than air moving through a hole.

The midwife pushed herself to her feet, slowly and fully this time. It looked exactly like watching a tired woman stand up from a chair. She did not come over. Her eyes went to the peg rail, now missing its ribbon. Then to the ribbon lying on the floor by the imaginary hearth. Then to the sampler and its flowers. Then she sat again, easing down with a breath that sounded like something finally finishing.

The rocker tried one last time to be the star of the show. The lullaby dropped out of the vent and into the rails. The creak tried to line up with its own version of the tune, like the chair was getting ready to sing harmony. I gave it one good shove, sent it swinging higher and quicker than it wanted to, then stopped it hard mid-swing with my hand. The crack of the rails snapping back to stillness rang off the walls. After that, the creak was just wood.

The window glass pulled one more sad little trick. The clerk came back holding something smaller this time. A hospital bracelet, white plastic turned gray by time, too long for a newborn, too short for anyone grown. My brother's name sat on it in lettering that nearly matched my mother's hand, but not quite. The "C" in Cross looked right. The rest did not. As soon as my brain recognized what it was supposed to be, the bracelet dulled, frayed, and slipped out of sight like someone had dropped it into deep water.

The room finally started feeling like just a room again. Warmth rose in a faint line where a real hearth would have been built. The tag on the ribbon stopped twitching. When I looked at it sideways the letters held clear for one inhale, then relaxed into blur again, like the house was giving me the chance to choose not to know. If I wanted that name, I was going to have to go over there and pick it up myself. That would make it mine. I left it where it was.

"Not singing," I said, out loud this time, so the room could not pretend it had misheard me. "Not holding."

The reply came from small things. Dust at the thresholds shifted, pulled away from the cradle instead of toward it. The dark oval on the tiny gown dried from the outside in and stopped just shy of vanishing, leaving a faint mark like a scar that had decided to be honest instead of dramatic. The vent's tune thinned into plain air movement. The hum in the baseboards kept going, steady and low, but it felt structural now, like part of the bones of the house, not like fingers on my lungs. The midwife rested with her hands folded and her eyes on the ceiling, the way you sit when you are listening for trouble in another room and not hearing it.

Near her chair, a scrap of thermal paper stuck out from the gap between the baseboard and the floor. I bent and worked it loose. Same hand, same heavy pencil lines, same stubborn intent. If it asks you to carry, make it carry air. J. L. at the bottom in small, plain letters. My chest hurt for one solid beat. I folded the note and slid it in with the others. Paper against paper. Small things against larger ones.

Before I stepped out, I went around and opened every little door again. Wardrobe, built-in, the shallow cupboard that had pretended to be wall until I found its edge. None of them hid anything new, but the air shifted in tiny ways every time one opened. Pressure eased. The room felt less clenched. The cradle stayed where it was. The rocker looked like what it was. The sampler stayed flowers. The midwife watched me with that steady, tired focus people use when they are making sure you remember the exit is behind you.

At the threshold I glanced into the glass, but I looked at my own reflection instead of waiting for tricks. I did not see a woman who had been singing to anybody. I saw a woman who had been working through a list. That was important.

The narrow panel door stood open onto a side hall I had not walked yet. The air there had a different feel, less haunted and more practical. Hot dust, warmed pipes, the steady hum of something that burned fuel and turned it into heat. A pencil arrow on the baseboard pointed down that hall, left stroke longer, point sharp. Same wrist as J. L.'s notes, stubborn right to the end. It felt like someone had stood where I was and decided to leave a sign for whoever came next.

I left every door in the nursery open behind me. I took the little wooden block from the rocker, because wedges were turning out to be more useful than any charm. The spoon stayed under the cradle runner. It was still on duty. I was not going to take away the only guard in this house that never asked me for anything.

The lullaby did not follow me out. It did not even try. Without my breathing to latch onto, it had nothing to work with. The nursery breathed on its own. The midwife sat her invisible shift. The tiny gown on the peg rail stayed dry.

I stepped into the side hall and let the new hum under my feet announce the next part. The boiler waited where the plaque said it would wait. I put my hand on the stair rail and felt how solid the wood was. That helped. If I was going to step down into the organ room of a house that thought it fed everyone here, I wanted at least one ordinary thing holding me up.

BACK AT THE NURSERY threshold, the limewashed walls held that same faint chill, the same bright, careful stillness, like the room had been dusted and then told to behave. The cradle sat motionless with the spoon wedged under its runner. The rocker looked patient and old, too quiet, like it was waiting to see if I would change my mind and use it. The vent above the chair hummed its low, wrong note, just enough off that it made my teeth want to clench. The lullaby was not a song anymore. It was a habit hiding in a single pitch.

I stayed standing. That was rule one. I put my fingers on the back rail of the rocker again, close enough to feel the smooth grain, not enough to let it claim my weight. The wood had that shine that comes from years of being a handhold for people who needed something to hang on to. The chair read my posture like it was waiting for a cue, ready to match me if I let it. I did not. I kept my knees loose, my shoulders unlocked, my breathing mine. In for four. Hold for four. Out for six. The vent listened and tried to slip into my rhythm, but it stayed a half step off, the way a bad karaoke singer always misses the note no matter how hard they try.

The index card in my pocket rasped against the lining when I shifted. I could feel the little stack of rules like a solid, square spot over my ribs. Break rhythms. Keep your breath. Do not describe the noise. Open every door. Do not carry what it hands you. Make it carry air. I whispered them once, more to remind my body than the House. They sat in my mouth like a coin. Useful. Heavy. Hard to swallow by accident.

I moved through the room and opened everything that could open. The wardrobe door creaked a complaint and then swung wide. Inside, folded baby clothes sat in neat stacks that felt more like props than possessions. The built-in cabinet's latch stuck for a second and then gave, revealing shelves lined with cloth, pins, little jars, tiny tools that had not been touched in longer than my parents had been alive. Each time a door opened, the air shifted along my wrists, small currents pulling toward the new gap, like the room exhaled in installments. Dust along the floor stirred and drifted toward the hall. It looked like stitches getting picked out of a hem.

The House noticed. Of course it did. The rocker creaked a little louder, trying to offer me its rhythm in a more obvious way, like a host patting the only empty seat in the room. The vent warmed up its note and, for two breaths in a row, it matched me exactly. The sound had my cadence, my timing, even the way my breathing sometimes hitches when I am trying not to cry. My throat wanted to fix the flat note, wanted to sing the lullaby right, because that is what you do when a song lands crooked. I let the urge sit there and did not give it a voice.

The midwife shifted in her chair, the bare minimum it took to unfold her hands. The red skin on her wrists looked angry and used. She did not look at my face; she looked at my hands, then at the sampler, then at the blank spot where a hearth would be. Her attention felt like directions. Put your effort there, not where the House wants you.

I went to the peg rail and took the ribbon down again. The tag fought my focus, letters sliding and jittering when I tried to pin them in place. From the corner of my eye, they behaved, forming something that might have been a name if I had been willing to read it. I was not. I cupped the ribbon in both palms and carried it back to the same hearth-spot on the floor, laying it there like I was putting down something breakable that needed to be exactly where it was.

"You can rest," I said, same words as before, steady and simple. No story attached.

The warmth in the boards spread out from my hands, a faint line that ran toward that invisible hearth, then out under the cradle and into the corners. The vent's tune cracked a little, dropping flatter. The cradle shuddered once against the wedge and quit like it had been reminded that there were limits now. The rocker creaked twice in protest, as if the chair itself thought I was being rude, then quieted.

The lullaby tried a different tactic. Instead of meeting my breath head on, it came at me from the side, vent to window to rocker, out of sync with itself. The sound bounced around the room like two phones on speaker playing the same call. I planted my feet and kept my count. In for four. Hold. Out for six. I let my body own the beat. The song hunted for it and kept missing. The baseboards throbbed with the deeper hum from below, but it was not in time with my lungs anymore. That mattered.

The sampler jumped like it wanted to be dramatic about it. Letters splashed across the linen so fast the thread looked like water, forming and unforming in a blur. I refused to lean closer. I let my eyes hit it only at the end of breaths. A first name arranged itself again, careful stitches fighting a shaking hand. Elenor. I did not chase the last name. It rose and faded back into flowers almost in the same moment. That was fine. Names do not need my tongue to exist.

The rocker, annoyed that I had not used it, tried to move without my help. The creak had a new pattern now, a more deliberate rhythm, like somebody tapping a beat on a table. I gave in just enough to set it rocking once, twice, and then caught it on the forward swing with my hand, hard enough to slam it still. The crack of wood landing startled me in a good way. It made me jump out of the lullaby's timing and back into my own.

The clerk made his move again. The window showed wall for a heartbeat, then shifted. He appeared like a reflected person in the corner of my eye, wearing that same neat shirt and blank name tag. This time he held a smaller document, something with boxes and lines, the size and shape of a birth certificate or maybe discharge papers. You dropped something, his mouth shaped. On the line where my mother's name should have gone, mine sat in tidy letters. Below that, a date that belonged to a month that had not happened yet. I kept my gaze on the rocker arm under my hand. In the glass, the paper yellowed at the edges and then powdered into dust. The clerk's outline thinned and dissolved back into a reflection that could have been anything.

Half the fight in this room was not letting the House talk me into naming things. The other half was refusing the props.

The vent's note wavered one more time, then sank into the background. It still hummed, but now it sounded like any old duct in an old house. Not special. Not magical. Just air going where the heat told it to go. The cradle sat steady on its wedge. The rocker creaked once, a regular, boring furniture noise, then nothing.

The middle part of the work was done. The part where the House tried all its tricks at once and found out I was not interested in being a stage.

I climbed up on the rocker seat again, balancing one hand on the plaster near the vent, careful not to grip the grille. The warm air pushed around my fingers, nothing more than moving heat now. Vinegar, cold fat, old smoke. Kitchen ghosts, not personal ones. I exhaled long and steady, let the breath ride right into the vent, then did it again and again until it felt like the ductwork had no choice but to take the rhythm I was giving it. My lungs were not there to carry the room. The room could carry my exhale and like it.

The midwife finally stood all the way, not the half-lift of someone clinching a decision, but the real thing. Her weight shifted, skirt falling back into the shape it must have had when she walked these floors alive. She did not approach me. She scanned the room instead. Peg rail. Ribbon on the floor. Sampler with flowers. Hearth spot with invisible warmth. Vent going quiet. Then she sat again, settling into the chair with a breath that sounded like she had been waiting a long time to hear the room sound like this.

The lullaby tried one more time to live inside the rocker. The creak took on that almost-singing rhythm again, the rails and joints trying to rise and fall in something like tune. I did not let it go on long. One smooth push sent it swinging in a pattern that made no musical sense at all. I stopped it hard, hand braced on the arm, so the sudden stillness hit like a door slamming. The sound bounced off the walls and came back clean. After that, the chair stayed still when I left it alone.

In the window, the clerk switched tactics. He flashed another item at the edge of the glass. This time it was a hospital bracelet, the cheap plastic kind, slightly too long for a newborn, a little too short for an adult wrist. My brother's name was printed there in letters that mimicked my mother's handwriting, close but not exact. The C in Cross had the right loop. The rest felt wrong. As soon as my brain recognized what it was supposed to be, the bracelet grayed out, frayed at the edges, and vanished from the pane.

The air in the room changed, small and real. Heat crawled along the floorboards from the imaginary hearth. The tag on the ribbon lay still. When I glanced at it sideways, the letters held clear just long enough for me to know I could read them if I wanted to. I did not want to. If I picked that name up, it would be mine. The House would not own it anymore. Right now, it was better to let it lie there midway between us.

"Not singing," I said again, because there is power in repetition. "Not holding."

Dust along the thresholds, which had been pulling toward the cradle the whole time, finally shifted in the other direction and forgot the habit. The stain on the tiny gown dried into a lighter shadow, like the memory of a touch instead of the touch itself. The vent sounded like any old vent. The baseboard hum stayed, but it felt less like fingers on my ribcage and more like the regular throb of infrastructure. The midwife put her hands back in her lap, eyes turned toward the ceiling in that way you see in waiting rooms, listening for trouble and hearing none for the first time in a long time.

I spotted another piece of thermal paper at the edge of the room, half-hidden where wood met wall. I crouched, pinched it out, and flattened it between my fingers. If it asks you to carry, make it carry air. J. L. again. The same hand that had drawn the arrow in the hall. I folded the note and put it with the others. It felt right having them all together. Little rules from people who had done their own hard work down here.

I took one more lap around the room, double checking every door. Wardrobe open. Built-in open. Small cupboard open. The panel that had concealed the side hall still ajar. Every opening changed the airflow just a little more, turning the room from a closed loop into a space things could move through. The cradle stayed quiet. The rocker stayed put. The sampler stayed flowers. The midwife watched me go with the calm patience of someone who has finally seen people leave the room without carrying extra weight.

At the threshold I let myself look directly into the glass. My reflection stood there, not stretched or blurred, just me. No song in my face, no hollow eyes, no haunted tilt. I looked like a woman who had followed a checklist. That was better than any other version I could have imagined.

The little panel door that led to the side hall gaped in the wall like a secret passage revealed in a kid's mystery book. The air beyond it had that hot metal smell of boiler rooms and utility closets. A simple hum ran along the baseboard, steady and uninterested in drama. A pencil arrow pointed the way down, drawn in a hand that had been tired and clear-headed at the same time. I could almost picture J. L. kneeling here, pencil in hand, making sure the arrow would outlive them.

I left every door open behind me. I took the rocker block, solid in my palm. The spoon stayed under the cradle, doing its job. The lullaby did not try to follow. It could not. There was nothing in me left for it to match.

The side hall's hum waited. The boiler room waited. I put my hand on the stair rail and felt the weight of my own body settle into the wood. The house thought it fed everyone who crossed this threshold. It was already deciding how it wanted to feed me. I was going to have a say in that.

THE SIDE HALL HAD the feel of a service hallway in an old school or hospital. Narrow floorboards. Paint thicker here from years of touch-ups, layer over layer. The air moved in one clear direction, from behind me toward whatever waited at the far end. The hum in the baseboard rolled along beside me, steady and low, like a generator running in the next room. It was the most honest sound I had heard in this house.

Behind me, the nursery held steady. Every door I had opened stayed open, no quiet clicks trying to close them when I looked away. The ribbon lay on the floor beside the pretend hearth. The sampler stayed flowers. The midwife sat her post in a way that looked less like being trapped and more like finally being allowed to sit. I left the spoon where it was, wedged under the cradle. I had no intention of removing the one piece of hardware in this place that refused to negotiate.

At the doorway, I pulled the index card out of my pocket again, even though I could have recited the lines in my sleep. Break rhythms. Keep your breath. Do not describe the noise. Open every door. Do not accept returns. Do not let other people name it for you. On the back, in smaller letters but harder pencil, my newest rule waited. Do not carry what it hands you. Make it carry air. I read them all twice and put the card back, pressing it flat against the notes from M. E. and J. L.

The arrow on the baseboard pointed down the hall, left stroke longer than the right, the point dark from a pencil that had been pressed too hard. The graphite sat in the brush strokes like it had been there for years. J. L.'s wrist, tired and careful. I ran two fingers along the paint just beside the mark, enough to feel the ridge of it without smearing anything.

After about three paces the smell shifted. The lemon cleaner faded, and the hot, dry scent of warmed wood and metal took over. Under that, a wet iron smell floated up from below, the particular scent of old water sitting in pipes that have just been told to wake up. The wall on my right held a small, chipped wooden sign at shoulder height, the word Boiler painted on it in blocky letters. Whoever had lettered it had not cared about style. They had cared about being understood by tired people on stairs.

The door under the sign was hardly a door at all, more of a hatch. The frame had sunk and been forced back into square at least twice in its life. The latch gleamed where countless hands had grabbed it. I slid the wedge block I was carrying under the nursery-side door to keep it propped. The instant both doorways were truly open, the air moved better. A soft pressure eased off my ears. The hum under the floor dropped a note, adjusted, and kept going.

I put my hand on the boiler latch and did not lift it right away. I listened. Sound from the other side came in layers. A deep steady vibration that belonged to a big tank. Lighter taps where pipes expanded and contracted. The occasional dull knock of old metal changing temperature. None of that sound was trying to line up with my breathing yet. Good. I opened the hatch a little and let warm air roll out, thick and dry and slightly dusty, like a basement that has never really cooled down.

Stairs dropped away steep and narrow, the steps cut short, as if the people who had built this part of the house had been shorter than me or just cheap with lumber. A simple rail had been bolted into the wall, sturdy and plain. I put my hand on it and tested my weight. It held like it meant it.

I went down two steps and paused. In for four. Hold for four. Out for six. I walked the breathing pattern into my body again before I went any further. Then I stepped back up one stair, just to prove to myself and the House that direction was mine to choose. The hum stayed where it was. It did not chase my heart rate the way the lullaby had. That felt like another small victory.

At shoulder level on the wall, pencil marks notched the paint in a vertical line, the way people mark kids' heights over the years. Alongside each notch were initials instead of ages. M. E. appeared several times, at different heights. J. L. showed up lower, once, with a notch that looked like the last effort of a shaking hand. A third set of initials I did not know made a single mark and then never appeared again. There were no dates, only labels. Pantry. Parlor. Nursery. The last box beside them was blank except for the word Boiler, printed faintly as if waiting to be traced over. I did not give it my initials. I knew exactly what it meant to let a house keep your name on a list like that.

I slid the wedge all the way under the hatch so the door could not swing back down on me by surprise. Air from the nursery and the hall flowed down past my legs, cool mixing with warm. Dust lifted in thin lines along the baseboard and drifted toward the opening, like stitches unraveling. The pressure in the stairwell settled into something that felt normal, or at least familiar.

The hum tried one little trick. At the top of each inhale, it seemed to rise half a beat, nudging my lungs to follow its timing. I felt the push and answered by extending my exhale, making the out-breath longer and heavier than the in. The hum fell behind. It did not change tactics. The rail stayed solid under my palm. The wood, at least, had made its choice about who it was going to support.

Halfway down, another smell layered in on top of the hot dust and metal. Cooked plastic. Old wire insulation. That faintly sour tang that means a breaker has been stressed more than once. Somewhere below me, there were panels and switches and labels, and I could feel, in the same way I had felt the clerk's glass, that the House wanted to walk me through them. It wanted me to pick what each control meant and name the dangers for it so it would not have to.

I stood still on the step and let that idea cool down until it no longer felt persuasive. Labels have power when you say them out loud. Maps matter when you agree they are true. I had walked through too many rooms in this place already, letting it show me how it saw things. Down here, I was not accepted as a tourist. I was a potential operator. I did not owe the House that job.

Above me, wood creaked once. Not the rocker. This was the sound of the midwife's chair shifting weight. The noise was small but distinct, like someone adjusting themselves to keep listening. The nursery stayed quiet. No crying. No rocking. Just that sense of someone waiting to see what I would do next.

I flattened my palm over the nearest stair post and felt the wood grain run under my hand. "My name is Riley Cross," I said, the same way I would have said it to a bored intake worker behind bulletproof glass. "I will not sing. I will not hold." No drama, no shout, just facts stated for the record.

The hum did not drop, but it stopped feeling like it was flexing against my ribs. It became what it should have been all along, the sound of a big mechanical thing doing its job somewhere below.

On the riser in front of me, another pencil arrow pointed down, smaller than the one in the hall but shaped the same. The point was darker, the graphite dug deeper into the paint and the wood beneath it. Beside it, J. L. had squeezed in one more line in tiny, stubborn handwriting. Hums like a vent. Do not sing along. The pencil strokes had cut into the grain. I tapped the mark once with my fingertip, an acknowledgment, then lifted my hand before the gesture turned into anything ritualistic.

I went down two more steps and paused. Then back up one. If the House wanted me to rush, it could wait. The midwife did not call. The nursery stayed open and bright behind me, doors propped, air flowing.

I leaned into the rail for real then, trusting it, and started down into the boiler room. The hum grew louder, the hot dry smell of machinery wrapped around me, and the rules card pressed against my ribs like a second spine. The House believed it fed everyone under this roof. Deep down here, it wanted me to agree. I was going to find out what "feeding" meant on its terms and then decide how much of that I was willing to let it have.

Chapter 7
BREATHING BELOW

THE HATCH LIFTED ON a breath that belonged to heat. The air that rolled up was the kind that never cools, old brick warmed so long it had started to think it was its own little sun. I set the block under the hatch and waited through a full count to see if the door meant to pick up any tricks while I watched. It did not. The hinge clicked once and settled. I took the first two steps down and let the handrail tell me if it was going to hold. It did.

The heat tried to climb into my lungs and set the tempo. The first inhale came short, because that is what rooms like this want, the thin top of your lungs where panic sits. I flipped the habit without asking anyone's permission. In for two. Out for six. Long, not deep. The air went out of me like water poured slow from a pitcher. It kept my chest from grabbing at the room. The next breath came up short again on reflex. I fixed it. Long exhale. Long inhale. The count laid a plank across the top of the heat and gave my body something solid to walk on.

Bricks crowded in closer as the stairs turned. The boiler sat in its pit like something that had gotten used to being worshipped, new steel dropped into old walls, a skin and a skeleton from two different centuries. The sightlines bent and lied the way fever lies, stretching the back wall farther away when I looked at a dial, squeezing it closer when I blinked. Pipes ran out of the top like a rack of ribs, all of them sweating, all of them labeled in a neat little hand I did not trust.

RETURN JOY. CARRY LOAD. RELIEF. STREET. BREATH.

83

The gauge closest to my shoulder twitched. The needle did not move up or down. It jittered sideways in tiny nervous kisses, as if it were trying to write something that was not there. R C. The needle snapped back to zero and stayed there, almost shy. In the narrow sight glass below it, the water line showed a stripe of bubbles and, for one beat, the blurry shape of a baby hand. When I blinked it was only foam and air.

"Of course," I said, and that was all I gave it. Talking is a tool. You do not hand over a tool unless you are sure you are going to need it back.

I crouched and reached for the floor with the back of my hand. Low brick keeps an honest temperature when metal has reasons to lie. Warm, not burning. Safe to kneel. I traced the main line out of the top of the boiler with my eyes first, then with my hand hovering just above the pipe, an inch off the steel, feeling for the kind of heat that teaches you a lesson you remember forever. My fingers learned what the labels refused to admit. BREATH was the feed. STREET bled off to outside. RELIEF was the only valve with a cage. Someone had painted that cage the cheerful safety-poster kind of red. That did not make it honest.

A pencil tapped above the burner inside the sheet-metal shroud. Three beats. Pause. Three beats. The Auditor had found a duct down here too. I ignored the rhythm and flattened my palm on the brick so my skin could cool before it started pretending to blister.

I pulled the card from my pocket to read the rules out loud, because saying them had been working. The paper gave way between my fingers, soggy from sweat, breaking down into pulp that smelled like skin salt and pencil lead. Graphite smeared across my palm, a little gray map that meant nothing. If I were a different kind of person, I might have cried from how small and stupid that felt. Instead I rolled the wet mess into a ball the size of a cough drop and set it on a hot pipe so it would dry down into a husk I would not be tempted to touch again.

The J. L. note had pulled in damp along the corners, but the ink still held. The words were clear in the firm hand that had written them out three times to make sure they lasted. If it asks you to carry, make it carry air. I slid the note inside my shirt, where my ribs would keep it flat against me. The diary on the hall shelf had carried the same kind of warnings. Do not ring. Do not describe. If you must sign, sign only your name. Mara's rules had gotten me this far, but they read different down here, in front of a machine that would happily cook a person and call it a lesson. Instructions can be a kindness, or they can be the long way around to the edge of a hole. If the only end of the path is a fall, then the person who drew the map is not on your side.

"Noted," I said to nobody in particular, and got to work.

A valve inside the red cage twitched a quarter turn on its own. RELIEF, said the placard. Helpful like an unfamiliar hand on your back at the top of a staircase. The hiss that followed had the sound of something getting ready to go bad. I wedged the little rocker block into the cage door so it could not swing shut and slipped in sideways, shoulder and hip, the way you slide around a car with the hood up while the fan is still going. A rag hung from a nail, left behind by some earlier caretaker who had decided to be kind. I draped it over the valve wheel to kill the shine. The metal under my fingers felt wrong for a pressure release. Too cool. The real feed sat one pipe over, unmarked steel with a wheel worn matte by hands and years. I turned that wheel one notch and stopped.

That became the new rule, because you learn rules one at a time, down here.

Change one thing, then wait.

Waiting in a hot room is its own kind of test. The dial shivered. The sight glass settled. The hiss did not build. I marked the wheel's position with the bolt I had picked up off the floor earlier, a rough scrape of dirty metal against dirty metal. That mark belonged to me. The room could paint over it later. It was not going to while I was watching.

The emergency cord hung from the ceiling in a cute little loop that had once been a perfect circle and had sagged with age. The placard above it read PULL ONLY WHEN READY TO WALK IN THE DARK. The red paint had faded toward sidewalk chalk pink around the edges. The cord hummed when I touched it, like a bug was living under the braid. It ran over to a lever across the way, with a black bakelite handle and a stamped plate that dried my mouth out just to read.

BREATH.

Three screw heads held the plate in place, painted over so many times the slots were ghosts. Nobody wanted this to be simple.

On the far wall, a diagram was trying to pull itself together. Lines lifted out of the paint and arranged into tidy boxes with little labels. Ease. Burden. Green. Joy. None of those words had ever carried current. I kept my back to that drawing and listened instead. Real load sings in plain sounds. A clean sixty-cycle buzz in one panel. A flatter, off note along the return path. The wrong hum was the House. The right one belonged to the parts a person could actually fix.

I mapped what I could with heat and sound, and what I could not I mapped with distance, counting the space between things and then counting again with my eyes closed to see if the numbers stayed the same. Twelve steps from the hatch to the main. Seven from the main to the mouth of a concrete throat that led away into cinderblock and painted lines and whatever lies this place told when it wanted company. I took the bolt and scratched those numbers into the brick at knee level so I could find them again by touch instead of sight. "Count steps, not doors," I said out loud, because putting it in the air laid down a track for later, when the room would be loud and I would need to hear myself.

Condensation kept trying to write messages on the pipes while I moved, little half-words smeared onto hot steel with a fingertip of water that boiled away before they meant anything. I saw my last name once in the curve of an O that leaned toward a C, then decided I had not seen it. Above the burner, the pencil kept its rhythm long enough to be funny and then cut off. The silence inside the shroud rang.

The diary in the hall had an entry about the basement that came off like a dare. Hate this part of the house. Soon as I located the breaker I reset and went back upstairs. Note to self, send an electrician next time. Someone could follow that advice straight to their last day. Reset and go upstairs. Leave the machine humming a tune that matches your lungs and let it kill you slow. It was not a manual for staying alive. It was a list of ways to die gradually and call it courage. The House had been chewing on that kind of bravery for years.

"Not a martyr," I said, and found the conduit that led toward the panels. The painted cinderblock throat that took the wires away was ten degrees cooler. Stale cold breathed against my shins. Stencils on the wall pointed both directions. STREET, arrowed left and right. RECORDS twice, one of them with a crooked R. COMFORT marching straight ahead into the dark. Three colored lines ran on the floor in the kind of logic hospitals use when they think color will save people. Red, yellow, green. Green went both ways and doubled back near my boot without ever admitting it had turned.

I stood at the mouth and let my body remember the heat behind me, the hum of it, the surfaces I had already touched and could find again if I had to. I laid my palm against the wall and glanced at the graphite smeared on my skin. The words had turned to bruised shapes. They would not last. That was fine. If I could not keep four rules in my head without a card, I had no business going where I was going.

New rules, said in my own voice so the House could not claim I borrowed them:

Breathe long, not deep.
Test with the back of the hand.
Change one thing, then wait.
Count steps, not doors.

The cord behind me hummed like a live animal at the end of a leash. The bakelite handle waited with the calm of something that would never move by accident. I would deal with it when my feet knew the way back in the dark. I slid the bolt into my pocket and stepped into the throat.

Heat at my back. Stale cold ahead. The House had started labeling everything because labels make people feel safer than they are. I kept my hand on the brick and counted under my breath. Twelve to the main. Seven to the turn. I did not look back. The diary did not have a page for this. Good. I did not want it coaching me on how to fail politely.

Behind me, the boiler settled a pocket of steam somewhere deep and sighed. Above me, the house that pretended to be mine listened hard to see if I would start to sing. I filled my lungs just enough to keep moving and let the rest of the air belong to itself.

THE CORRIDOR TOOK THE heat in my back and turned it into a story I had already heard once. Cold, old and stale, breathed out in front of me. The cinderblock walls sweated the way walls do when somebody has trained them to keep secrets. Three stripes ran along the floor, red, yellow, green. The green one forked and doubled and turned until it brought itself back to my boot like it had never gone anywhere. The thin echo of my footsteps bounced back, cheap and hollow, and tried to pass itself off as directions.

The lights flickered in their own little pattern. One, two, three, dark. One, two, three, dark. They wanted my eyelids to fall into step. I picked a slower rhythm and stayed with it. The dizziness slid off by half. Rhythm is a mouth. It eats whatever you feed it.

Panels lined both walls, close enough that I could have touched metal on both sides and pretended I was being held by something. There were no circuit numbers. Just stamped steel with room names from different decades. PARLOR. PANTRY. NURSERY. RECORDS. STREET. HALL. SLEEP. A smaller faceplate at eye level read EVAN in tidy letters that sat a little crooked on the screws. The metal behind that one hummed like a stage amp. The cover was colder than the wall. Cold is a tell when the rest of the room is warm. Not mine.

Another schematic was crawling into being near the ceiling, still arguing with itself about what to call things. Lines sharpened into ladders with steps and little landings. Ease. Burden. Green. Joy. The font was that friendly print you see on insurance forms. I turned my back on it and listened instead.

Real load sings at a true sixty. The air handed me two different choirs. One with steady, clean pitch, work actually being done. One a half step flat, the House humming under its breath in a wire coat. I crouched and set my knuckles near each panel seam, one at a time, left hand tucked behind my back the way you do when you do not want a shock crossing your chest. Warm faces with real load. Cold faces with the House's full attention. I followed the clean buzz until I found RECORDS. Its handle sat full on. The flat choir hid in there like a radio tuned just wrong.

"Do not carry," I told my hand, not the hallway, and pulled the handle down. A damper somewhere in the duct above me sighed. Upstairs, the friendly voice on the office printer cut off mid-pitch and the fake lemon in the air thinned down to real dust. The flat hum clinging to that panel peeled back like a note somebody finally stopped holding.

The pushback came right away. Two EXIT signs woke up at opposite ends of the aisle and glowed a believable red. They asked me very politely to trust them. I looked at the one on the left, then the one on the right. The left exit took two steps backward every time my eyes went to it. The right stayed put. I dropped the bolt on the floor and scraped a long mark toward the right exit, kneeling on concrete, the sound too loud in the tight space. I stepped around the painted lines. If there were marks down here, they were going to be mine.

A damp gray patch spread across the concrete under SLEEP. The panel itself was warm in a mild way. The handle sat halfway out of its slot, like a choice that never quite finished. When I got close, the lights rolled forward and went black in a wave. The two separate hums leaned together and turned into one long, ugly chord. Conduit popped and settled like teeth closing. I pressed my back to the wall and recited in a voice I kept small on purpose, not from fear. "Count steps, not doors. Twelve to the brick. Seven back." I found the handle by feel and shoved it fully off with the bolt. No half states. The blackout paused like indecision hurt. Then the emergency strips lit up again and went right back to their little pattern. One, two, three, dark. I let my eyelids do whatever they wanted. I did not match them.

The EVAN panel tried a sweeter hum when I went by. The painted nameplate flaked under the kind of breath I did not give it. Under the chipped paint, the metal tag actually read EVENT. Cold air seeped from the seam. I pressed my palm to the brick below and felt it hold me up without asking for anything in return.

"Not mine," I said, and kept walking.

The graphite from the ruined card still stained my palm. The words I had written there were already fading toward bruise colors. BREATHE LONG. BACK OF HAND. CHANGE ONE, WAIT. COUNT STEPS. I pressed my thumb over each line, then took the bolt and traced them darker right into my skin. It hurt. Pain is a kind of ink.

A painted arrow on the floor slid just a fraction along the concrete while I watched it. I focused on the noise instead. The steady sixty-cycle at the STREET panel, the thinner off note twined through it, trying to convince the real load it had company. I shut STREET off at the subfeed. Somewhere far above, a crosswalk chirp cut out in the middle of a fake bird call, saving a pedestrian who did not exist. The little sound the kids used as a game had been coming from my wire. The House had been using it to get my rhythm. Not anymore.

The hallway tried to redraw itself with light. The strips went out of sync. The green floor line bent up into a loop that crossed right over my scrape mark and tried to cover my line without using paint. I knelt again and used the bolt like a piece of chalk, dragging two more scars into the concrete at an angle that made letters only I would care about. R for return. C for count. They looked like the gauge needle had looked when it spelled my initials and then pretended it had not.

Around one bend, a conduit sat at head height with a bare nick in its insulation where a metal strap had bitten in. The air around it prickled with static waiting to go somewhere. I turned sideways and ducked under it, palm on the brick, head down, mouth shut. Whatever I would have said in that moment would have been the wrong word, and the House would have kept it.

At the end of a short side run, a floor chase lay open. The dust inside had its own swirling weather. A pencil stub lay there, chewed until the wood looked like teeth marks. Next to it, a scrap of paper no bigger than a matchbook carried a single line in tight, serious writing. Boiler + Street + Records, then Breath. The letters had been pressed so hard they cut the fibers. M. E., maybe. Or J. L. The pencil snapped between my fingers when I tried to lift it. The scrap tore and the half with the important words slipped under the metal lip, into a slot too narrow for my hand. I held onto the useless half until the heat curled it like a leaf, then let it go. Notes are a trick when the place they live in uses them as props. I had already done two of the three things that little script was ordering before I ever saw it. That would have to count as faith.

The emergency strips settled into a rhythm that dropped me into shadow every third step. I walked anyway, counting out loud. My voice came back flat and practical. Twelve to the last elbow. Four to the wide bay. The hum shifted shape the way a body does when it takes a breath it did not really want. The caged lever waited on a small stand painted the same washed-out red as the cord. BREATH was stamped on its plate in letters that had lost their crisp edges under too many coats of paint. The three screws holding the plate down were buried in layers. The cord from the boiler looped up and over a pulley and down to this, braided and neat, humming under my hand like it had its own ideas about timing.

The placard above the stand was written in the same heavy capital letters as the old signs elsewhere in the house. PULL ONLY IF YOU CAN WALK TO LIGHT WITH EYES CLOSED. The word ONLY had been underlined twice, and then again later, darker, by somebody with a different pen and a shaky hand. Little ovals from two fingers showed where someone had held the top edge and said the sentence out loud, trying to be sure.

I stood there in the hot mechanical air and watched the lights run through three full cycles without lying to me. I opened every little gate and vent nearby that would move under my hand. One tried to swing back and pretend it had not. I jammed the bolt in as a wedge. Change one thing, then wait. I changed nothing for five long, slow breaths and let the room show me whether it was going to shift. It did not. It wanted to sell me a choice.

For just a blink, the list on my palm looked wrong. The lines had moved. BACK OF HAND had slid to the bottom, BREATHE LONG had climbed up. Maybe it was sweat. Maybe it was the way I had retraced the letters and left graphite free to smear. Maybe the House had learned a new trick and was trying it out on a small scale. I blinked again and the list sat back where I had written it, except the O in LONG looked a little thicker than before.

"Later," I told whatever future version of me was going to check these words and find them scrambled. "Not now." Right now I had heat and a cord and a rule written down by somebody who cared enough to grind that underline into the board.

I wrapped the red cord once around my wrist, a promise to the part of me that wanted to drop everything and run. The braid hummed against my pulse like it knew my heart rate. I tested the bakelite handle with one fingertip. It gave just enough to let me know it would move when I was ready. I picked the dip in the light cycle. I breathed out for six counts and let the air go the way you step into cold water when you have already decided you are doing it. Then I wrapped my hand around the lever and got ready to shut down the breath of a house that had been trying to borrow mine.

I LET ONE WHOLE dark stretch go by just to learn how long it was. One, two, three, gone. The heat leaned in like a big dog that had decided not to bite, just breathe on me until I panicked. I tightened the cord around my wrist, palm down so the braid lay right over the bone. The hum in it climbed up toward my elbow, small and steady. I closed my fingers around the bakelite, breathed out for six until my ribs unclenched, and pulled.

The world did not exactly go off. It folded in. The light disappeared into someplace I did not have access to. Sound flooded in to fill the gap. Steam stretched itself out into one long, aching vowel. Water rushed back into pipes it had been encouraged to leave. Brick snapped and clicked along hairline cracks. The cord burned a neat line around my wrist and then settled. The handle locked down low and stayed there. Nothing triggered. No alarms. No shrieks. Somehow, that was worse.

Panic came up fast, like a hand over my mouth. I answered it with the one thing that had held all day. In for two. Out for six. Long, not deep. There was no outside pitch trying to drag my lungs into rhythm. I supplied my own and held onto it.

I shut my eyes on purpose. The dark you make for yourself is cleaner than the dark a room makes for you. I braced my knuckles against the cinderblock and read my palm with my thumb. The graphite had sunk into the lines of my skin like a map pressed into soft clay. BREATHE LONG. BACK OF HAND. CHANGE ONE, WAIT. COUNT STEPS. I touched each word in turn to make sure it was still in the world in a way I could feel. Then I started walking.

At the second step the floor dropped an inch, as if the room had taken its own breath and forgotten to hand it back. I let my knee bend and took the change as normal ground, not a trick. A warm breath grazed my cheek and vanished. It did not feel human or mechanical, just the space itself expressing a thought. A pipe ticked out four pulses in a row that wanted badly to be a name. I flattened my palm against the wall and counted. Twelve to the elbow. Four to the bay. My boot found the scratched line in the concrete and something in my throat loosened. That ugly mark felt loyal.

Something brushed my calf. Paper-thin, with a crisp little edge, clinging and then letting go. It slid away like a label that had missed what it was meant to claim. I kept my hand on the wall. I did not give it a second touch.

The big hum was gone. No whole-house breath trying to make my lungs match it. Only local sounds were left, making their small, honest truths. The faint sugary tang of hot dust fell out of the air. If the EXIT signs still glowed, I could not see them. The flicker pattern lived only in my memory now. Heel down, roll forward, do not speed up.

At the nicked conduit I ducked on instinct. Cool static nipped the air just above my scalp. The lights did not swoop back on. The schematic on the wall might as well have been a mural of clouds. I found the floor chase again by the gritty air and the thin cold line of the slot at my ankle. Left turn. Four steps. The scratch mark. Seven steps to brick. My shin clipped the wedge block at the base of the hatch and

I made a noise that almost came out as a laugh, and almost as a sob, and finally decided to be just another breath.

Up the narrow stairs, the heat thinned as I climbed, shifting from furnace to bathhouse to that homey warmth that lingers under a stove after dinner. The handrail under my fingers felt like someone else's hand on my arm, steady but not possessive. At the top I shoved the hatch and it opened without drama. The block toppled and skittered away across the floor. The air from the kitchen slid around my shoulders like a shawl still thinking about what color it wants to be.

The ceiling light was out. The window showed a wash of early blue that made the dark soft instead of sharp. The fake lemon smell that had been hanging around all week had faded back to the more honest stink of old smoke. The refrigerator motor did not chew at the quiet. The quiet did not have teeth.

I put the chair back where it belonged, under the pantry knob, without even looking. Its legs dropped into the grooves they had worn in the tile. My hands knew the little twist it took to make the back sit snug against the knob. I kept my eyes off the pantry door. I looked at my palm instead. The words still clung where I had pressed them in, grubby and normal. For one heartbeat they slipped around, BACK OF HAND climbing up, BREATHE LONG dropping down, COUNT STEPS trying to sit first in line like a kid at ballet practice. Sweat, I told myself. Fatigue. When I blinked, they lined up the way I had written them. The O in LONG was definitely thicker.

I crossed the kitchen toward the far wall, ready to lean my shoulder against cool plaster, and found that I did not need the support because the plaster was not cool. The paint had puffed out into a rectangle that did not belong there, the exact proportions of a door panel pressed from underneath. Raised lines I could feel, built by pressure, not brush strokes. In the center, a knot in the old wood bulged in the shape of a knob, about half the size of my fist. It looked exactly like the shape a hand makes inside a wall when it does not want to be moved. The bulge swelled once in a slow inhale and then held. The pantry was not going to be the only door for much longer.

"This is starving," I told the room. It was not a question. Starved things learn how to follow food. Doors are just mouths with hinges if you let them be.

The window brightened by one shade. Down on Weaver, the first truck of the morning took the hill and ground through a gear change. The house pipes did not mimic the sound. The baseboards did not offer me a beat to walk to. I wiped my palm on my shirt and the letters stayed legible. Then I picked up the bolt again, knelt by the pantry molding, and scratched a new sentence into the paint at eye level, where I would see it every day until I packed a truck and left.

Kill and relight in your order.

The tip of the bolt dug through layer after layer of color and bit wood. Paint dust packed under my nails.

I stood up and gave the dark one more line, said the way you say somebody's name at a closed bedroom door when you want them to know you are not going anywhere.

"I will choose the light."

The house did not argue. It did not have to. It had already found a fresh spot to grow a new door. I could feel the wall picking up the idea, the way a sponge soaks up anything you pour on it. I wedged the chair under the pantry more firmly and walked to the window. I stayed there until the sky committed to morning and the glass gave me back the shape of someone who had walked in the dark with her eyes shut and knew she could do it again.

In the hall, somewhere past the shelf where the diary waited, a pencil ticked once and then stopped.

MORNING WORKED ITS WAY in thin and slow, like milk through dusty glass. The fridge stayed quiet. The baseboards did not try to rise and fall with my lungs. I made coffee because rituals give your hands a job and because heat in a mug is an answer your body understands.

Steam fogged the window and then forgot what it had been about. Outside, Weaver Street held onto its gray the way a person holds their breath.

The crosswalk bird stayed silent. The light at the corner flipped through its colors with no sound at all. A truck fought its way uphill and the engine brake laid a long sigh over the rooftops. No other hum reached for me. The silence had weight, but it was good weight, like a blanket. I let it lie over my shoulders and did not ask it how long it planned to stay.

The pantry chair held its post. The back still kissed the knob in that exact way it knew, solid and stubborn. Across the kitchen, the far wall had been busy overnight. The bulge that had been only a hint now had full panel seams pressed up into the paint, raised shapes like a door trying to remember itself. In the middle, the old knot had swelled into the outline of a knob the size of a heart. When I stood close enough to feel my own breath bounce back, the paint was warm under my hand without any shine. That heat was not from the sun. Not at this hour, not on that side of the house. Hungry things move toward whoever feeds them. The House had built itself a new mouth.

I ran cold water over my wrist at the sink. The cord burn circled it in a slim red ring and stung under the tap. The words on my palm blurred in the water, swam, then settled back into focus, shuffled once, then snapped into place. Breathe long. Back of hand. Change one, wait. Count steps. They held like a police lineup. I looked away and back. For one blink they reversed, then went still. Noted. Later. There is only so much structure a person can carry in her head before it starts to bruise.

I went to the hall and picked up Mara's first notebook like it was warm bread. The cover smelled like the house now, soaked clear through. My hand brought it up to my face without thinking. I opened somewhere in the middle and read until the sentences turned on me.

If you must pull the cord, do it at the top of the cycle so you do not fall.
If the dark scares you, pray until it speaks your prayer back to you the right way.

> If your breath gets too big, make it smaller so the room can teach you the right size.

Instructions can be kindness, right up until somebody starts using them to walk you to a hole. This did not feel like survival anymore. It read like choreography for a good death. I shut the book and spread my palm flat over the cover, feeling how thin even a thick journal is when the thing that wants you is a whole house and it wants your body more than it will ever want your thoughts.

On the inside cover, a page had been ripped out by the roots sometime years ago. The ragged edge looked like an uneven coastline. I took a pencil and wrote along the margin where the tear had left room, one line that belonged to my mouth and nobody else's.

> Do not die beautifully.

The pencil bit deep. The words held. Seeing a sentence there that had not come from Mara or the House put a little steel back in my ribs. I slid that notebook to the bottom of the stack so I would have to move weight to get to it next time.

Outside, the scooter kids had gathered at the end of the block. They kicked one foot against the curb and watched the silent traffic light, chins up, brave in that way morning gives everyone for free. The smallest boy caught me in the window and raised his hand. Not a warding gesture this time. Just a wave. I raised mine. The girl made a little rectangle with her fingers like she was framing a door, mime-opened it, then shook her head, like: not yet. Their wheels clacked away over the same cracked line in the sidewalk. The sound had no extra echo hiding inside it. I listened until even that went quiet.

The mailman came early, his safety vest bright as a bad joke against the washed-out sky. He tucked a stack of letters under his arm and shaded his eyes at my house like a person checking for a big dog in a half-fenced yard. When I opened the door he held out a window envelope like it might shake in his hand. Another lawn service flyer. Service postponed, again. Other checked in the reason box, again. The red stamp in the corner had softened under the thumb that hit it every time.

"Sensors are up this way," he said, trying on a smile. "They get jumpy when the street power is off." He looked past my shoulder and then apologized to my shoulder for it. "You got it quiet in there."

"For now," I said, taking the envelope and adding it to the little pile of ignored bright print. He nodded like we had just traded an opinion about the weather and walked on.

I ate toast at the counter and left the plate in the sink without letting that become a new ritual. Words from the diary sat under my line and rubbed at me like sand in a shoe. Pray until it speaks your prayer back the right way. Make your breath the right size. The more I looked at them, the more they felt like a mirror held at a bad angle so you could watch yourself drown and call it grace. I pressed my thumb against the burn at my wrist until the sting washed the sentences clean in my head.

In the dining room, my folder of printouts waited on the table. The Sanborn map slice with the old service lane. The meeting minutes from the clerk's office, with Mara's looped M in the margin. The missing person notice, initials that had a face if you were alive in the right year. All of it felt thinner than it had the day before. If the House wanted me to carry real weight, it was not going to be sheets of paper. It was going to be a door. The bulge in the kitchen wall flexed once and settled, like it agreed.

I took the bolt to the pantry molding where I had carved my new rule last night. In daylight, the letters looked rough and honest. Kill and relight in your order. I set the tip again and added the word I had only said in my head before.

Only.

The paint curled under the metal and peeled back, showing raw wood. The grain ran in little rivers my fingertip followed without thinking. The lines you can trust are the ones you make yourself, with your hands, when your face is not on display.

In the living room I tugged the sheet off the old armchair and let it drop. Dust rose in a soft brown cloud and settled again, like a breath the house did not get to keep. The bay window showed the same old street, plain and small-town. No extra doors. No extra people. The kids' chalk hopscotch grid on the sidewalk had faded to a ghost. I stayed there and watched Weaver Street until the light finally decided to be day and the everyday sounds of a weekday came on one at a time.

In the kitchen, the new panel lines in the paint stayed still while I watched. That was polite. It would not last. I laid my palm against the warm shape and kept it there until my hand learned the truth that warmth is not always an invitation. When I took it away, the knot that wanted so badly to be a knob wore a faint dark ring I did not remember leaving. I wiped at it with a dish cloth. The ring stayed. Heat can write as well as water can.

In the hall, the pencil inside Mara's second notebook tapped once, so soft it could have been my imagination, then went quiet in the way small animals go quiet when they hear a bigger one.

I stood still and let my breath go long, not deep. The quiet settled around me. It felt real enough to trust for an hour.

The card in my pocket was gone. The rules on my palm would fade. The diary would keep offering me pretty little ways to fail. I rinsed my mug, set it upside down on the rack, and told the room, "Not beautifully," because putting the words in the air meant the House could not pretend it had come up with them later.

The far wall did not respond. The paint swelled just a little and went still. The chair leaned into the pantry door like a stubborn friend who refuses to go home. I left both doors alone and went to look for shoes that could handle a whole day in a town that was going to look at me and at my house with the same careful interest they saved for sirens in the middle of the night.

Chapter 8
FALSE EXITS

MY PHONE BUZZES ITSELF across the floor until it taps the baseboard like a stupid little bug. The vibration makes the water glass on my nightstand rattle against the wood. I wake up slow, the way you do after a bath you stayed in too long. My wrist throbs when I reach for the phone, a clean red ring where the cord burned me last night. I smack the alarm off. The silence that follows feels like regular silence again. It has room in it for trucks grinding up the hill, for a dog three houses over to bark a few times and give up, for some bird to decide if sunrise is worth its time. It is not that tight, staged quiet the House likes to press over my ears.

I stay flat on my back and count four slow breaths to remind my ribs they belong to me. Long, not deep. In for two, out for six, until the sting climbs down a notch and turns into something I can just carry around. When I roll my head toward the door, I can see into the kitchen. The chair is still braced under the pantry knob, shoulder-to-shoulder with it like a friend who refuses to move. On the far wall, the paint bulges where it should be flat. It has not grown overnight, but the surface has a soft glow that is not coming from the sun. I know if I went over there and pressed my palm to it, the warmth would meet me like a hand pushing back through a thin door.

The diary is on my bed.

I did not put it there. I remember very clearly how I did not put it there. I shoved it under a stack of other notebooks in the hall, on purpose, to make sure Future Me would have to dig to get at it. Now it sits on the quilt with the ribbon marking some page I have not seen, acting like a cat that wandered in and decided my stomach was home.

There is a faint dust ring on the nightstand in the exact shape of a book. That ring was not there when I set my glass down last night. Books do not get up and walk. Houses do.

I touch the ribbon with two fingers the way you touch a dog's ear when you are not sure if it is in the mood to bite. The fabric is warm. I open the diary where it wants me to open it. This handwriting is not Mara's, and it is not mine. It is clean print, the kind you see on brochures that pretend to be on your side while they steer you into signing something.

> Sing softly until you feel calm.
> Match the nearest steady sound so you can learn the room's mood.
> If your breath grows too large, make it smaller so the room can teach you the right size.

In the margin, thin pen has circled the line I wrote last night, the only one that had felt like it came out of my own bones. Do not die beautifully. Next to it, in that same neat stranger's hand, someone has added: Beautiful deaths are tidy.

I close the book before my hands decide to throw it against the wall. Dust sighs out of the quilt. It smells like old cotton and old wood, boring and real. I tell myself today is a work day. Today is coffee, keys, the lock at the library door that sticks a little, the sidewalk crack I step over without thinking. I tell myself I am not bringing the diary. I am not bringing any cards. The rules I scratched on my palm have already faded to a faint gray blur and then to nothing. Good. If the House can rearrange a list behind my eyes, then the only rules that matter are the ones I can feel in wood and heat and air.

I get three steps toward the kitchen. Then I look at the shelf. The shoebox sits where it always sits, pretending to be light and harmless. I tell myself no. Then I tell myself just once. I carry the box back to the bed because if I open it in the hall it will feel like I am sneaking.

It smells like dust and old glue. The first Polaroid is the sunroom, lace curtains lit from behind, a wet ring on the little table where a glass sat too long. The second is the stair hall, frames lined up straight, the handrail dulled by years of careful hands. The third is the kitchen pantry, the chair jammed into place under the knob, the tile shining in the way honest tile shines when you actually clean it. My breath stays long on purpose. It is the only thing that keeps the house from sniffing around my lungs and deciding I am dinner.

Then everything flips. Not a flicker. A clean swap, like someone slid one stack of cards over another.

In the sunroom photo I am there now, caught in a blur with my shoulders up and my face wide open, the way people look when they open a door without thinking first. In the stair hall shot I am bent wrong at the knees, both hands clamped on the rail like a puppet that someone dropped. In the kitchen picture I am on my hands, palms flat against the tile, staring straight into the camera the way you beg a phone because you already know you cannot beg the room. Outside the edges of the flash, the daylight in the pictures matches the light in my actual house. No harsh glare, no night shadows. Morning light.

The whole stack slides out of my fingers. Plastic frames slap on the quilt and tumble, then clatter onto the floor like a bunch of dropped fish. I grab one at random because I need one of them to be regular, just to prove I have not lost my grip on reality. Plain living room. Couch a little off-center, sun making a bright square on the rug. I blink. Now I am on my back in that patch of light, arms thrown out wide like somebody surrendering to nobody at all. I blink again. The room is back to empty. Same couch, same square of sunlight, no body, no me. The white border of the Polaroid feels oddly warm along my thumb, as if someone else just put it down in my hand.

I really hate that.

"No new rules from pictures," I say to the bed, the box, and the morning air. Saying it builds a tiny shelter big enough to breathe in. I gather the photos in a loose mess, tuck the worst of them facedown at the bottom as if weight will keep them from rearranging themselves, put the lid on, and slide the box back onto the shelf. My hands are shaking just enough to count. I stop it by flattening both palms over the quilt and smoothing until the stitches lie straight and the fabric reads the message that I am not leaving.

In the kitchen the kettle sounds like patience when I set it on the burner. The gas circles the metal in a neat blue ring and behaves. Steam ghosts up against the window and writes nothing important before it disappears. The bulge in the far wall warms the air just a little. That is all. When the kettle whistles, I pour. Coffee does not fix anything that matters, but it gives my mouth something to do besides argue with the House. I drink half a mug because routine is a rope you can hang onto in the dark. I rinse the cup and watch one drop crawl down the inside and pick its route.

The chair holds the pantry knob like it was born there. Tiny half-moon dents in the paint show where the back has bitten in over and over. I believe those marks more than I believe half the words in this place. I stuff the diary into a pillowcase and knot the top, then wedge the bundle behind my winter coat in the wardrobe. Cedar and old soap hit my nose, bright and simple, like a memory from a house that actually loved people. The wardrobe door closes with a soft, tired little click that sounds like someone saying fine, I will help. If that book ends up back on my bed, I want to know which thing in this house picked it up.

Keys. Wallet. Phone. The front latch sticks in cold weather. You lift from the bottom and nudge it with your hip. My body remembers without thinking. The door opens onto a small-town morning that knows how to start off gray. The grass needs mowing and is not going to get it today. The crosswalk light at the corner flips red to green in absolute silence, because I cut Street off at the breaker. I count steps anyway. Counting feels like talking in a language the house does not speak. Twelve to the curb. Three down. Seven across. The scooter kids stare like they have front-row seats at a show. The smallest one makes a rectangle with her fingers, opens it toward me as if she is drawing a door in the air, then closes it again and smiles a little too big. I lift my hand. Hands feel safer than any piece of paper ever has.

I do not look back at the bulge in the wall. The air at the back of my neck does not change temperature. That feels like a small kindness and a big setup. I take the kindness and keep walking.

I TELL MYSELF I will not open the box again. Then I open it again, because I do not want to be the kind of person who looks away and calls that bravery. I want to be the one who looks and still manages to stay on her feet.

Inside, it smells like dust, old glue and a perfume that sank into the cardboard sometime in another decade. The top photo is the sunroom, clean and simple, lace shining in the light, the thin scratch in the wood where a vase once got dragged instead of lifted. I hold my breath through the first three pictures, like a kid racing across the shallow end of a pool. Then I make myself breathe, long, not deep, until my chest stops acting like I am under water.

These pictures do not change with time. They change with me. With how I look at them.

One second the stair hall is just a nice composition, rows of frames, straight rail, the runner carpet doing its job. The next second I am there in the frame, on my knees with one hand pressed to the runner like I am trying to comfort the rug. The pantry shot is just a pantry, chair braced under the knob like a sensible habit. Blink, and then there I am again, head turned toward whoever is taking the picture, my expression all the way past patience, almost to begging.

Blink and the room is empty. Blink and I am there, mouth open in a silent O that might be somebody's name or might be the sound a body makes when it forgets how to breathe. The edges of the Polaroids carry a low, steady warmth now. If I closed my eyes and ran my thumb along the border, I know I could tell which ones were just handled by whoever decided what I should see. I do not give them that test. I keep my eyes open and let them sting.

"No new rules from pictures," I say again, this time with more weight. I can feel my brain trying to write guidelines about blinking and attention and timing. I refuse to let it. I am not going to let paper train me. I slide the ugliest snapshots face down to the bottom of the stack and put the lid on with both hands, like I am tucking in a kid that never learned how to sleep on her own. The box goes back onto the shelf. The shelf holds it like this is all normal.

In the wardrobe, the diary sits behind the coat with a patience you can almost taste. It feels like heat through the fabric. I pull it out anyway, just to see if my own sentence is where I left it. The pillowcase knot gives with a dry hiss. The book is warm like a person, not like paper. I open it near the middle and find a ripped-out page, an uneven bite through the paper that looks exactly like the coastline of a place I do not want to visit. The fibers along the tear are fresh enough that my fingertips itch. Around the gap, Mara's handwriting shows up and disappears. Her long-tailed g, her looped capital M, then suddenly the stranger's tidy script again.

> Sing along softly until you feel calm.
> Match the nearest steady clock so you can learn the room.
> Sign both names if you are not sure which one is yours.

It is the tone that makes my stomach turn. That patient, fake-friendly clinic pamphlet voice that wants to hug you and lead you straight into the worst decision of your life. On another page, the breath sentence shows up with its meaning sanded down. If your breath gets too big, make it smaller so the room can teach you the right size. In Mara's voice, the idea had been about not hyperventilating. In this voice, it sounds like "Shrink yourself so the house does not have to try very hard."

The line I wrote last night is missing from the page where I put it. But later, in the margin of another entry, I find my own words scribbled in the thin ink of that third hand, circled like a bug under glass. Do not die beautifully. Next to it, the same pen has written, Beautiful deaths are tidy.

I close the book before the anger has time to spill over my fingertips. Anger is loud in this house. Loud things slip and trip and the House likes to be waiting for that. I knot the pillowcase tighter than before and jam the diary deeper behind the winter coat, until the smell of cedar and old soap eats the smell of paper. The wardrobe clicks shut in a softer way this time, like it is trying to be on my side.

One Polaroid has slid under the bed. I get down on my knees and reach under with my palm flat so I cannot accidentally read it with my fingers. The scrape of cardboard is something like relief. I pull it out and hold it face down while I count my breath in and out a couple of times. Then I flip it over.

The kitchen stares back at me, plain as ever, except the far wall has grown up. Now there are full panels, rails, stiles, and a knob that catches the light in a wet, bright oval. My hand is on that knob. I do not remember doing that. I do not remember anyone taking this photo. I blink, and in the next instant the wall is back to its bulge, the knot in the board just a knot again. I slide the photo to the very bottom of the stack when I put the lid back on and leave the room without saying a word about it to the air.

The floorboards are at least honest about their history. One long gouge where something heavy got dragged in a bad mood. Two round dents where a bed leg sat too long and a dropped hammer left its mark. I put my palm down on one of the wider boards and feel the coolness soak into my skin. You cannot change wood without leaving sawdust somewhere. Ink is a coward compared to that. Even photos change their mind in total silence.

I take a dull pencil from the kitchen drawer to the nightstand and write a single line on the back of an old grocery receipt. Not a rule. Just a warning to myself as an animal that keeps trying to be trained. If it is printed, assume it is bait. The pencil bites down hard enough that the letters shine at the bottom where the paper is pressed flat. The eraser breaks off in crumbly pink bits that look like chewed candy. I fold the receipt and tuck it into my front pocket so it lives against my leg instead of on a wall where the House can start treating it like one of its own notes.

In the hallway, I hear a tiny tick from inside Mara's second notebook, the sound of a pencil touching down and lifting with care. I do not open it. I stand and listen until the silence feels normal-sized, like our world and not the House's version.

The chair still has the pantry door locked into its shoulder. The scratches in the paint line up and make sense. The warped wall stays calm while I stare at it, which is exactly what liars do. I turn away first, on purpose, so at least that choice is mine.

Coffee is done. Keys sit where I left them. My shoes know how to move quiet over tile. In the bathroom mirror I check my reflection, not for anything supernatural, just for proof that I am still a person.

Both eyes blink together. My mouth looks like my mouth when I am not talking. That will have to be good enough.

WEAVER STREET LOOKS LIKE a weekday pulled out of a dream and set back down almost right. Sprinklers overdo it on somebody's lawn, throwing a fine mist across the asphalt and making the road shine. Tires hiss through it like the sound of a skirt across tile. A dog barks three times, then decides it has done its job and quits. The traffic light at the corner changes color without any chirping from the crosswalk bird, obedient and quiet. I count steps because I am not letting a light bulb make my choices for me. Twelve to the curb. Three down. Seven across. The pavement under my shoes feels familiar and says nothing new.

The scooter kids have migrated to the low concrete wall outside the bakery. Their scooters lean in a row, handlebars touching like gossiping neighbors. Their skinny knees knock together with the solemn pride of uniforms. Two of them stare openly as I pass. The smallest makes a rectangle with her hands, like she is framing a shot, then opens it toward me as if she is opening a door. She closes it again and gives me a big, all-teeth smile that is almost reassurance and almost warning. I lift my hand in return and get a little nod that feels like a temporary truce.

The library smells like it always smells: cleaning fluid fighting with old carpet glue, layered over a hundred years of dust that settled into the cracks of the windowsills and gave up. I turn the deadbolt and the front door opens without a scene. OPEN flips around to face the street. The overhead lights hum to life one bank at a time, finding their usual pitch. True sixty. No weird wobble. I let that hum sit between my ear and my jaw like a coin I know by touch. It does not ask me to match it. It just keeps the building steady.

The computers wake one after another, steady and forgiving. Logo, spinning circle, desktop. It is like watching a little staircase build itself out of light so I can walk into a normal day, one step at a time. The book return bin is full of ordinary stories. Romance paperbacks that lost their battle with time. A gardening guide out of season that still smells faintly of dirt and plastic pots. A beat-up true crime book held together with tape that dried out two patrons ago. Each book lands on the rubber mat with a solid little thump that means gravity still works the way I remember. It is a rhythm that expects nothing from my lungs.

I shelve local history first because it feels like putting my hands on something solid. Binders full of old plat maps, photocopied church picnic photos, marriage announcements, shots of men standing next to fish that look like lies. The county binder is heavier than it should be when I lift it, lighter when I set it back. I do not open it to check. I just slide it home like someone laying a baby down and then take a step away. Some things have to choose you first.

The corkboard by the door has healed where the mystery book club flyer used to sit. No torn bits of paper, no leftover staples. The cork there looks almost new. I press my thumbnail into it and feel only cork. I smooth the corner of the summer reading poster that has curled, because corners like a little attention.

A guy in a faded baseball cap comes in looking for tomatoes. Not recipes. Plants. He says "greenhouse" like he is confessing and then laughs and asks for something for beginners anyway. I find him a book full of pictures of hands in soil and little seedlings that look braver than they have any right to be. He thanks me like I just gave him a secret. The receipt printer gives its usual cough and spits out a strip of thermal paper. I tear it off and hand it over and refuse to see anything mystical in a machine that jams twice a week.

At the children's table, a girl leans over her paper and draws a door with serious care, slow line, careful knob. When she is done, she marches it over to the return slot, feeds it through and says "for you" without actually looking at me. The rubber flaps close with a clean little click that sounds like a thank you all by itself. I fish the drawing out and tuck it into the growing pile of grocery lists, receipts and kids' art that end up here. Crayon is honest. It does not pretend to be more than wax and color and pressure.

In the staff bathroom I look at my face and blink to make sure the timing still lines up. For one heartbeat my left eye falters. In the next they are together again, synchronized like old friends. I touch the red ring on my wrist. It stings like a normal burn.

By noon the light from the high windows goes white. Dust drifts through the beams over the front display table, tiny pieces of other people's houses and clothes and skin settling into this building because everything ends up in a library sooner or later. I eat a yogurt at the desk while a woman in the corner reads the same paragraph in the local paper three times, folds it, then tears it out to take with her. Some paragraphs are like that. They live better in a pocket.

A teenage boy shows up with a blue-stamped envelope and a list of years that make him happy. 1896 through 1902. He wants birth announcements. I show him the microfilm machine, the way the focus works, and the mercy of low light when you are trying to read bad scans. He leans too close, corrects himself, then jabs a finger at the screen and grins as he finds what he wants. He copies one line in big, careful block letters into his notebook. He does not bother printing a physical copy. Not every truth needs a piece of paper to exist.

The phone rings once in the normal rhythm, then again half a beat wrong. I pick up and say "library," and hear nothing but that hollow hush that does not belong to this building and the soft shape of a sigh. I hang up. I make a dot with my pen on the desk blotter, rip that corner off and throw it away. I do not intend to build a new counting ritual around wrong rings.

Afternoon settles in gently, like a shawl someone lays over your shoulders without asking. A couple whisper about a dog they found on a website, then stop whispering because it is dumb to whisper in a public building that welcomes talking. A high school kid checks out three musician biographies I am pretty sure he is not going to read, scanning each barcode with the detached skill of someone playing a game he has already beaten. He leaves with his chin up like he did something important anyway. A retired man camps in the back with the obituaries and underlines ages that match his with a yellow highlighter. I walk the aisles, straighten spines with two fingers, and listen. Just pages rubbing, dust shifting, bindings creaking the way they always creak. No breath tries to sync with mine. No hidden hum rides underneath the fluorescent buzz. I let the library be itself for an hour.

Close to quitting time I stop at the corkboard and push a thumbtack into that healed corner to see what will happen. When I pull it out, the hole stays. That simple, ordinary little wound in cork makes me stupidly happy.

Outside, the sky dims and leans against the windows. I lower the blinds a third of the way, just enough to tell the night that it can look in but not move in. I log the computers off and shut them down. Their screens flash my reflection for a second, then fade to black. I flip the sign to CLOSED and hear it settle against the glass. Bathrooms checked. Lights off in a staggered pattern so the building does not feel like someone flicked all its nerves at once. The fern in the corner drinks its water without any obvious gratitude. That is plants for you, and some people, and my house. I actually like that the fern will make its own mind up in the morning about whether I did enough.

I wrap my fingers around the keys and rest my other palm on the inner latch of the door. Floors tell the truth when you give them a chance. The boards under my shoes carry the weight like they always have. The air in the little entryway holds the temperature you would expect from a mild day that never committed to warmth. There is no lemon sharpness from cleaner. There is no weird flat chord pressing under the background hum. Just dust, just evening, just a town deciding whether it wants to go to bed early or stay up late.

"Home," I say, and let the word go ahead of me like a scout. I wait a second to see if anything tries to grab it. Nothing does. I lock the door, slide the keys into my pocket, and open the door to step outside and pull it shut behind me.

I HIT THE LAST light switch. The monitors blink off and give me my own face for a heartbeat before they give up the room. I flip the OPEN sign so CLOSED faces the street and it hangs there with that tiny metal clink that always feels like a period at the end of a sentence. Bathrooms checked. Lights turned down in steps. Keys warm in my palm. The front vestibule holds a perfectly normal evening, glass cool under my hand, the sidewalk washed in thin color and sound from the street.

I put my hand on the latch and listen the way I have been training myself. The floor does its regular creaks. There is no lemon in the air. No extra hum. Just dust and a town pulling on its night clothes.

"Home," I say again, out loud, to see if the word still works.

I turn the lock, pull the door open, and step straight into a different room that smells like shellac and old cigarettes.

The wood grabs me in one piece. This is not the library foyer with the map case and the bulletin board and the faded welcome mat. This is a paneled study, close and warm, lined with books that have not been opened since somebody wore hats to work every day. The door shuts behind me with a crisp little click that does not belong to my deadbolt. The air slides across my face like somebody trying not to laugh through their nose.

A green-shaded desk lamp throws a circle of yellow light on a heavy desk. The lamp itself is the plain banker kind you can still buy, but the light feels theatrical, like a spotlight. Everything inside that circle is a little too sharp and a little too staged. On the blotter, a metronome swings its arm back and forth, ticking with the kind of confidence people have when they think they own time. It is almost right. Almost. The beat sits just flat, off by a hair in a way that would drive a piano teacher crazy. I feel it put out little feelers toward my heartbeat and miss.

In the corner, a grandfather clock keeps its own slow count. The tick lands on fifty-nine, the tock on sixty-one. It never hits the number clean. There is a tiny, uncomfortable room between the two sounds. I decide I am not walking into that space.

The books in here wear cracked leather like thin skin about to crack open. Their titles are stamped in gold that has dulled to tea brown. The smell is old varnish on oak, dust warmed by the lamp, and a faint ghost of tobacco from people who smoked when smoking indoors still counted as classy. On the floor, a velvet rope lies coiled in a perfect loop. When I glance away, it shifts the tiniest bit, then pretends to be perfectly still when I look back. There is a brass hook at one end and a brass ring at the other. Thresholds love props.

On the wall hangs a framed map under glass, one of those detailed block maps surveyors used to carry, all inked boxes and careful street names. The old service lane that used to run behind Weaver Street runs straight through this study, as if the room arrived later and draped itself over the path. A red thread stretches from a pin stuck in 112 Weaver to a penciled label in the margin: STUDY (YOURS). The head of the pin is glossy red, like a dried drop of blood. I do not touch the glass. Things that want fingerprints have a look.

The desk holds a big ledger with RECORDS spelled across the cover in brass. The kind of book offices used when they wanted people to believe the words inside would last forever. The clasp is already open, the little tongue of metal lifted, waiting. A fountain pen lies on its side with the nib just close enough to the paper to be rude. If I were the kind of person who straightened other people's pens, I would move it into its groove. I do not.

I say my name out loud like I am correcting someone behind a counter. Calm and flat. "Riley Cross. I did not sign anything." My own voice sounds like it has to push through glass to reach my ears.

The ledger opens on its own to the first page. The paper is thick enough that the movement makes a sound in my chest. Two neat columns, ink in steady hands that change style every few lines as the years roll. The left column holds words pretending to be dates but not bothering with numbers. Pantry. Parlor. Hall. Records. Street. Sleep. Study. The right column lists names across decades that do not care about each other. My eyes go straight to Mara Ellison without waiting for permission. Beside her name, the left column reads Study, Street, Breath, the ink lighter in the middle where the pen had run dry and been dipped again. Two lines below, the writer has only put initials: J. L. Some people turn themselves into initials when they are done trusting full names to paper.

Fresh ink lifts off the page and hangs there for a heartbeat, then writes itself in that neat, third-hand print. CROSS, RILEY — ENTRY PENDING. The dash is too perfectly straight. The letters take exactly the space they need and nothing more. The fountain pen rolls toward me, slow, until the nib taps the side of my wrist like it is nudging my attention.

I keep my hands down by my thighs and let it tap. Once. Twice. I give my eyes to the metronome instead because it is very eager to collect them. It keeps chopping the air and never quite landing where it should. I keep breathing long and even and refuse to let any clock in this room catch the rhythm. Habit wants to turn those breaths into a rule. My mouth stays shut.

Behind me, the door I came through has grown into the House's style. Tall stiles, raised panels, a round knob about the size of my heart. It sits a little too high for comfort. I have to try it, because pretending it is not there would be worse. The latch turns easily. On the other side is a short hallway with green-painted walls and soft, patient lighting, like a quiet hospital corridor. At the far end sits the library vestibule, looking exactly like it should. The distance is small. I walk two steps forward. The vestibule slides back two in a smooth, polite way, as if it is trying not to crowd me.

I step backward into the study and close the door, palm flat on the panel instead of on the knob. The wood is warm. The warmth feels like it belongs to something more alive than furniture. The burn on my wrist throbs under my sleeve and reminds me that touch can be a brand.

On the blotter, two faint signatures shimmer when the lamplight hits them right. One might be Mara's, if you are the kind of person who can recognize her loop on an E. The other is my name, written in a hand that is not my own. The letters are clumsy and upright, like a little kid learning to write Riley Cross for the first time and waiting for someone to say good job. I cannot tell if those ghosts were written in this exact room or in some cousin of it decades ago. The House does not bother with that kind of detail. Neither do I.

The velvet rope uncoils one extra loop and stops, like a trained dog that tenses before the trick and then freezes when nothing happens. I nudge the rope lightly with the toe of my shoe. The pile flattens and rises again. The brass hook gleams. My muscles want to hook it across the door to the hall, to make the doorway look official. I let it stay where it is. I am not here to accessorize the House's traps.

The metronome keeps throwing its crooked beat at me. I do not take it. I walk the room instead and check the other lamps. One on a side table. One on a shelf. I flip them on in an order I choose. One, two, three. Three separate cones of light, each set by my hand, not by some dramatic plan. I pause between each one and let the air settle. Change one thing, then wait. Not a rule written down anywhere. Just a habit that has been keeping me alive.

The ledger almost sighs. Another line appears underneath my pending entry, same neat handwriting, arrows laid out like instructions on a fire drill poster. Study → Hall → Nursery → Breath. My chest pulls tight. Those four words want to slide together into a sentence. I put a wall up in my head and do not let them. I pull open the right-hand desk drawer instead.

Inside is a little collection of obedience tools. A paper knife. A stamp pad still a bit wet. Sealing wax in calm committee colors. A tiny bottle labeled Soot Eraser. My fingers twitch with the urge to throw the whole drawer out onto the floor. I close it gently. Anger is loud. Loud is useful in some houses. Not this one.

I lay my palm flat on the desktop. Wood tells the truth when it can. The varnish is smooth, worn down by years of elbows and papers and someone's favorite mug. There are little nicks along the edge where a bored person tapped their pen. A round shadow where that same mug once sat over and over. Under my thumb, hidden under the shine, is a shallow groove where somebody pressed a pen too hard and carved right through their patience. My finger fits that groove perfectly. It feels good. Too good. I take my hand away. Comfort is a story this place would love to sell me.

I look at the map without really seeing the streets. My focus goes to the blank edges of the paper instead, where there is nothing written yet. The red string waits there like a fishing line that has already hooked something heavy. I pick up the fountain pen, because never touching it at all would be its own kind of choice. The nib is sharp and ready.

I set it in the brass rest where it belongs. The move means nothing to anyone but me. It is me saying that a tool does not get to assign me a job.

"Not beautifully," I tell the room, because I want those words living in this wood as much as they live in the diary. My voice fills up the corners. The clock keeps missing the beat. The metronome keeps pretending it knows what time it is. The ledger sits there with my name, pretending it is keeping track in some fair way.

I do not pick up the pen again. I do not touch the page. I slide the ledger closed with my fingertips barely touching, then take my hands away so I do not leave any oil on the brass. The clasp clicks shut, a tiny sound that belongs to me.

The green hallway beyond the fancy door shows me the vestibule again. This time it looks closer, and the green on the walls looks a shade lighter, as if the distance got shortened when I was not looking. I ignore it. I walk to the other door, the one tucked flush in the paneling with almost no trim at all, like the architect got bored and gave up. Behind it is a narrow aisle of books and a blank board, nothing more. No hallway, no exit. I close that door and look at the velvet rope resting exactly where I left it and let it rest.

The clock hunts for sixty and forgets it again. The metronome swings and swings, always a little off, like a grasshopper trying to decide where to land. I draw three long breaths of this room's air. It tastes like old finish and dry paper and something sweet that might be mildew. I quietly rehearse my own order a second time. Lamp, lamp, lamp, door. I put my hand on the knob and wait. I do not turn it until the waiting feels like a chosen pause and not like fear pinning my feet.

When I am sure, I turn away and look at the ledger one more time to make sure it has not changed the rules under my nose. CROSS, RILEY — ENTRY PENDING. The ink still shines a little wet. The second line under it has rearranged itself. Study → Records → Breath. I hate that it moved. I hate that I saw it move. I do not write that path on my skin or on a card. I keep it only long enough to recognize it later and refuse it.

"Later," I tell the ledger. Not yes. Not no. Just not now.

I open the door to the green hallway and walk forward one step. The vestibule stays where it is. Another step. Still there. I do not hurry. Behind me, the metronome ticks like an insect that no one invited. The grandfather clock drifts over fifty-nine, lingers, then slides toward sixty-one.

I do not look back until I am standing right at the threshold to the real library. When I do, the study is still lit by the lamps I chose. The rope is still coiled on the floor. The ledger stays shut. The red thread on the map has not moved. I step through. The glass of the library door is cool against my palm, clear and honest, and my reflection sits where it ought to sit.

I turn the key in the lock and hear the real deadbolt throw with a sound I know as well as my own name. Ordinary metal doing its simple job. I stand there with my hand on the door and hold one more long breath to see if the room behind it wants to laugh at me.

It does not. That is not the same thing as mercy.

Chapter 9
ROOMS OUTSIDE THE ROOMS

I TRY TO SLEEP like a regular person in a normal house that has my name on the bills. Phone facedown. Hall light off. Quilt up to my chin because my body remembers how comfort is supposed to work even when my brain keeps side-eyeing everything. The window sneaks in a draft I do not recognize. October in Bakersville should have a real bite to it. This is just cool air without a season.

The fridge never kicks on. No clunk, no rattle from the ice tray that has outlived three owners. I listen for trucks grinding up Weaver and get nothing but the crosswalk cycling colors with no little bird sound to mark the change. The quiet has a polished feel, like something that has been practiced in front of a mirror.

My palm on the headboard should give me the usual mess of wood grain, all random lines and knots you can trace when you are bored. Instead the pattern repeats. The same pale ribbon of grain passes through two knots, then shows up again three inches away, copied and pasted. I close my eyes and go back to the one thing that has never lied to me. In for two. Out for six. Long, not deep. The cord burn at my wrist tugs once, like it is checking if I am still here, then calms down. The house keeps its best neutral face.

Sleep comes thin and light. I hover on top of it and drift in and out, aware of the room even while I am technically not in it. I surface to the sense of light shifting softer without asking permission. I miss the ugly noises of my life. The printer at the library with that little throat clear before a page. The fridge's stubborn hum. They should not be here, but my ears look for them anyway. When I finally drop for real, it feels like stepping off a curb I did not see.

Screaming hauls me back.

I bolt upright too fast. The room goes grainy at the edges, then pulls itself together. The scream has direction but not a throat. It is that long, tearing sound a pipe makes when it wants to be a voice. I say my name in my head first, then out loud in a small voice, to mark the fact that this is a new moment and I am in it. Riley. My tongue sticks to the roof of my mouth around the word. I touch the floor with the back of my hand before I commit to standing. Cool wood. Honest.

The hallway is longer than it has any right to be. The light out there bends toward a color I do not have a label for. I did not turn any lamp on. The picture frames I hung perfectly level now all lean to the left by the same amount, like they agreed to a dress code. I keep one hand on the wall as I walk. The plaster has that faint tack of too many paint jobs layered on top of each other. My fingers slide, but come away clean. No dust at all. That is wrong for a house this old.

The scream pulls me toward the spare rooms. It repeats in the same breath shape, same length, every time, like a recording. Each one ends flat, like a hand slapped over a mouth right at the end. I count my steps because counting is the only thing that calms anything right now. Nine to the bend. Four to the landing. Six to the first door. None of those numbers match any of my normal house numbers. That tells me more than the noise does.

The room I open smells like a hospital that has been mopped with water that should have been changed an hour ago. A metal bed stands under washed-out light that has no obvious source. Machines cluster around like staff who stayed after the patients left. Their cords dangle unplugged, but every small screen holds a faint gray glow, like a thought not fully formed. The floor sounds hollow under my bare feet, the way floors do in rooms that get moved into and out of so often they forget who they belong to.

My brother lies in the bed.

He is twenty forever, stuck in the year the car took from him. His hair is almost right. His mouth still has that stubborn crookedness I grew up arguing with. The sheet fusses at his collarbone, the way it does when a nurse has just been by and left everything neat. I touch his arm the way you touch someone you love when you do not want to scare them. Cool. Not the cool of a nap. Cool like a pillow that has been empty for hours. His eyelids flutter. He does not answer to the shape of his name, but I say it anyway because I do not know how to keep him without saying it.

The scream runs again and I feel it along my spine more than in my ears. It is not his. It belongs to the walls.

"Wake up," I say, and my voice falls into the exact rhythm I used that first week after the accident. The night we came home. My mother stood in the doorway with both hands on the frame like she was holding the house up and pretended it was just how she leaned. My dad stood behind her, practicing how to be in a room without catching or throwing emotions. They wore those faces for cousins and neighbors and casseroles. Those expressions took rehearsal.

I turn and there they are in the doorway.

Same clothes. My mother's right shoulder sits a little lower, like it always does when she has driven too far in one day. My dad's jaw has that one crooked line where he always misses with the razor. "You have to rest," my mother says in a voice that does not fog the air. "You are scaring us," my father adds, gentle in that tone you use on a dog wedged under a table. Their mouths move, but the air in front of them does not. They are the version of them my memory polishes when it feels like hurting me on purpose.

"I am not the reason he died," I say. The line I learned in therapy, the one I hold like a smooth stone in my pocket. It comes out too fast. "It was not my fault," I say again, slower, letting it settle in my mouth like a prayer. The room tilts left a little, then right, as if it is trying out sympathy. The gray screens on the machines show a soft horizontal stripe and nothing else. No beeping, no helpful numbers.

The truth sits down right next to my denial and looks almost the same. I was at the wheel. I chose that road. I kept going with my life. The House adjusts around that truth the way water adjusts around a stone, changes its shape without ever arguing.

"I have to go," I tell them, and step forward. They do not move. My shoulder meets my mother's arm and passes through with the faint pressure of cold paper against skin. The part of my body braced for impact just stands there confused. Their faces stay fixed. They hold

119

the doorway like a photograph hung in a museum that you can walk through by accident when the projection bleeds onto the wrong wall.

I put my hand on the door and close it carefully, like I worry about pinching their fingers even though they are not really there. My forehead rests against the wood. Cool. True. The scream slides down the hall and rises up from the floor at the same time. That is the thing about this house. It loves straight lines right up until you need one.

I put my palm back on the wall and let the tacky paint guide me to the bend. The mirror finds me from the wrong side. When I pass it again, my mouth looks softer than it should. I do not trust that. I choose left and the runner shows a stain, loses it, then shows it again like a heartbeat under cloth. I choose right and end up at the same mirror, the same light, the same pretend mercy.

"Riley," I say, just to prove I can still get my name into the air. The sound comes back, but the voice that returns it is mine from a different age. I stop saying it.

Back in my bedroom, the bed is made. The headboard still wears its repeating grain like a glitch. My jacket lies where I left it because I only own one that fits, and the world is not kind enough to misplace it for me. I know the clock on the stove downstairs is showing a time that does not match the rest of town. I can feel that without checking. My hands itch to write a new rule on my skin. I do not let them.

I go back to the spare-room doorway with the metal bed and my brother asleep in it. Leaving anything half done in this house is like leaving a form half filled. It will finish it for you, and you will not like how. My parents stand in the doorway again with the same careful faces. The House likes this scene enough to hit replay.

"I was at the wheel," I tell them, and myself, and the plaster around us. "I took him there. I did not save him." I keep my voice plain. Not dramatic. Not pretty. The words do not unlock a secret compartment. The faces do not melt into sympathy. The machines do not flicker awake to applaud my honesty. Fine. I do not need a grade from this place.

"I am going," I repeat. I walk through my mother's arm again, through my father's stance, through the wash of light without source. Their weight is the weight of paper. The hall breathes in the wrong spots. I spread my fingers on the wall and keep moving because forward motion is the one thing this house cannot fake for me.

I do not run. Running would let the House pick the tempo. I walk. I walk until the corners decide to bend in new directions. I walk until my own breathing gets louder than the pipes and the scream and the memory. I walk until I reach a door that is not a bed, not my parents' frozen faces, not a mirror trying to flatter me.

Then I open it and step through.

THE HALLWAY HELD ITS breath when I closed the door on my parents' cardboard faces. That was the detail that finally clicked into place. People talking should move the air. They had not. The scream had never come from them. It was the plumbing all along. I had never made it out of the pantry. Not the library. Not Weaver Street. Not the clean little story I told myself about opening on time and shelving romance novels. I was still inside, and the House was playing dress-up with my life.

I started walking and the floor decided it was bored. It stretched under my steps without adding boards, the way a dream neighborhood stretches a block until you have to trot to keep up. The runner squeezed tight to the baseboard and puffed wider where my heel hit, like asphalt waving in a heat shimmer. Picture frames leaned in toward each other like they had gossip. I straightened one just to see. The glass fogged for a heartbeat, like someone breathing on it from the other side. I put it down without checking the photo. Photos tell you only what they want you to see.

Left took me to the bend with the mirror. Right took me to the bend with the mirror. The third time through, the mirror threw back a slightly softer version of my mouth. I touched the plaster with my palm the way you might rest a hand on a skittish horse, then opened a door I knew should lead to the linen closet.

Instead I got a stairway that stepped down twice and then back up four times to the same little landing, just from the opposite angle. The light in there had a weird tint, like someone had picked a color that does not exist yet. The scream ran along the baseboards, ignored the steps completely, and went upstairs.

"Fine," I told it. "We will play your way for a minute."

I ran. Not flat out, not so fast I would slam into a wall, just fast enough that whatever rhythm the House wanted to set for me went out of tune. Doors trapped me in corners that barely existed. One opened onto a long narrow room filled with nothing but chair legs. No seats, no backs, just rows and rows of legs cut clean and stacked, like someone had harvested history for parts and then gotten distracted. Another door opened onto a closet deep enough to have its own weather. Cold wind pooled at the bottom and lifted my hair right at the crown. I shut that door on the wind and heard myself laugh. It was small and wrong. That scared me more than the screaming did. Laughter is a gate you do not remember opening until something walks through.

The hallway with no windows ended at a room with four doors, one in each wall. I stepped inside and the pressure on my skin changed, a soft push over my arms like someone had opened an airplane cabin half an inch off normal. The sound in here was not quite sound. It was more like the feeling of someone else's breath, a hush that knew how to lean on your lungs. The walls did not move, but I could feel them working.

"Not this," I told myself out loud, because rules behave better when you say them where they can be overheard. I took Door One. It opened onto the same room, turned ninety degrees. Door Two. Same deal. The House admired its trick and nudged the light a little warmer, like it was setting up for a good photo. I stood still and refused to be tuned. My heart, for once, did not immediately jump to obey. In for two. Out for six. I counted. I hummed one line of a song I barely remembered, just enough to give myself a beat that did not belong to any metronome.

Nothing changed.

The pressure in the air learned my pulse. It pushed harder. My body wanted to match it. I held my rhythm, and the four doors stayed identical, and the air thinned by a hair. Panic came up like water in a glass, just to the brim and curving. The oldest rule I know came back, the one that kept me alive in other people's houses when I was a kid. Sometimes you make yourself smaller so you can slip out of a trap that wants you to push back. I hate that rule. Hating it does not make it useless.

I lowered myself to the floor and spread my hand flat to feel the boards. Old wood, wide planks, a splinter waiting for someone careless. Honest work. The hush in the room tapped my wrist like a stranger asking for a dance. I let my pulse fall in step with it.

It felt like letting someone who cannot count lead. My heart slowed to match the room, then overshot, then stumbled back, then finally synced. My head went light. My ears burned. I kept my hand on the floor and let the House have this one small win if that is what it took to open the next door.

A hairline crack appeared where two wall panels met, a seam that had not been there before. Not a trick of the eyes. A real line. The hinge exhaled, quick and pleased, as if it had been waiting for somebody to stop performing and just go with it. I took one breath in the room's borrowed rhythm, exactly one, then pushed myself up too quickly on purpose and felt my heart stutter back into my own pattern.

I put my hand on the new door and felt heat under the paint.

"Once," I said to the room. "You do not get to do that twice."

I stepped through the narrow seam as it widened for me. It tried to hold onto my breath like fabric catching on a nail. I pulled free. The hush behind me let go. When the door closed, it stopped being a door and learned how to be wall.

THE ROOM ON THE other side had low rafters and a slanted ceiling that understood the idea of an attic but had not quite nailed the math. The seam behind me closed with the quiet of a mouth deciding it is done talking. I stood in a space that wanted to be an attic without earning it. The rafters leaned low over my head, but there was no stair to explain how I had gotten here. The air smelled like old dust that remembers real winters and a cedar chest that has been locked since some forgotten wedding. Light was just there, no lamp, no window, with the flat, pale quality of a January noon. Every speck of lint showed up like it had been invited.

Toys waited everywhere, too clean to be normal. A tin carousel turned itself slowly with no key in sight. A scatter of jacks lay in a perfect star pattern, no hand to set them. A rocking horse sat dead center on its curved runners, totally still, as if it was holding still for a portrait. A dollhouse with a hinged front wall showed tiny rooms inside, each one furnished exactly right. Two chairs at every table. No shadows deep enough to hide anything. None of it looked abandoned. It all looked staged.

In the middle of the floor, a small table stood set for two. The kind of table you expect to see in a children's book. Two porcelain cups on saucers, steam curling up even though there was no kettle and no smell of tea. A little teapot in a fabric cozy printed with strawberries that never go out of season. A porcelain doll sat in the chair opposite mine. Her dress was cream with tiny blue flowers. Somebody had arranged her light brown hair in a perfect coil that would take patience and time on a real child. Her glass eyes were aimed just to the left of my face. Steam rose and drifted right through her cheek.

"Sit," she said.

The voice did not come from her plastic throat. It lived inside the ring of the cup, inside the porcelain and the steam. When the word came, it vibrated the surface of the tea that was not there.

Every rule I had set for myself screamed no. That was the trap. I pulled the chair back anyway. The small wooden legs made the right sound on the floor, that light scrape of wood over wood. I sat and laid my fingertips on the table edge to feel the grain. Old pine, nicked and worn. Honest.

"Sugar?" the doll asked. Again, the voice came from the cup, not the painted mouth. A tiny spoon rested across the saucer, ready for me like someone had set it down a minute ago. The spoon was warm when I picked it up. I held it over the cup and did nothing.

"We can talk without pretending," I said. My voice sounded too big in the little tea circle for half a second. The air adjusted around it until we matched.

"That is what the last one said," the cup murmured. The doll's painted face stayed frozen. Her eyes did not fix their aim. "She told the same story three times and never used her real name. I put her in the nursery until she remembered."

"I have seen the nursery," I said.

"I know," the cup answered.

We sat in the quiet with the fake steam between us. My heartbeat started to feel like a clock wedged in my throat. The tin carousel turned another lazy notch. The painted horses lifted their legs in the air they had been given. The rocking horse behind me stayed locked in place.

"Ask," I said. Playing along had opened the last doorway. No reason it would not work here.

The dollhouse door clicked as if something tiny was closing a cabinet inside it. No big move, just the little respectful sounds of a house that knows someone is listening.

"Who drove," the cup asked. The steam lifted and held steady. A fine mist gathered on the spoon in my hand, making it slick.

"I did," I said.

"Who died."

"My brother."

"Was it your fault," the cup asked. No anger in it. Just curiosity, like a kid asking why a bird cannot live inside a backpack.

I could have spit out my usual. A drunk driver crossed the line. I had the green. He had the blood alcohol level. His car was a weapon he aimed, not a punishment I earned. All true. It would not be enough for the House, because the House does not eat data. It feeds on the way your mouth moves when you say things you hate saying.

"It was not my fault," I said anyway. My hands needed to hear it once. "He was drunk. He came into our lane. He killed himself and my brother, and he lived long enough to complain about his back." The temperature of the room dropped just a little. The steam thinned. The carousel slowed almost to a stop.

The doll's chin seemed to lift by the smallest bit. Or maybe the light shifted on her. Either way, the feeling was the same.

"Try again," the cup said, softer.

I set the spoon down. My fingers shook, so I laced my hands together in my lap so they would have to work harder to show it. I lined up the words in the plainest way I could.

"I was at the wheel," I said. "He was in the passenger seat. I chose to take that road, and I did not think about turning around when the weather went bad. I saw the headlights and I picked the shoulder and it was not enough. I did not save him. I did not bring him home."

"Whose fault," the cup asked for the third time, not like a judge, just like a door that needed the right key.

"I am the one who lived," I said. "That is the part that belongs to me. It is not the whole story. It is the part that keeps me awake."

I did not dress it up. I did not try to wring tears out of it. I said it the way it sounds in my head at two in the morning when my body forgets we are in a bed and not a ditch.

The steam stopped. Both cups went from breathing to still between one inhale and the next. The doll's eyes, still not quite meeting mine, seemed less off. Something hidden in the teapot dropped, a soft clink like a tiny metal ball falling into the one right slot after running a maze.

"Better," the cup said. Not sweet. Not cruel. Just satisfied. "You may go."

I waited for the twist. The House loves a near miss. Nothing moved. The carousel stood still. The rocking horse stayed frozen. The dollhouse door crept open a finger's width, like it was reacting to a draft. I stood. The chair legs made that same honest scrape on the floor. I nodded to the doll because it felt like the right thing to do, even though it made me feel ridiculous.

"Thank you," I said. Manners are a kind of weapon when most of the rules are for show. My voice did not echo. It just landed and went quiet.

Across the room, a long narrow panel in the wall had learned how to be a door. Not painted. Real. A new seam ran along the place where plaster met the lower wainscoting, and a small latch glowed faintly with warmth, like a hand had just left it. I set my palm on the wood. Wood will tell you things. The grain under my fingers rose the way real boards do when they have been cut from a real tree. I could feel the drag of a saw. There was dust in the seam that no one had wiped away. That was enough evidence for me.

I did not look back. The doll kept her glassy stare. The cups stayed cold. The pretend tea did not come back. I opened the panel and found a steep, narrow stairwell, the architectural version of a throat.

The steps were painted a soft, sad gray. The paint had worn down to smooth curves at the edge of each tread where real feet had stepped over and over. The air below me smelled like a kitchen that had been used to feed grieving people for years. Soap, coffee, something always left simmering on low. It tugged at me the way every kitchen pulls people in when they do not know what else to do with their hands.

There was a latch at the top of the stairs that matched the one I had just opened. That felt like a joke the House expected me to notice. I wrapped my fingers around it, listened for the way my own heart was beating now that it had let go of the House's tempo, and started down.

The staircase hugged me tight. Close walls. Paint worn smooth anywhere a hand might have slid. It smelled more like a working kitchen with each turn. Three turns down. A soft draft moved up past me, gentle enough to lift the hairs on my arm. It did not feel hostile. Just present. My fingers followed a baluster sanded down by decades of hands that had nowhere else to be. Every touch said people had used this passage, whether or not their names ever made it onto paper.

At the bottom, another latch waited, same as the one at the top. That felt like a punch line and a warning. I set my palm on it, heard nothing but my own pulse, and opened.

THE PANTRY DOOR MET me like a room that had been waiting to see if I would make it back, not like it had been spying. The chair still leaned shoulder-first into the knob, doing its little job. When I slid it aside, the legs squealed against the tile in exactly the same voice as always. The fridge hummed, reliable and plain. The air smelled like dish soap, yesterday's coffee, and my own skin. The light from the window came from the correct angle for the time of day and did not ask permission from anything under the floor.

I put the chair right back where it belonged, exactly under the knob, and pushed until the fresh crescent marks in the paint lined up with the old ones. Seeing that layered damage steadied something inside me in a way that made me both embarrassed and grateful. I would take any honest record the world was willing to give me now. Scratches, dust rings, scuffs. The grit under the cabinets that never quite sweeps out.

I crossed to the sink and turned on the water. Cold, with that metallic bite and chlorine edge that says city pipes, not some old trick. I drank straight from my cupped hand until the taste of porcelain and steam finally washed out of my mouth. I put two fingers on the inside of my wrist. My pulse answered in my rhythm, not in any beat the House wanted to share. It stuttered once, then evened out and stayed mine.

The bulge in the far wall was just a bulge, at least for the moment. Warmth lived behind the plaster like a secret. "Not now," I told it. The paint stayed cool to the touch. I counted that as a temporary agreement.

My phone waited on the shelf under the counter like a pet that is not sure if it did something wrong. I pulled it out. The date on the lock screen flashed up in my face like a challenge. The clerk at the library had left two voicemails and one short text. Everything okay? I typed back, Library opens at ten. My thumb shook once, then stopped.

The kitchen looked almost right. The ceiling light fixture sat just a hair off center from where I knew it had been, but it did not move when I stared at it. The same pale ribbon in the floorboards repeated near the threshold, but only once. That felt like a compromise.

I slid down the front of the cabinet until I was sitting on the cold tile, because tile has no plans beyond being hard and cold. I kept one hand hooked over the back of the chair. While the coffee maker puffed and chugged, I told the room out loud what I knew for sure.

I am here.
The fridge is on.
I am breathing.

I did not say safe. Safe is a word that racks up interest.

Dark came in from the edges the way tide comes in, slow and steady, retaking shoreline. I let it. The wood under my fingers stayed solid. The tile did not change under my weight. If the House wanted to try something else, it was going to have to come through the most ordinary parts of my life to do it. I closed my eyes and let the day decide if it was going to give me another shot.

I WOKE UP ON the kitchen floor with a square of honest sunlight crawling across the tile toward my hip. Late afternoon had climbed in through the window and settled in like it was paying rent. My hand was still hooked over the chair back. My fingers ached from clutching it like the wood might wriggle away if I let go. The refrigerator kept humming its plain old tune. The clock on the stove said 5:42 in green numbers that had no idea what I had been doing with the hours.

I sat up slowly and let the room correct into place. Tile, cold and hard. Cabinet face, with that crescent-shaped nick at knee height I always mean to sand. A trace of stale coffee in the air, a little sweet. My wrist throbbed where the cord burn circled it. I pressed the faint ring to the cool metal of the fridge door and counted until my pulse stopped trying to make a point.

The pantry door showed the gouges I had made, little bites from the chair back. I pulled the chair away just enough to see the knob. It looked too clean. Someone, or something, had wiped off the smear of gray paint my hand left earlier. My heart skipped. I pushed the chair back until wooden back met metal again and those new crescents landed in their old home. The sound of that contact steadied me more than it should have.

Water from the tap tasted like pennies and cold pipes. I drank it anyway, rinsed my mouth again and again until I was sure there was no ghost of porcelain left. In the living room I closed the curtains halfway and checked the front door twice. The deadbolt thunked into place, then thunked again, happy to be useful. Outside, Weaver Street looked exactly like itself. A man walked a dog the color of tea with too much cream. A kid carried a plastic sword and jabbed at invisible enemies with serious form. The crosswalk at the corner flipped its lights on schedule and did it without noise.

The phone blinked at me from the counter. I finally let it run its mouth. The clerk's second voicemail came first, worry shoved under a brisk tone. A calm voice I did not know wanted to confirm story time for Thursday. A teenager with a new number asked if the musician biography he liked had returned. The date still sat on the lock screen, calm and rectangular. I wrote back that the library would open tomorrow at ten, then slid the whole phone under a coaster. It was petty. It made me feel better anyway.

Upstairs, the wardrobe waited with the pillowcase I had tied like a bad magic trick. The diary sat on the bed again, ribbon neat across its cover like we had an appointment. I did not touch it. I grabbed a laundry basket, flipped it upside down, and dropped it over the book so it was caged like a turtle shell. It looked stupid. That was part of the point. This house likes clever. Sometimes the answer is dumb and heavy and plastic. I left it there.

In the bathroom, the mirror showed exactly what I expected. A woman who had slept on tile. Eyes puffed at the edges. Hair crimped in an odd wave from where it had dried against grout. I showered until the steam fogged the glass and the red ring around my wrist faded from angry to just noticeable. When I wiped the mirror with my palm, a faint circle showed in the steam, the exact size of a teacup. It blurred and ran when I dragged my hand over it. I made a low sound in my throat that might have been a laugh. That sound scares me more than crying does.

I made the easiest dinner I could talk myself into, with the fridge wide open beside me because I liked feeling the cold on my legs. Toast and eggs. Food that tastes like you have decided to keep going, nothing more dramatic than that. I ate at the counter and kept an eye on the pantry like it was a dog with a history. The chair kept its lean. The far wall held its bulge without growing. If anything was watching, it was doing it behind the disguise of plain surfaces and old paint.

Dusk folded gently around the house. The first porch light down the block clicked on. The sound of the street settled into the right key, like a guitar string someone had finally tuned correctly. I made up the couch as if I were a guest in my own house. Blanket, pillow, one good lamp on low, mug on the table. I set a kitchen knife within reach, blade flat on the coffee table. I am done pretending the thought never crossed my mind. The chair in the kitchen sat where I had left it, turned so its back blocked the pantry door. The sight almost made me smile. Almost.

I walked the house the way a farmer walks a fence line before dark. Check every gate, every post. Windows latched. Back door snug. The main bedroom stayed shut. The spare room that had held a metal bed and my brother's body now just held the usual clutter. A folded comforter. A box of winter clothes. The sheets in the closet smelled like the ghost of someone else's powder. The mirror on the landing returned my face at the right angle, nothing softened, nothing borrowed. The second time I passed it, my mouth looked exactly the same. I counted that as a small win.

I settled into my little camp on the couch. Blanket over my legs. Lamp dimmed to something my eyes could let go of. Mug within reach. Knife handle turned my way. The chair in the kitchen was visible through the doorway if I lifted my head. Its back leaned into the pantry door like a tired friend guarding a secret. I let my jaw unclench.

Sleep tested the edges of the room like a cat peeking around a doorway. I let it come. The house made the familiar pops and groans of wood cooling and air shifting. Underneath those, I heard something else. A faint tick, like a metronome winding down, out of rhythm and far away. It did not come from the kitchen or the stove clock. It came from some other layer of the house. I counted under it. In for two. Out for six. Long, not deep. The tick did not catch me this time.

When I woke in the dark, the lamp had turned itself off. The chair in the kitchen still pressed its back against the pantry. The tiny pencil mark I had drawn on the baseboard to line it up with glimmered, catching stray streetlight like graphite does. The ticking had stopped.

The house held me the way a tired adult holds a sleeping child. Not loving, not cruel. Just careful enough not to drop me.

I slept again. If I dreamed, the House did not keep a copy for me to find in the morning.

Chapter 10
RISING DREAD

MORNING SHOWED UP IN pieces. A square of sunlight climbed the kitchen wall. The refrigerator kept doing its job. The little pencil notch I carved last night sat exactly where the chair back met the baseboard. I laid my palm over it and felt the faint grit of graphite. The world did not flinch. That was enough for now.

Shower. Coffee. A clean shirt, because fabric tells the truth even when people do not. I did not look at the diary under its upside-down laundry basket in the bedroom. I glanced at the pantry and kept my mouth shut. At the corner, the crosswalk went through its colors with no chirping bird to go with it. I counted twelve steps to the curb, three down, seven across. My shoes met the pavement and reported nothing new.

At the library I unlocked the door and waited to see how the building would breathe. Cold air slid in and touched my face the way it always does when you open a public place in the morning. No fake lemon scent. No strange extra hum hiding under the regular one. I flipped the sign to OPEN and the metal tapped the glass with that soft, bossy sound that only signs and paperweights have. The overhead lights came up to their usual tone. A clean sixty-cycle buzz. I let it sit between my jaw and my ear and refused to build my heartbeat around it.

The first patron through the door was a woman with a stroller and the wrecked look of someone who slept in shifts. I crouched to the baby's level. The baby blinked off-beat, one eye then the other, like her eyelids were practicing. A bubble of spit sat on her lip and a smear of dried milk streaked her cheek. All real. The mom asked for weather books. I gave her one with big pictures that show clouds building up before storms. Her breath fogged just a little when she laughed about "cumulonimbus" being too much before noon. Fog shows up when it is cold enough. You can depend on that. I pocketed it like loose change.

I checked in the returns. Every spine has its own little groan. None of them had learned a new language overnight. A gardening guide sighed down its glue line. The date stamp ink bled a little because someone refilled the pad too hard yesterday. The receipt paper came out warm. I pinched the slip and felt the heat leave in a straight line, like a tiny life doing exactly what it is meant to do.

The copier jammed with its usual moral outrage. Red light blinking, machine offended. I opened the front and teased out the twisted page, all crimped and crushed. Hot dust and plastic hit my nose. The paper left a gray rash on my fingers where the toner had smeared. I wrote "service soon" on a sticky note and stuck it where the staff would see it, not where a house might get any ideas.

A teenage boy came in humming some song too new for our shelves. He asked for a drummer's biography and tried not to act relieved when I knew which one he meant. His fingernails were chewed raw. He smelled like laundry done late at night, half dry. He said thanks without looking up, all long limbs and awkward kindness. One hundred percent human.

At ten-thirty the accountant sent the usual all caps email about mileage. SUBJECT: MILEAGE. The body was just a reasonable checklist with empty boxes waiting for marks. I watched the cursor blink. It did not try to match my pulse. I filed the email in the folder where I keep things that want me to prove on paper that I exist.

A man in a ball cap came in asking for "tomato books again, but for inside ones this time." He lifted his cap to scratch at an old burn scar on his neck, shiny and roped. Scars are terrible liars. I walked him to the gardening section and pulled the book with actual dirt under the illustrated fingernails. His thanks landed heavy in the air, the way gratitude does when it costs someone pride. I added a flyer about saving seeds to his stack. He did a whole performance of pretending he did not see it, then carefully tucked it inside the book.

At the cork board near the entrance, I checked the pinhole I punched in the corner last week as a private joke. It was still there. When I pressed my thumb to it, the cork crumbled under my nail the way cork should. The board had not healed itself. The town never minds being a little messy. The House, on the other hand, likes things too neat. I decided that was one point for the town.

The microfilm kid came back with a new project. Death notices this time, for a school chart nobody will read twice. I set him up at the machine, watched him lean in too close, watched him correct himself. Then I watched his face shift when he finally found someone he knew, or someone his parents talked about. People get that soft, stunned look when they bump into their own dead on a screen. He did not print anything. He wrote the dates down with careful numbers. His pen smudged because his palm was sweating. Skin always tells on us in ways we need.

After lunch, the copier worked on the first try. I did not like that at all. A machine quietly saving its tantrum for later feels like the kind of hospitality a haunted house would fake. I printed a month of the calendar just so I could touch the paper and feel the warmth leave. Then I folded one corner on purpose, a small, ugly crease. Faking that level of boring detail would bore any predator, even a patient one.

All afternoon, people threaded through the building in the right rhythms. A retired man ran his finger down the obituary column and stopped on a year that matched his brother. A kid dragged a stepstool across the floor with full volume and then said sorry like he meant it. A woman copied recipes longhand from the internet because she said food only tastes right if she writes it herself. The room smelled like ballpoint pens, winter coats, dust, and the stubborn plant in the front window that only wants water every third day. I watered it on the pattern someone taught it, even though I do not agree with plants having pride.

I tested what I could without turning myself into something measurable. I said hello to a man and watched him do that half-startled flinch and then pretend he had not. I handed a laminated card to a girl and watched her immediately pick at the edge, because plastic begs for it. I opened the back door for a minute to let in real cold. The alley smelled like wet cardboard and exhaust. Exactly the smell an alley should have on a nothing-special day.

Near closing, I stood at the front windows and watched the crosswalk. The light went through its little routine and never chirped. A woman in a red scarf waited, then stepped off on yellow because she was done waiting. Her boots squeaked on a wet spot and she swore under her breath and laughed at herself. Her breath fogged. She was not listening for anything but her own timing. That helped.

The overhead lights kept their note. The floorboards complained in the same familiar way when I did my last walk around. I turned off one lamp, waited, then another, waited, then the next. Gave the building a breath between each, like you do with a nervous animal. The copier stayed quiet. The receipt printer did not spit out anything dramatic. The desk chair refused to roll smoothly and let out its little gasp.

At closing, I put my hand on the front latch and listened for that wrong kind of hush. Nothing. I locked the library like a person who had been allowed to keep a full, normal day.

On Weaver, the bakery was exhaling the last of its sugar air. The scooter kids had swapped boards for mittens and walked home stiff and proud in their coats. One of them said my name with that solemn little nod kids give adults they have decided can be trusted. I lifted my hand. They waved back.

I did not look behind me. I did not count to twelve. I knew exactly how many steps it took to get from the library door to the point where my life bends toward that house. I took them with my breath long, not deep, and thought, If this is a set the House built, it did a good job. If it is not, then this is my actual life, and neither of us is going to be the first to look away.

GROCERY MART SMELLED LIKE oranges, floor cleaner, and the kind of sugar that lives in bakery cases after lunch rush. The fluorescent lights hummed overhead in a high steady whine. I grabbed a cart for the formality of it and rolled slow through produce, filling it like I was setting a stage. Apples polished a little too well. A bag of mixed greens to pretend I eat them on purpose. Carrots clipped short at the tops, lined up like recruits. Bread, milk, eggs, pasta, a jar of sauce with a picture that promises more than reality. Enough that my cart said, This person plans to stay alive here for a while.

I watched people like I was looking for a bad edit. A teenage employee misted the lettuce and flinched when the spray blew back into his face. He wiped his cheek on his sleeve, the exact sleeve he probably got told not to use, then looked around for witnesses. A man stared at the endless cereal wall like he was cracking a code, then grabbed the bright sugar bombs he clearly wanted the whole time. A woman read off the ingredients on a can with her lips moving, patient and precise, then set it back with a tiny shake of her head. Up front, the scanners chirped nice clean beeps. A baby in another cart tried out a long vowel and cracked himself up.

In the dairy aisle, one of the cooler fans stuttered for a few seconds, then found its rhythm again. That little stumble was exactly the kind of failure a normal building makes by itself. I stood there and let the cold wash over my face. When I turned, I noticed a cardboard soup display had been spun around the wrong way, all labels facing the shelf instead of the aisle. Somebody would fix it. The world messes up and then corrects itself, no big speech. I filed that away where I keep the reasons to keep trusting anything.

At the meat counter, a guy with a fresh razor burn under his chin asked if I wanted my pork chops thick or thin. He delivered the question like it mattered. I said thin. He smiled like that proved something for him. The brown paper packet he passed over had a real weight, nothing sneaky. I pressed it lightly. Felt the give of the meat, the little cold pocket where juice wanted to gather. The kind of food you cook when you are trying to feel like a person again.

At checkout, the line looked like every Tuesday ever. The lady who used to drag me to church and does not go anymore waved with two fingers from the next lane. A little kid in a puffy coat dropped a handful of coins, then watched them roll away with absolute heartbreak.

An older man who knew everyone in town lined his groceries up by height and kept one hand on a jar that wanted to tip. The clerk at register three had hair dyed the exact shade of bottle auburn that glows under fluorescent lights. Her glitter nail polish belonged under stage lamps. Her name tag said BRITT in block letters that had been wiped and re-markered too many times.

When it was my turn, I put a divider on the belt because that is how the ritual goes. Britt gave me the customer smile that makes the day move along.

"How are you," she asked, in the way of someone who wants the short version and really hopes you stick to it.

"Good enough," I said. Which is most of it.

She started scanning. The little beeps sounded pleasantly bored. She moved with the practiced speed of someone whose muscles know the order of events. Milk. Bread. Pasta. The sauce jar with the fake basil on the label. The herbs I had grabbed because they smelled like something living. The codes rolled under her fingers.

"Address?" she asked, eyes on the screen.

I rattled it off without thinking. She typed, hesitated, glanced up at me, and finished it with a tiny, knowing half-smile.

"Weaver," she said. Not a question. "That old place near the curve."

"That is the one." I kept my voice steady. A plastic bag sighed open under her hand.

"You bought it?" She made bought sound like a dare.

"Renting," I corrected. "Brave bank. Braver security deposit." My laugh sounded like I was just chatting. It felt more like wearing a coat I had not broken in yet.

Britt set the egg carton aside and wrote "EGGS TOP" on the bag in squeaky marker. "You are brave," she said, with the kind of emphasis people use when they do not mean it as an insult. "Last woman there had a rough time."

The hairs on my arms woke up. "Oh?" I kept it light, like this was gossip and not a report from the future.

"She came through here every week," Britt said. "Always bought candles. Said the power went weird. I told her to call the city, and she said it was the house, not the lines." She scanned the carrots, then stopped to double-check the code list taped under the register. "She got thinner that last year. Wore two sweaters when it was barely fall. Smelled kind of like wet cellar sometimes. If I asked if she was okay, she would laugh. Not mean. That laugh people use when they are about to cry and refuse to do it in front of you."

"How long ago?" I asked. I already felt myself bracing.

"Couple years," she said. "Before that winter when the plows were late every storm. She stopped coming in around then. Bank notice went up. Heard she was in a place." Britt's voice softened on those last two words. In a place does a lot of work in a small town. "She said the house was alive. That it moved doors on her and counted her steps. Said it took her music away." Britt handed me the bread like she was handing over part of the story. "You do not look like someone who scares easy. That is meant as a compliment."

"I leave lights on," I said. "Helps a lot."

"Same," she said, and that grin she gave me was pure human, no gloss. The scanner chirped one last time. The total popped up, just numbers doing math. "That place is pretty, though. Good bones. They do not build like that anymore. Maybe you will fix it up right."

"Maybe it will fix me," I heard myself say. It came out too easy. I swiped my card. The machine beeped its approval. Britt tore off the receipt and passed it with a pen. The whole little ritual of paying, signing, and being allowed to leave played out like it always does.

"Welcome to Weaver," she said, like she had some say in it.

Outside, the air had that sharp parking-lot-cold taste. One cart wheel caught in the gap where two slabs of concrete met. I bumped it free with my hip. I took a second with my hand on the car roof, just letting the metal pull whatever leftover static I had out of my fingers. I checked my hands for shaking. None. Checked my reflection in the window for any weirdness. Both eyes blinked together. Mouth lined up right. Fine. Enough.

I loaded the groceries like someone who lived here on purpose. The drive back was uneventful in all the right ways. A pickup took the hill too fast and then slowed at the top. A dog barked twice at nothing and gave up. A guy maneuvered a ladder through a too-small gate and almost dropped it, then saved it with muscle memory. Nobody turned into a ghost. No street melted into a hallway. The town behaved like itself.

At the house, I pulled in and made two trips because sometimes you have to let pride do something simple. The porch boards complained at the same places, the second board from the step creaking louder like always. Inside, the air had kept our uneasy truce. Coffee, soap, a hint of cooking, me. I dropped the bags on the counter and looked at the pantry out of the corner of my eye, the way you look at an animal through slats. Chair in place. Pencil mark there. The bulge on the far wall was not bigger, which was not the same as good, but it was something.

I heard a tiny laugh slip out of me, quiet and wrong, a sound that could belong to the woman Britt described if it wanted to. I shut my mouth, turned to the bags, and started putting things away. Eggs on top shelf. Herbs in a glass with water, pretending I am the kind of person who keeps them alive. Milk where the cold hits hardest. Bread in the old bread box, its hinges still moving on oil someone else rubbed in ten years back.

"Alive," I said to the empty kitchen, testing the word. The room did not react. The chair did not move. The wall bulge sat there like it had been carved in. I pulled a skillet from the cabinet, lit the burner, and listened to the gas catch. Fire said what it always says, and for once I believed it.

The receipt had warmed against my leg. I pulled it from my pocket and laid it flat under the fridge magnet shaped like a fat little dog. The paper cooled under my fingers. I felt that last bit of warmth leave. That small, simple thing ending exactly the way it should. I let myself stand there a little longer than made sense, looking at that magnet and that receipt. Ordinary life doing its job. That was the whole point of leaving the house. That was the test.

It did not make me less scared. It just meant the fear had to share the room.

I COOKED BECAUSE COOKING is a good lie and a better distraction. Heat, salt, garlic in oil, all the things that make a kitchen smell like someone plans to keep going. The burner lit on the first try and stayed steady. Oil slid into a smooth oval and shivered when the onions hit. I stirred and watched the steam fog the window glass, not the whole room. The pantry stayed at the edge of my vision, quiet and solid. Chair braced. Pencil line true. The bulge in the wall kept the same shape, not bigger, not smaller.

I ate at the counter. Nothing fancy. Thin pork browned in the pan, noodles, herbs thrown in at the end for the smell. A TV show murmured in the background, some narrator talking softly about how bridges want to sway and how engineers talk them out of it. His voice stayed inside the speakers. It did not drift over from the pantry door. I still kept one ear tilted that way and resented it.

I did the dishes. Hot water, soap, plates clacking into the rack. That sound always feels like a bell in a small space. I made myself let it be just that. The faucet gave its usual high squeak at a certain angle. I shut it off and wiped down the counters until the dishcloth grabbed on clean surfaces instead of crumbs. The chair still leaned into the pantry. I laid my hand on its back, felt old wood, and that was all.

My legs ached, so I ran a bath. The mirror in the bathroom fogged over politely and kept its opinions to itself. I slid into the tub and let hot water creep up my skin a little at a time until my body unclenched. I leaned back until my hair fanned out. The tile around the tub held the warmth the way old houses do after a long summer. I closed my eyes and counted the drip from the faucet. It skipped every now and then, a little honest mistake in the rhythm. My breathing did not match it. I kept it long and steady and let the water pretend to be neutral ground.

I drifted, not all the way to sleep, just far enough that sounds felt softened. My ear filled, then cleared. The world narrowed to the quiet slap of water against porcelain. I raised my arm and watched a bead of water crawl from my wrist toward my elbow.

Halfway there, the bead went red.

I blinked. The surface of the tub darkened like someone had tipped ink into it. Color spread from under my skin, slow at first, then more sure, curling into lines. I know the smell of blood from hospital hallways and bad nights. That smell crawled into the back of my throat. Another ribbon of red unrolled near my knee. The tub seemed to tilt. The drain tugged at the water but never got ahead of it. The color climbed as if the tub were filling with something thicker than water.

Get up, I told myself. My body disagreed for a second. The red crept up my chest, circling my collarbones. The smell got hot and sharp. I grabbed for the rim of the tub and my hand slid. Felt like someone had oiled the porcelain. My head knocked the edge. A white flash snapped across my vision. Somewhere in the noise, a tiny metallic clink sounded, like a spoon hitting tile.

Then I was on my knees on the bathmat, both hands gripping the outside of the tub. Water poured down the sides and soaked into the rug in an ordinary, cold, miserable way. My chest heaved. My head throbbed at the spot where it had hit. I touched my hairline and checked my fingers. No blood. Just clean water. The air smelled like soap and steam and hot ceramic. Nothing else.

I backed up and sat on the lid of the toilet, breathing with my mouth open. The water in the tub was clear. One hair floated. The drain did its job. The faucet dripped once, then not again. I let out a short, broken laugh, that same wrong laugh, and the room accepted it without echo.

I stood, slowly. The bruise made itself known, a neat pain under the skin, already building color for tomorrow. I shut the taps and wrapped up in a towel. The mirror was a haze of steam. In the fog, a circle started to form around forehead height, the size of a teacup. Before it finished, gravity dragged it down and it split into two harmless streaks. I wiped the glass with my whole hand and left the kind of print anyone would expect. I kept my palm there until the warmth made my shape clear, five fingers, no tricks.

The house answered with the usual little creaks and sighs of old wood. Nothing spoke my name. In the bedroom, the laundry basket still sat on the diary like a dumb helmet. It had not shifted. I pulled on soft clothes, avoiding the sore spot on my head. My eyes in the dresser mirror looked tired, but they were both mine, both responsive, both blinking when asked.

I walked through the house setting it up for night like I was closing the library. Curtains halfway. One lamp in the living room turned low. Blanket and pillow on the couch. The bed in my room looked nice and neutral, but it felt like making a promise I was not ready to make. In the kitchen, I filled the kettle just enough to hear water hit metal and set it on the burner. When it started to whisper, I switched the flame off. I did not want steam climbing the walls tonight.

I checked the front lock and laid my palm flat against the door. That small ritual felt less silly now and more like a contract. The wood did not answer, but it did not pull away either.

The pantry sat where it always sits. Chair pressed to the knob. Pencil mark on the baseboard. The bulge on the far wall existed at the edge of knowing. I nudged the chair out one finger-width, then shoved it back into place so the paint picked up fresh arcs. Layers of marks, proof that I had been here more than once. I told the wall good night under my breath in the same tone people use with a tied dog. Not loving. Not threatening. Just clear.

I put on another easy show. Something with cooking and a host who pretended to forget ingredients so strangers at home could feel smart. I let that harmless noise fill the room. I folded laundry that was already folded. I laid my keys out on the table where I could see them in the morning, even though I knew the house did not need doors to move me. Before bed, I shut the TV off myself. I did not want to give anything the chance to take credit.

I went through the little shutdown routine. Kitchen lamp. Hall light. One more drink of water. One last stop at the pantry to set my hand on the chair back. Wood against skin. No heat. No hum. Just contact.

I stretched out on the couch with the living room lamp low. The house made the minor sounds it always makes when air cools and wood settles. I counted my breath because I do that now whether things are calm or not. Long, not deep.

Sleep slid in from the edges. I shifted and the bruise on my forehead complained, a small sharp ache. I took that as proof of impact and stored it with the facts. Outside, a car rolled down Weaver in second gear. The crosswalk changed colors without singing. A dog, somewhere, half-barked, thought better of it, and quit. I wondered how hard it would be to move out. Then I wondered if I had any guarantee the House would let me go. Then I shut that line of thought down, because that is how it steals your hours.

Sometime in the middle of the night, I woke up. The lamp was off. I decided I had been the one to switch it off, even if I did not remember. The chair in the kitchen was a dark shape leaning where it was supposed to lean. The tiny pencil line on the baseboard caught a strip of streetlight and looked like a seam in reality. My heart tripped once, then found its pace again. In for two. Out for six.

I fell back asleep with my open hand resting on the blanket over my ribs, like I could hold onto a promise I had not actually been given. The house seemed to hold its breath with me. It felt patient. It felt like a clock that had decided not to tick out loud.

Chapter 11
NEW RULES

THE DAY SLIPPED ON without catching, like glass that has been sea-worn until it cannot hold a fingerprint. Morning light came in pale and even. The pencil notch I had made at the baseboard still sat where the chair back kissed it. I pressed a thumb to the graphite and felt the small grit that proves a mark is not a memory. Coffee, clean shirt, keys. I did not lift the laundry basket off the diary. I looked at the pantry and let my face stay empty.

Weaver Street behaved as if it had rehearsed. The crosswalk cycled its colors with no tin bird to sing the count. I refused to look for it. Twelve to the curb was there under my feet if I wanted it. I did not want it. The library unlocked without conversation. Cold air touched my face the moment the deadbolt gave. No lemon. No hidden chord. I turned the high lights and listened for a pitch that did not belong. True sixty laid itself between jaw and ear and stayed politely out of my pulse.

The morning patrons were soft at the edges, like people in a dream you are almost done having. A woman with a stroller mouthed thank you and her lips were a half-beat off her sound, then caught up, as if the world had cleared its throat. The baby's blink was messy and perfect. One eye, then the other, then both. A teenager in a hoodie asked for the drummer biography and the word biography came out a little tired, the way teachers say it in May. He chewed his nail, felt it hurt, stopped, then forgot and did it again. Real. A man in a cap wanted tomatoes indoors and touched the scar under his chin with the practiced gentleness of someone who owns his old injuries. Real.

Receipt paper came out of the printer warm and then cool before my fingers found it. I held the strip anyway and watched the heat leave a second time that could not exist. The copier jammed and I opened the belly and found no paper. The red light scolded me as if the crime were in the room and not in the machine. I closed it and it purred and behaved. The clock over the desk ticked 10:01 and then breathed and showed 10:01 again. Two breaths later it offered 10:03. I did not write any of that down. I had decided before I unlocked the door that I would not carry notes today. No cards. No rules. If the House had been reading my handwriting this whole time, it could read air for once.

By noon the copier had forgiven me without saying why. I watered the plant on the sill because it prefers a schedule that would annoy a saint. The counters smelled like books and winter wet wool and the old plastic of a keyboard that still pretends it is new. Email blinked its cursor with no desire to own my heart. I closed it. The room breathed like a building that holds its occupants without needing applause.

Closing came on the hour and gave me permission to move like a person who knows the steps. I took one steady walk around and touched what needed touching. Spines aligned with two fingers. The copier belly shut. The microfilm carriage returned home with its small accepting click. I turned three lamps down one by one and gave the room a breath between them. I did not wait to see if it wanted to keep me. I flipped the sign. I locked the door. I let Weaver Street take me back like nobody's problem.

Home smelled like soap and yesterday's coffee and the corner of the house where sun gets stuck. The chair sat in its post against the pantry. The pencil notch looked smug and right. I lifted the chair and set it aside and did not make a new mark. I put the phone in my pocket, flashlight in my hand. No diary. No cards. I touched the door once with the flat of my palm because wood tells the truth even when the person touching it is about to lie to themselves. Then I opened and went in.

The kitchen blinked away behind me like a stage with the curtain dropped. The thin woolly hush arrived at once, the way attic air settles when light touches dust. The flashlight's beam bowed at the edges as if the air were thicker by a degree. When I lifted the phone to check the camera, the preview lagged one frame behind me. My face moved and then arrived. I put the camera away and kept the light.

Speed, I told myself. Like a kid who knows the dog is asleep and wants to cross the room before it decides to be awake. The first corridor tried the trick where it presents three versions of itself depending on which foot you step first. I did not give it the time. Long breath, not deep, only because my lungs have their habits. I took the left and walked through before the wallpaper could decide on its pattern.

The ledger study tried to dress itself in importance. The banker's lamp glowed the green it thinks means authority. The ledger lid sat open like a mouth ready to teach. I entered and set the triangle of light in my order, lamp, lamp, lamp, and did not let my eyes land on the page where tidy print pretends to care about me. The clock in the corner missed its sixty on purpose. The metronome on the blotter made a show of getting things almost right. I ran my fingers over the desk edge because wood is honest in the ways it aches. Then I took the far door and did not ask to read my name.

The heartbeat room waited with its soft push under the skin. I stepped inside and the pressure set itself like a hand on a shoulder. Last time I had fought it the way you fight a poor dancer who wants the lead. Today I put my palm to the floor and matched the room for a single count, only as long as it took for the seam to appear where no seam had lived. A lip opened, as if I had spoken a secret and the wall had done me the courtesy of hearing. I stood too fast on purpose so my heart would stumble back into me. Then I moved through and let the seam seal itself as if it had never been a favor.

I ignored the nursery corridor where tiny shoes always line themselves up in neat, scolding pairs. I did not look at pictures. The House loves to put its hand on your face and make you see the thing you already spend nights avoiding. I did not participate. The phone in my pocket chimed once with a sound that belongs to a message. No banner. No sender. When I woke the screen it was empty and polite. Battery at sixty-six percent. I did not like that number. I did not have time to offer it a story.

Ear pressure changed the way it does in an old elevator that pretends there are only two floors. The flashlight dragged a little in my hand. The beam bent over trim that had been painted too often. The smell here was always soap that never finished rinsing and the idea of dust more than dust itself. I moved through a narrow throat into a hall that did not want me but did not yet ask me to leave.

I passed the second study without giving it the power of a name. Past the cold closet that collects small winds. Past the turn where the mirror waits to catch a version of my mouth I do not recognize. The glass tried and met nothing it could sell me. My breath kept to its long shape and did not try on the room. The hush around me thickened as if a crowd had gathered just outside my hearing. I did not stop. I did not write a rule. I did what you do when a strange dog is on a porch and you are not its business. Keep walking. Do not make yourself interesting.

The corridor pinched and then opened on a landing I did not remember, a small square of floor with nothing to justify its existence. Three doors faced me. The left had the House's good wood and proud stiles. The right had paint that carried too much ambition. The middle wore the glossy beige of apartments, the color landlords choose when they cannot choose anything else. It had a peephole that threw back my flashlight in a mean little fish-eye.

I felt the long breath arrive and resisted the habit of counting it. I held the light steady. The phone in my pocket gave me the small vibration that means someone wants to be known and then changed its mind. Ear pressure eased the way it does when a car crests a hill and gravity remembers you. I put my palm on the middle door. The gloss was warm in a way that did not belong to this house.

"Noted," I said to the wood I did not trust.

I tried the knob. It turned. The smell that breathed out was stale tobacco and old carpet and rot with sugar in it. The hinge did not complain. The light fell into a room I wanted to call mine and did not allow myself that comfort.

I stood in the threshold with my light angled down so the beam would not pretend to flatter anything. Behind me the House watched with its practiced silence. In front of me the beige door waited to be closed like a bad habit I have never successfully given up.

I stepped through.

THE DOOR OPENED ON my old one-bedroom as if a landlord had polished a memory and missed the corners. Beige walls. Thrift couch with arms that sagged inward like tired shoulders. The rug I bought at a church sale, but the stain it always hid had migrated three feet left. The lamp had the shade I once threw away. My keys should have been in the bowl by the door. They were, two of them, even the one I lost for a week that turned up under the radiator. The air carried sweet rot, not fresh, the smell that comes when fruit dies slowly in a warm room.

I stood with the light low and let the beam slide across surfaces the way water slides along tile. The flashlight showed ordinary. The phone camera offered mildew in the grout that crept in the preview when I panned. I switched to selfie and the wall behind my head breathed in an easy rise and fall. I turned the camera off and the breathing stopped. I turned it on and there it was again, a ghost chest lifting under paint. Battery at sixty-six percent. Still.

The television faced the couch with a frozen weather crawl for a storm three years gone. The channel banner was right, font almost right, the date not. The clock in the corner of the screen ticked forward and then corrected itself back. The remote on the coffee table had a ridge worn into the plastic from my thumb, but on the wrong side.

The kitchen corner offered a crooked magnet shaped like a dog pretending to be a potato. It held a rent notice with the right number and a font that belonged to a different decade. The fridge hummed a familiar key and vibrated under my palm like a cat purring through a cough. A photo strip was pinned by another magnet, four frames from a mall booth I had avoided for years. Me and my brother in the last good week. Goofy faces in the first frame. A true laugh in the second.

The tenuous pride of getting through in the third. In the fourth he looked past me at something outside the booth, the exact shape a person makes when a stranger touches their shoulder. I blinked and the last frame was blank. I did not blink again. I folded the strip and slid it into my back pocket like a fragile coin.

Water tapped in the bathroom, slow as a heartbeat that is bored. I found the sink dry, the faucet closed, the drain singing its own drip. Three drops in rhythm and then nothing, the silence as deliberate as a held breath. The mirror tried to fog and could not find enough heat. I raised the flashlight and watched the silvering at the edges chew at the glass.

I walked the perimeter because that is what you do in a space that wants to pretend it belongs to you. The bedroom showed my old bed frame but shorter by an inch. The window faced a street that did not belong in Bakersville. A bus in the distance glowed the number of a route I have never seen. The closet smelled like cedar and cigarettes and the sour nap of coats that do not fit anyone now. On the shelf a shoebox labeled WINTER held a single mitten and a dead moth that looked like a leaf with ideas.

I kept the light on the floor and followed the boards to the place a door should have been. The apartment's front door had always been a straight shot from the couch. Here there was wall. Not honest wall. Timid trim that wanted to be a frame but had not admitted to it. Paint sagged at the seam, thick with too many layers, the way a lie gets heavier each time it is told.

I could have backed out and let the House take what it thought it had earned. I put my knuckles in the seam and felt the soft give of paint over the stiffer give of wood. I set my shoulder and breathed long, not deep, because breath that does not match anything survives pressure. I pushed. The paint cracked in a clean little sigh. The wood beneath it answered with a hollow that told me space waited.

"Open," I said, because words are tools when hands tire. I levered the trim with the flashlight body and felt the hinge line wake. A narrow hatch shaped itself with shy edges, the smell of cedar and dust breathing out as if someone had opened a trunk. The rot retreated down the hall behind me. The new air tasted old and dry and careful.

The opening led into a throat. Boards close together, pale where feet had not known to walk. I slid the phone into my pocket and went in with the light gripped low. The passage pinched at the shoulders and then widened by a hand. My clothes brushed raw wood that felt polite about splinters. The floor under my knees changed twice, laminate to rough plank to a smoother board I recognized by the long, generous grain I had felt under my palm once before.

I crawled toward that familiarity because habit is a compass when maps lie. The smell of cedar deepened. A draft rode past my cheek with the patient temperature of a room that likes winter. My breath hushed against the wood and the hushed sound did not echo back. I listened once for my own heart to offer a trick. It kept its shape. I kept moving.

The throat let me go. I pulled up onto floor I knew in my hands before I saw it. Old pine with a scar diagonally across one plank like a thin white river. The attic had been here the whole time over my shoulder, only a wall away, waiting with its hard work and its little theater.

The playroom had set the table again.

Two cups steamed on the small round. The doll sat in her chair in a dress with tiny blue flowers, gaze aimed just to the left of my face. The rocking horse centered itself without rocking. The tin carousel stood with the horses poised between lift and rest, a very long in-breath.

I stood, dust on my knees and cedar in my mouth, and the light threw my shadow against the rafters like a puppet someone had forgotten to put away. I lifted the cup to eye level and saw the steam travel through the porcelain cheek that had never learned to be opaque. I sat because the room had already decided there would be a conversation.

"Hello," I said to the rim, because that is where the voice lives.

The doll's head tipped a degree that cannot be measured, only noticed. The steam bent. Somewhere below us, in a lower room, wood remembered a bang. It arrived like a promise with a long walk ahead of it.

I put the light on the table. I kept my hand on the handle of the cup without lifting it. The attic felt the way a stage feels a heartbeat before a curtain rises. I was where I needed to be. The House had made certain of that without ever admitting to the kindness.

"Hello," I said to the rim because that is where the voice lives. Steam rose, thin and steady, and licked the porcelain as if it knew a script.

"Sit," the cup said, breath living inside the lip the way sound lives inside a bottle.

I sat. My flashlight lay on the table, beam trimmed down so it would not bully the room. I kept my eyes on the cup because speaking to a face that does not move is a way to give yourself to a trick.

"What are you," I asked. "What do you want. How do I end this."

"Pretty questions," the cup murmured, almost pleased. "Useful answers are ugly. You will not like the shape."

Something shifted. I looked up. The doll's chair had angled itself a finger's width toward me. Her painted hands had moved closer to the saucer, as if she meant to touch it and thought better of being caught. I stared. Glass eyes, unblinking, aimed just to the left of my face. Dress quiet. No movement.

I dropped my gaze back to the cup. "Mara wrote rules," I said. "The House shuffled them. Tell me the rule that matters."

"Rules are how people put their fear in straight lines," the cup said. "This place eats straight lines. Do not give it tidy food."

A small sound, cloth against wood. I looked up again. The doll's head had tipped the smallest fraction toward the door I had crawled through, the difference between polite and paying attention. Her right hand rested on the table now, one finger extended, touching the sugar spoon. When I kept my eyes on her, she became a perfect object again, trapped in the stillness that pretends to be innocence.

Back to the cup. "What is in the middle of this. What is the heart."

Steam cut. It did not fade. It stopped between one breath and the next. The cup went quiet, a vessel that had never known speech. The attic seemed to listen past me, down through its spine. Dust settled on the beam of my light in a slow drift.

When I lifted my eyes, the doll had moved. Her hand had pulled the sugar spoon closer to my saucer, handle aligned with my thumb, as if she meant to set me into the old game again. Her head was turned a degree toward the hatch, a child's idea of a warning. Porcelain lips stayed closed. The room around her looked the way a stage does when the actors are late, props too patient to be kind.

"I am not playing," I told the cup. "I am asking."

"Deaths are so beautiful when they are orderly," the cup whispered, steam remembering itself in a thin thread. "Yours is not beautiful yet."

The doll's chair had crept a finger backward when I glanced up, a tiny brace as if she expected impact. Her left hand had lifted and hovered near her mouth, not quite touching her lips, the way a child shows shh and hopes to be obeyed. I watched for breath. None. When I held my gaze she froze into porcelain again, all virtues of arrangement and none of intention.

"Names," I said to the rim, "Mara's, mine, the ones in the ledger. Do they open anything."

"Names are locks you put into your own doors," the cup said. "Do not admire your keys."

Wood answered from below, a heavy report that began as a knock and landed as a blow. The attic floor flexed under the chair legs. Dust fell in a soft curtain from the rafters and hung in the light like ash. I did not look away from the cup. The next strike came up the house like a fist moving rung to rung on a ladder, deliberate, angry, sure of its route.

My eyes lifted before I could stop them. The doll now faced the hatch completely, a precise quarter turn that would have scraped if she were anything but porcelain. Her right arm had extended by a breath and her tiny finger pointed at the panel seam as if her joints remembered a language they should not know. The tea trembled by a ring as if sound had learned to be water.

"Who," I asked the cup. "What do you mean by He."

The cup did not answer. My phone in my pocket vibrated once, a small animal's shiver, and showed no message when I dragged it awake.

Battery stuck at sixty-six, the icon smug in its green. The light on the table narrowed as if air had thickened by a fraction. Another blow, lower now, as if something had chosen to strike at the base of the house to prove that it understood load.

"Tell me," I said, and heard the little knotted thread in my voice that knows begging when it hears itself. "If there is a heart, point me to it."

"Do not say heart in here," the rim breathed. The steam faltered. "Do not push. Pushing makes the rooms bruise."

I looked up because I could not help it. The doll's hand had found the sugar tongs and placed them delicately on my saucer, a host arranging pieces for a guest who is failing her part. Her head had dipped, not in courtesy, in warning. In the corner of her mouth a hairline crack had appeared, running up toward the cheekbone, a flaw the room meant me to notice. It looked like a drawn line to show where a face might break.

The next strike became a run, four in fast measure that traveled up the walls under us, each one a little closer in the way a thunderstorm picks a house and comes for it. The hatch behind me breathed inward and then held. The rocking horse rolled forward a whisper and returned exactly to center without rocking, a ceremonial motion too practiced to be comfort. The tin carousel turned a quarter without music.

"Stop helping me only when I am not looking," I said, and let my eyes rest on the doll. She stopped at once. Stopped the way a child does when the game requires invisibility to count. I looked deliberately back to the cup. Porcelain on my breath, heat at my chin.

"Why warn me," I asked. "If you belong to it."

"Do not flatter this place with belonging," the cup said, dry now, the sound soft and hard together. "It keeps what is useful. It shows what will feed a pattern."

Another blow. Then another, and this one under the attic floor itself, a hand slamming the hidden underside of the table we had all agreed to sit at. The tea rippled and touched the rim and left no mark. The ladder of sound reached us and stood one tread below, deciding whether to climb.

I raised my eyes. The doll had turned back toward me by a degree. Her left hand still hovered near her mouth, halfway to shh. Her right had shifted from the tongs to the cup's handle, porcelain fingers curved like a person inviting a friend to take the thing they are refusing. The chair had inched closer to the table, its legs now planted in dust ovals just ahead of the ones they had left before. She had pulled herself into the ceremony with me because it was the only grammar she had been allowed.

"I am not playing," I said again, and my voice did not believe me.

The cup's breath came plain for the first time since I sat. No riddles. No pretty shape. "He is here."

The hatch drew in a long impatient breath and let it go. The floor answered with a deep, wooden throat sound. Dust lifted from the seams and floated. The flashlight flickered once and steadied. My phone offered me its dumb green sixty-six. I felt the house set its teeth around the moment the way a jaw sets around a bite.

I kept my eyes on the cup so the doll could move if she meant to save me from myself. I listened for the foot I knew would find the rung. I held the long breath that belongs to me and not to any room. The blow that came next did not knock. It landed, directly beneath us. The table trembled. The steam tore and vanished. The cup went silent as well.

"Who," I said into the rim, softer than a whisper.

The cup did not answer. The doll had turned her whole face toward the hatch, one perfect line of intent, porcelain mouth parted by the width of a breath.

Chapter 12
DOWN THE RABBIT HOLE

THE HATCH IN THE attic pulls a breath like it owns the room. Dust lifts off the rafters in a slow sheet and hangs there. The little teacup on the kid table goes quiet. I press my palm to the attic window. The glass is cold enough to sting.

"No more," I tell it. I say it to the room. I say it to myself.

The latch is painted shut. Of course it is. I choke up on the flashlight like a hammer and pop the corner pane. One quick hit. Spider crack. I knock the rest out with my sleeve over my fist and the folded edge of my coat. The glass comes loose in small bright pieces that tinkle on the sill. Winter air slides in, clean and sharp. Somewhere below, something hits wood hard enough to make the floor under me answer with a low, angry groan.

I swing a leg over the sill, then the other, and flatten out on my stomach. The gutter bites under my ribs. The clapboard feels like dry skin under my hands, chalky paint flaking into my palms. For a second I am seven again on the roof of my parents' ranch, told to get down, pretending I cannot hear. Then I look over the edge.

It should be two stories to the yard from here. Three if you count the attic. It is not. Windows drop away in stacks, one tier and then another, each one reflecting my light back in a mean little blink. Four levels. Five. It feels like standing on the edge of a parking garage and realizing the ground moved while you were thinking about lunch. My stomach tries to climb into my throat. I pull a breath in for two counts, out for six. Long, not deep. My heart tries to catch the beat of the pounding below. I tell it no and mean it.

I inch sideways along the clapboard, shoulder to the frame. The flashlight rides between my teeth. The beam bows at the edges like the air is thicker than it should be. Paint grit grinds into my hands. My fingers find a drainpipe a few feet left, old metal banded to the wall with straps that have given up on being straight. It is not where logic says it should be, but it is there.

I hook my left arm around the pipe and test it with my weight. It groans like a grandpa leaving a recliner, then holds. The pounding moves up through the framing as a steady pressure. Not steps. Impact. Measured and confident, like someone who knows this staircase in the dark.

I slide down the pipe hand over hand. Boots feel for seams where boards overlap. Two spans. Three. My arms shake, not from fear, from work. A window one level down sits cracked an inch. Warm air breathes out of it, carrying dust and something sweet that does not belong to houses that are safe.

The pipe shivers against my forearm. Another hit from below, closer now. I swing for the sill and miss. My knuckles ride paint. I swing again and catch the bottom lip with three fingers. The sash sticks. I shove it with my forearm and it jumps up like it meant to help all along. I fold myself through the gap like a letter being pushed into the wrong mailbox, hip scraping the frame, boots thumping carpet. The room takes me in without a fuss, like it has been waiting for me to choose it.

First things first. I slam the window shut and set the latch. It clicks, polite and neat, like a smart appliance. That bothers me more than if it had argued.

I stay on my knees a second and let my body report in. Hands on carpet, not splinters. Ribs sore where the gutter dug in. The bruise at my hairline throbs like a coin under skin. Breath steady enough. I pick up the flashlight and tighten the cap. Nothing against me but friction and dead batteries, and I can manage those.

I do not look back out the glass. I do not give the House that drama. I check the wall where the attic hatch should be. Smooth paint. No seam. No draft. The opening sealed itself like a mouth that does not want to be part of the conversation anymore. The House shuts doors fast when it wants quiet.

The air in here has a thread of sweetness under the dust. Old cigar smoke. Leather warmed by bodies that think they are important. Down in the bones of the building the pounding climbs a rung and pauses. Listening, maybe. Counting me. I keep my breath long and quiet. I pull my phone because the habit lives in my hands now. Battery at sixty-six percent. No notifications. Screen looks normal. I put it away. No diary today. No index cards. No rules to read. If the House wants to cheat, it has to read my mind, and good luck with that.

My fingers find a light switch. I leave it alone. Last thing I need is a friendly lamp deciding to act like a throat. I keep the flashlight low and run the beam along the floor. The carpet has that dead feel from years of feet, soft on top and compressed underneath. The baseboards have paint layered on paint until the corners are rounded off like the whole place has been blurred by an app.

I listen at the door. Nothing but warm air. No breath. No whisper. Just a room holding its own breath. The knob fits my palm like money. I look back at the window once. Streetlight pushes at the glass and fails to make a shape. The cold line from the gutter still sits under my ribs. I feel awake in a way caffeine never manages.

"Not yours," I say. I am not sure if I mean the room or my heartbeat. Probably both.

I turn the knob. The latch gives a small, mannered click. The door opens on warm dust, a banker's lamp glow, and the edge of a heavy desk. The flashlight picks up green glass, polished wood, a leather chair that probably has its own opinions. The smoke smell sits under everything, sweet and stale, like a party that ended ten years ago and no one bothered to air out.

I do not step through yet. I stand in the doorway with the beam low and let the pounding count another rung. It does. One hit. Then another. Each one precise, like a hand that never misses the rail it wants. The sound rides the framing more than the air. It feels close without being here, the way thunder makes the window shake when the storm is still down the street.

"All right," I say, not to be brave, just to get my mouth working again. "Come on then."

I walk into the room that wants to be a study. The window clicks behind me like it just remembered how.

THE ROOM SMELLED LIKE old cigars and leather, that sticky sweet note that clings to your throat even if nothing is burning. A green banker's lamp threw a pond of light onto a desk the size of a small boat. The shade hummed at a pitch you feel in your molars more than your ears. Books climbed the walls in tidy ranks, heavy spines picked for how they look from across a room. The carpet had that plush give that says stop moving and be impressed.

"Riley," a voice said, steady and practiced, like someone calling roll.

The big chair turned. My grandfather had the kind of presence that made furniture feel like part of his body when he was alive. The House got that part right. Suit tailored, tie clean, cuffs framing his wrists like they were evidence. His skin had the flat paper look of old letters. His eyes were bright the way glass reflects daylight. Not alive. Not gone. Something in between that knows which words land.

"You threw it away," he said. The sentence arrived like a pronouncement he had been waiting to deliver for years. "We built you a name. You made yourself a clerk. You put the family in a ditch and called it a choice."

I set my flashlight on the blotter and turned the beam down to the corner. No halo for him. The light caught a notch in the wood where a pen had tapped for three decades. It found the dark ring from a glass someone should have used a coaster for. It made my hands look steadier than I felt.

"Afternoon," I said. "Not staying."

He rolled right through that. "You destroyed the line." His jaw moved on the word destroyed like it had a taste. A coil of ash slid off the end of a cigar that was not lit. The ash fell into a cut-glass tray and did not break. The sound it made was soft and smug.

"You're not real," I said. "You're a house trick with good posture."

"If you'd had children, they would have corrected you." He leaned forward. The chair creaked like it was pleased to be included. "Children put a spine in a woman."

"My spine is fine," I said. I could hear my mother's tone in my own voice, that tight polite calm she used to get through family dinners. "I just stopped letting dead men grade it."

He looked at me like a judge looks over reading glasses, the kind of look that invites you to convict yourself. "You crashed a car and made your mother grieve. You lived and he did not, and you still chose small. Librarian small. Renter small. Easy jobs. Easy rent. Easy leaving."

"The drunk driver killed my brother," I said. It came out flat because truth sometimes does. "You liked the part where I carried the blame because it made your story tidy. Women make messes. Men sweep up. I remember the script."

The lamp's hum pressed a little harder against my teeth. The smoke smell thickened and then thinned. He did not blink. I hated how good the House was at building a quiet that works like a spotlight.

On the credenza, a silver frame faced the room. I did not look down. I could feel the weight of the photo anyway. Best clothes. Hostess smile from my mother. My father holding his shoulders like a coat hanger. My brother squinting because flash is rude. Me standing like a borrowed person. This is what the House does, it lays out a perfect dinner and waits for you to pick the poison yourself.

"You cannot kill a house," he said. "You could not keep a boy alive." He said it like he had paid for the words and meant to use them on every woman he met until the receipt faded.

"Watch me," I said. There are times when the shortest sentence is the only one that fits in your mouth.

There were three doors. The one I came through had already learned how to be a wall. The right-hand door was proud wood, glossy, carved to look like money. The left-hand door was cream paint scuffed at the latch, the color renters never get to choose. The pounding deeper in the house climbed another stair, not fast, just certain. It felt like numbers being counted without a voice.

I took the cream door.

The knob was warm in a way that made my skin want to pull back. The latch gave a soft, almost polite click. On the other side was a long hallway someone had kept ugly on purpose. Yellowed wallpaper peeling in thumb-wide strips. A runner with a busy pattern that tried to hide stains and failed anyway. Baseboards buried under too many coats of paint, edges softened from pretending to be new.

"You will come back," my grandfather said behind me, in the tone people use for sunrise and taxes. Not a threat. An appointment.

"Hard pass," I said, and shut the door with the same care you give a nice thing you do not want to break even while you are done with it. The kiss of the latch meant nothing. I did not give it a chance to mean something.

I ran my fingertips along the wall as I moved. Paint tugged a little on my skin, tacky in spots where the last coat went on heavy. The runner bumped at my heel the way cheap carpet always does. I walked the edges where wood shows through and the floor tells the truth. Frames hung at the right height for portraits. My light brushed the glass and got blur back. The House does that, turns faces to smears when you try to make eye contact.

Inside the bones of the place, the pounding moved like pressure. A blow. A pause. A blow. It traveled the rail too. Balusters made that small shiver you feel in your forearm when you set your hand on them. Somewhere a pipe knocked, and the rhythm tried to ride my pulse. I kept my breath long and quiet and let it bounce.

On the left, a mirror waited with too much gilt. It wanted to return me a softer mouth and a kinder brow. I skipped it and took the right turn toward a stretch of trim with sloppy paint. Perfect corners lie. Bad paint belongs to people. That has been true every place I have lived.

The runner ended in a ragged smile. Bare boards started. A knot in the wood looked like an eye and I stepped over it because I have learned not to donate symbols to rooms that already hoard them. Two doors faced me. One wore expensive wood like armor. The other had faint fingerprints around the knob you only see when a beam catches them. I picked fingerprints. Those belong to hands.

A small landing opened with a hairline crack tracing the ceiling. Someone had painted over it and the crack came back anyway. I liked that in a petty way. The hall beyond sagged a little in the middle where a joist had asked for help and been told to tough it out. I liked that too. Imperfect means honest. The House does perfect like it is a weapon.

I looked back once through the study. The cream door was an ordinary door again. The lamp on the far side haloed the leather seat. My grandfather did not get up. He did not need to. That had been his power when he had a pulse. He could sit and make you do the walking.

"Goodbye," I said, to him, to the smoke, to the part of me that still rearranges her face to be acceptable in rooms like this.

The pounding hit the next step. Dust loosened from the ceiling crack and snowed down in a polite sheet. That was my cue. I moved.

The corridor carried the old house smell I am learning, heat leaving paint, a ghost of soap, something like old raisins. A clock somewhere tried to tick and gave up. A vent hummed and changed its mind. The doors I passed learned to be small bathrooms, linen closets, utility spaces. The important door waited at the end pretending it was not important. Chalky paint. Knob brushed to a dull shine by worried thumbs.

I put my palm on the panel and felt good wood under too many bad choices. The pounding rolled a room closer. The air leaned toward the sound and fell back. I opened the door.

The hallway on the other side thinks it is a basement and a service corridor and a back alley all at once. Wallpaper hanging like tongues, a long stain down the runner like a river no one wanted to name. The smell kinked at the back of my throat. Wet plaster. Old steam. Something metallic in the dust that made me taste pennies.

Far down, out of sight, the pounding turned into a rhythm I could feel in my sleeves. He was close enough to enjoy himself. That is how it felt. Not a sprint. A hunter who likes the walk.

I started to run before the House could decide the pace for me.

Carpet tried to snag my heel again. I kept to the boards. A door on the left opened on a nursery that had learned props and not story. Shoes in judgmental lines. A crib with no mattress. A mobile turning on a room with no draft. I shut the door with my palm flat against it and did not look at the toys. The latch apologized for existing. I did not forgive it.

Half stairs that wanted to be up and down at the same time. My legs made the math work. The heartbeat room sat to the left with church manners. I felt the pressure at the edge of my skin, the polite hand that wants to set your rhythm for you. I did not match it. The far door in that room offered a seam for a single breath, then hid it when I refused the dance. I took the corridor and found my own seam two doors later where paint sagged over a frame. The latch let me through with a tired sigh.

The ledger study waited with its three lamps in triangle, ritual ready for me to perform. My name in tidy copy sat open on the blotter like someone had finally learned my handwriting. I cut across the rug and left a footprint down the grain on purpose. The desk reached for my hip with a corner that had bruised someone before me. The pounding turned that corner outside with a certainty that felt personal. I went out the far door and did not give the room my eyes on the way.

A kitchen that pretended to be clean. Enamel stove with a pilot that looked like a coin of light. The sink dripped in a rhythm that wanted my pulse. I twisted the tap until the drip stopped. The clock over the door read 3:11 and then 3:09 and then 3:11 again. I kept moving because conviction is how you get through rooms that take votes.

Dining room next. Chairs pulled out a hand width like they were being punished. A tablecloth that hung wrong because the person who set it had never met gravity. Plates with sugar-pink roses that made my teeth ache. I skirted the table and shouldered the servant door. It pretended to be a wall until the last second. It closed behind me and pretended it had never met me.

Narrow hall. Cedar and old coats. A window at the end that wanted me to go back outside where the floors multiply. The glass threw my light back at me and waited for me to make the romantic choice. I took the plain door with the cheap knob and the ghost of many hands. Hinges squealed like gossip.

A lounge spread itself out like a memory of someone else's better high school. Trophy case. Pool table. Lamp buzzing in an old key. The cue leaned in the corner, chalk worn to a perfect cone. When I passed, the balls settled with a click, a sound designed to slow you down. I did not slow.

The hallway tried the false outdoors again. Painted sky with a crack running through the clouds. A tree leaning away from the wrong wind. Gravel made of glued pebbles that scuffed under my soles anyway. The crosswalk light at the far end cycled through its colors without a chirp. I jogged past and did not step on it. Superstition or instinct, take your pick.

A door to the left tried on the shape of my kitchen. Pencil mark at the baseboard. Chair against the pantry. Humming that could have been my old fridge but the pitch was wrong by a hair. I set my ear to the panel and listened. The hum shifted toward the House's count like a singer with a good ear. I moved to the next door, the one that did not ask for my trust, and went through.

Stairs again. Down into air that tasted like pipes and old water. The rail warmed under my palm. The pounding arrived a room over my shoulder and considered. I felt it in the line of the rail, a small electric hum that had nothing to do with electricity. At the landing a nail head sat proud. I skipped it and took the corner.

A service corridor with tile that cracked in repeating squares. A plastic crate flipped on its side to be a shelf. A mop head in the corner that had chewed itself into a rag. The smell of old bleach and fresh damp fighting for the same space. The pounding entered behind me without hurry and tested the air the way a dog does at a screen door.

Right was a rectangle of fluorescent light. A vending alcove waited with two plastic chairs and a machine full of snacks behind glass. Every button said SOLD OUT in the kind of font that belongs in schools and laundromats. I pressed one anyway. The coil twitched and held. The chair agreed to carry me if I needed to sit. I did not.

Back past the crate. A gray fire door with a push bar. I pushed. It gave me the deadweight refusal of a door that has decided not to be useful. A sign beside it read STAIRS with an arrow pointing into a wall. I did not have the patience for the joke.

Utility room. Pumps talking to themselves. Mist in the air that catches a beam and makes a column. I touched a valve. It shivered like a living thing. I left it alone. I do not need to be brave in dumb ways.

Another flight, short and wrong. The window in the door at the top showed gray on gray, a hint of horizon that did not belong. I leaned my forehead against the glass for a second. The bruise at my brow announced itself. Sharp and honest. I took that pain because it was mine and it did not require me to learn anything.

Inside, a porch that thinks it is outside. Painted balusters. A rug that says WELCOME in a font that belongs to neighbors. Four doors, each with a wreath from a different season. The crosswalk light set at the steps again, cycling red to white to red. I stepped over it and took the second door because my hand moved that way without asking permission.

A parlor. Piano to the right, keys with a little dust line where no one has played. Hymn left open because someone wanted to suggest a personality. The bench had the exact crease an aunt would leave. The pounding reached the porch and pressed down through the piano. The strings sang without being touched, humming a note a hair off the one in my chest. I dropped the lid and cut the sound with a soft clack. The air took the message.

Rooms came in a chain after that. Sewing room with a machine that still smelled like oil. A pantry that was not mine, with tidy shelves that held nothing I wanted to eat. A study that tried to be the first study and missed the shade of green by enough to make my teeth set. A bedroom with my jacket on the chair and the wrong chair under it. A bathroom where the water flirted with turning red and then settled for clear because I had already told it no once today. My phone buzzed against my thigh. One polite pulse. I pulled it out. Sixty-six percent, like a joke stuck on repeat. I put it away and said a word that would have made my mother wince. The House swallowed the word and gave me nothing back.

The hallway bent and offered me three choices. Proud door. Modest door. Bare arch. I took the arch. You can see danger through an arch. You can negotiate with a door only if it wants to be fair.

Gallery. Paintings hung in ranks with their faces turned to the wall. Little labels with soft museum voices told me what I was choosing not to see. Maiden with Dog. Rider in Blue. Boy at Riverbank. The air tasted like glossy paper and dust. The pounding entered by another door and set the dust to lift and fall like someone shaking a blanket at the far end.

At the end of the gallery, double doors waited with brass rubbed to coin color by a thousand hands. I took both handles and pulled. The wood argued, then remembered it had to behave, then opened in a rush that made me stumble. On the other side, a kitchen that was almost mine, a copy built from memory and guesswork. Pencil line at the baseboard but too high. Chair in front of the pantry at the wrong angle. The fridge humming the wrong note, just enough to bother a person who listens for those things.

I backed out and let the doors fall. The brass shivered under my palms when the pounding hit the far side a second later. I felt it in my teeth again. I took the corridor that had not shown itself to me yet, because that has been the way through since the first night.

Stairs down into a concrete room that did not care about family photos. The bulb at the bottom decided to turn on for me. It lit a square of floor and a drain and a chalk line walked through so many times it had turned into a fog. The air tasted like cold water and iron. The pounding reached the top of the stairs and set its hand on the rail. I felt it in the wood as a small hum that knew my name.

A door waited on the far wall with a keyhole like a blind eye. I set my thumb to the hole and gave it a little skin. The metal bit and remembered how to be used. The latch pulled itself together and gave.

On the other side, more concrete. A pump somewhere pulling its weight. No piano. No chairs. No photos. No family. Just a room and the work of keeping a building dry. I stepped through and pulled the door until the latch caught.

I did not check the keyhole. I did not check my phone. I set the beam to a narrow line and started walking.

If I stopped, I knew what would happen. So I did not.

RUNNING IS THE ONE thing my body knows how to do without a committee. I get off the rug and onto the wood at the edge because cheap runners always try to eat your heels. The hallway breathes that damp paper smell. Wallpaper hangs in long tongues. A stain runs down the center like a bad river. The pounding behind me finds the stair and starts up again, not quick, just sure. Whoever it is knows this place in the dark.

Left throws a mirror at me with a flash of gold around it. It wants to hand me a nicer face. I do not give it mine. Right is plain paint and a scuff where shoulders hit. I take right, palm against the wall to feel the tug of paint. My light skates ahead. The beam bows at the edges like the air is tired.

A door opens on a nursery that has all the props and none of the life. Tiny shoes lined up like judges. Crib with no mattress. A mobile turning even though the room is still. The song it would play lives in the back of my throat. I shut the door with the heel of my hand and do not look at the toys. The latch gives a small sorry click and I leave it to feel bad on its own time.

Half stairs that want to be both directions. My legs make it work because that is what legs are for. The heartbeat room sits to my left with church manners. There is a push at my skin like a hand that means well and will not take no for an answer. I do not match it. The far door offers a seam for one breath and hides it when I refuse the dance. I keep to the corridor and find my own seam two doors later where the paint sags over a hidden frame. The latch lets me through with a sigh that sounds like someone who wanted to argue and did not.

The ledger study waits with three lamps in a triangle and my name open on a page that has never met me. I cut a diagonal across the rug and leave a footprint where a good guest would not. The desk reaches for my hip and misses. The sound behind me rounds the corner in the hall with a confidence that makes my teeth hurt. I take the far door and do not let the room have my eyes on the way out.

Next is a kitchen that cleans up nice in the places you can see. Enamel stove with a lazy blue pilot that watches like an eye. The sink drips in a rhythm that wants to pull my pulse into step. I twist the tap and stop it. The clock over the door flicks from 3:11 to 3:09 and back. I do not let it argue me into caring.

Dining room. Chairs pulled out a hand width like kids being scolded. A tablecloth that hangs wrong because whoever set it has never trusted gravity. Plates with sugar pink roses that make my molars itch. I slide along the sideboard and hit the servant door with my shoulder. It pretends to be a wall until I am halfway through, then acts like it has always been a door. It shuts behind me and plays innocent.

Narrow hall with cedar and old coats in the air. Window at the end that wants me to climb out onto the skin of the house again and play the height game. The glass throws my beam back at me. I take the plain door with a cheap knob crowded by ghost fingerprints. Hinges squeal like gossip and then pretend they did not.

A lounge opens up like a memory from someone else's trophy case. Pool table under a buzzing lamp. Cue chalk worn to a perfect cone. When I pass, the balls twitch and settle with a click that is designed to slow you down. I keep moving. I do not owe this room my nostalgia.

Another false outdoors. Sky painted on plaster with a crack right through a cloud. Tree leaning away from the wrong wind. Gravel made of glued pebbles that still scuff under my shoes. The crosswalk light sits at the far end and cycles red to white to red with no chirp. I run through the scene and do not step on the light. I do not need to find out what happens if I do.

A door to the left tries on my kitchen shape. Pencil mark at the baseboard, chair braced against the pantry, hum from the fridge. The pitch is wrong by a hair. I put my ear to the panel and listen. The hum slides toward the House's count like a singer sitting in on a song. I step away. The next door waits like a person who does not need attention to have worth. I take that one.

Stairs down into air that tastes like metal and old water. The rail warms under my palm as if it remembers hands. The pounding enters this level without hurry and tests the floor. I feel it in the line of the rail, a small hum that knows names and does not say them out loud. At the landing a nail head sits proud. I avoid it because I refuse to leave my blood where the House requests it.

A service corridor stretches on. Tile cracked in a grid. Plastic crate turned on its side to be a shelf. Mop head collapsed in the corner like a wet animal. Old bleach tang fights with fresh damp. I pass a vending alcove with two plastic chairs and a machine full of chips and candy behind glass. Every button says SOLD OUT in a font that belongs in high school gyms and laundromats. I press one anyway. The coil twitches. Nothing drops. The chairs look like they would agree to hold me if I sat. I do not sit.

Back across. Gray fire door with a push bar. I push. It gives me the dead weight of a door that has chosen not to help. Sign beside it reads STAIRS with an arrow that points nowhere useful. Cute. I do not clap.

Utility room. Pumps talking to themselves in a steady breath. Mist hangs in the beam. I touch a valve and it shivers like a living thing. I leave it alone. I am done being brave in dumb ways for rooms that clap when I hurt myself.

Short stair that wants to be longer. The window in the door at the top shows gray stacked on gray with a single darker line that might be a horizon or a trick. I rest my forehead against the glass for one count. The bruise at my hairline answers me like a coin tapped on a table. Pain is honest. I take it and open.

A porch that thinks it is outside. Painted balusters. Rug that says WELCOME in a font I do not trust. Four doors, each with a wreath for a different season. The crosswalk light sits at the top step and cycles its colors. The wood under my feet has that old house give, the kind that answers you back. The pounding arrives on the porch and the boards admit the weight without telling me what it is.

I step over the light and take the second door because my hand goes there on its own. A parlor waits with a piano and a hymn open on the stand. The bench has the dip an aunt would leave. Keys show a dust line where no one has played. The pounding lands on the porch again. The piano hums in sympathy, a half note off what lives in my chest. I close the lid and cut the sound. The room takes the hint.

Rooms chain after that like beads on a string someone pulled too tight. Sewing room with oil under the metal. Pantry in a different house with tidy shelves and nothing I want. Study that tries to be the first one and misses the shade of green by enough to make me mad. Bedroom with my jacket on a chair, wrong chair under it. Bathroom that flirts with turning the tap red, thinks better of it when I stare. My phone buzzes once against my thigh. I look. Sixty-six percent again. No banner. I put it away and swear under my breath. The House keeps the word. It gives me nothing back.

The hall turns and hands me three choices. Proud door. Modest door. Bare arch. I pick the arch because at least you can see through an arch. Gallery beyond, walls hung with paintings turned to face the wall. Labels do soft museum talk I do not read. Maiden with Dog. Rider in Blue. Boy at Riverbank. Dust shifts near my ankles when the pounding enters by a different door. It rides the air like a change in weather.

Double doors at the end wear brass rubbed to old coin by a thousand hands. I take both handles and pull. The wood sulks, then gives up and moves, then swings fast enough to make me catch myself. On the other side is a kitchen that wants to be mine. Pencil line at the baseboard, but higher than I drew it. Chair at the pantry, wrong angle. Fridge hum off by a hair. The light feels like my light and is not.

I back out and let the doors fall. A second later the hit lands on the far side and the brass shivers under my palms. It bites into the meat of my hand. My teeth answer with a buzz like I touched a live wire. I take the corridor that has not flirted with me yet. The ones that wait tend to be honest.

Stairs. Concrete air. A bulb at the bottom that decides to live for me. The square it lights holds a stain, a drain, and a chalk line walked through until it looks like fog. The pounding rides the rail behind me. I feel it as a small hum along the palm, too close to be a trick and still not a footstep. The door on the far wall has a keyhole like a blind eye.

I press my thumb into the hole and feel the bite of old metal. A little skin for a favor. The latch remembers what doors are for and lets me in.

More concrete. Pump breathing slow and steady like a machine that has learned to be a pet. The air is clean in a way that is not kind, just plain. No family photos. No piano ready to hum. No study that wants to teach me a lesson I already learned. Just a room doing its job.

I pull the door until the latch seats. I do not look back through the keyhole. I do not check my phone. I set the flashlight to a narrow line and start walking because the rule in my blood is simple now. If I stop,

I die. I say it in my head without drama. True things do not need big speeches.

The pounding hits the door once with the kind of pressure a strong hand uses when it wants to feel wood remember. The door holds. The sound climbs off the wood and into the slab under my feet. The pump keeps talking in its patient voice. My breath stays long and quiet because that is what I can control. Mine. Not the House's. Not his. Mine.

The room bends into shadow and I go with it. If the House wants me, it has to come get me somewhere that does not care about its taste.

Chapter 13
The Heart of the Matter

THE CONCRETE HALLWAY SOUNDED like a machine with sleep apnea. The pump in the back room caught, hummed, and fell quiet, over and over, until the silence between each breath felt like a dare. My flashlight threw a skinny beam along the block wall. The paint down here wasn't paint so much as a film of damp dust that never learned to dry. It tasted metallic in the air, like I had a penny on my tongue.

"Riley."

I turned so fast the light smeared across the floor. For a second my brain said it was a trick. Then my body got there first and just about folded in on itself.

He stood where the corridor bent, half in shadow. Ten, maybe eleven. Too-long hair because Mom always put off haircuts until the coupon came in the mail. Those beat-up sneakers with the duct tape smile at the toe because he swore they were still good. His coat hung crooked. His ears were red like we'd just walked in from the cold.

"You... you can't—" I had to swallow to get the rest out. "You can't be here."

He kept looking past me into the dark. His shoulders squared in that stiff, brave way kids learn from superhero movies. He didn't smile. "I can for a minute."

Behind me, something hit a door like a slow car. The metal sang through the cinder block. It vibrated in the bones of the hallway and then inside my ribs. I felt my heart try to match it like a dumb echo and made myself breathe long, not deep.

"What is it?" My voice came out thin. "What's behind me?"

"Don't look," he said, and his face worked around the words like they were too heavy for his mouth. He pointed with his chin at a rectangle sawed near the floor, low and mean. A contractor hole. Sheetrock ragged along the edges, line of conduit disappearing into it, yellowed insulation fuzzed like old bread. "Go through there."

Another hit, closer. Hinges screamed in protest, then remembered how to hold. I couldn't help it. I turned.

The door bowed. It snapped back. And then something squeezed through the gap, slow like a bad memory you've been keeping out with furniture.

At first it was just the wrong color. Gray that wasn't just lack of light but the kind of gray you get when water swells skin and makes it too smooth in all the wrong places. Hair stuck to scalp in wet ribbons. A shirt I knew like the back of my hand. Baseball sleeves, white body, red raglan arms, the little tear near the hem that he always said gave it personality. A dull silver glint swung under the collar, knocking gently as it moved.

My stomach went to ice, then to steam, then to nothing at all. I couldn't hear the pump anymore. I could only hear the blood in my ears.

"Riley." The boy beside me didn't take his eyes off the thing at the door. "Please. Don't look. Go."

I dropped to my knees and shoved the flashlight in first. The hole smelled like gypsum and mouse track, like cardboard after rain. I slid my arms in up to the shoulder. The concrete scraped my elbows. My backpack caught. I wrenched and felt the fabric kiss a nail head and survive by stubbornness. The floor was gritty and close and made me into a crawl I hadn't done since I was a kid under a porch looking for a cat that did not want rescue.

Behind me, wet footfalls dragged over concrete. Not fast. Not slow. That steady, awful rhythm of something that has decided it doesn't need to hurry.

"Hey," the younger version of him said to the shape in the doorway, planting his sneakers like a crossing guard. "Not her."

I glanced back, because I am a human disaster, because I was his sister, because I have never once done the smart thing first. My light caught the chain as it swung and the charm at the end, the tiny metal dog he got from a quarter machine that he loved way past the day it turned his neck green. My light skated over his face. What was left of it. Lips that didn't meet right anymore. Eyes that were open and glassy and not mine to meet.

"Go," the kid said again, more urgent. "Riley, now."

I shoved harder. The hole narrowed for a breath and swallowed me to the hips. The world shrank to the sound of my own air and the scrape of my sleeves. I could feel the cold off the concrete, a kind of clean cold that still felt filthy. A cable thumped my shoulder and then skittered past my cheek. My hip stuck on a two-by, a bad angle that made the breath punch out of me.

I heard it then. The other him. The corpse. It made a sound I felt more than heard, like lake water pushing through reeds. My scalp crawled. I yanked at my jeans and kicked, heel looking for anything. I slid forward the length of my forearm.

"Hey," the kid-version of my brother said again. He didn't sound scared. He sounded tired and brave. "I said not her."

The hole dropped without warning. Not far, but fast. I slid and hit an edge, rolled, and dropped again. The flashlight clacked against my teeth and spit light across a new room. I landed on a carpet older than me, dust coughing up around me in a gray halo. Above, the contractor hole showed a ragged mouth of light and the small black cutout of a boy with his arms spread wide.

"Thank you," I breathed, and it felt small to say it to a ceiling. "I'm sorry."

There wasn't time to be anything else.

I stood. My knees tried to second-guess me and I ignored them. The flashlight recovered from its tantrum and settled into a steady beam. The room had that weird, fat light that only happens around yellowed lampshades. It looked like a waiting room for people who never got called.

But none of that was the point of this scene. The point was the door behind me, the door I had just left, the door that was going to fail. The clang hit again, too close now to pretend. I didn't need to be told twice.

I ran.

The floor had the give of old houses, that helpful flex that isn't reassuring. As I reached the far arch I let myself look back one heartbeat. Just one. The light from the hole above cut a trapezoid on the wall. The smaller shape in it had dropped out of sight.

"Okay," I whispered to the air, like a promise. "Okay."

The corridor beyond angled down and to the left. Concrete again. Painted cinder. The flashlight caught a line of water along the base where the slab met the wall, a thin vein that didn't care about anything human. My breath came in long pulls that tasted like a coin. I could still feel that rhythm behind me, inside the block, inside the metal, inside me.

I cut the light and listened.

Dragging steps. Not an effect. A body that has forgotten how to be a body. The chain tapped something and made a small bell of sound that hurt so much I forgot to breathe on purpose.

I switched the light back on, dropped to my knees, and slid into another contractor cutout a few yards ahead, this one tighter, this one set wrong and low like someone did it after a fight with the foreman. Conduit shoved my shoulder. A splinter from the two-by stung the meat of my palm and I let it. I needed honest pain. The scrape of my coat sounded too loud. I moved anyway. Left elbow. Right elbow. Boots dragging. Hips in. Breath long. Panic short.

Behind me, the door I'd left finally gave up its job with a sound like a rib coming loose. I felt it even though I couldn't see it. That steady, patient thing stepped through what used to be a doorway and became a shape in my head again.

"Riley." The kid's voice wasn't in my ear but it might as well have been. "Keep going."

"Trying," I said, because talking gave my fear a place to go that wasn't my hands. "I'm trying."

The hole broadened and then found a vertical drop. Not far. Maybe four feet. I let myself go. It was either fall or get dragged out by the ankle and I knew which one I could live with. I dropped into dark and hit on my shoulder and rolled and came up in a crouch with the light already cutting the room. I don't know when my body learned to do that, but thank God it did.

I was in a different space now, and the smell told me before the beam did. Not damp concrete. Not mouse. Paper. Powder. Rose soap. That sugar-sweet old-lady smell that sticks to clothes for days. The light swept the floor and found a braided rug. A footstool. The corner of a china hutch. My heart tried to be a rabbit and bolt. I put my palm on my chest and pressed until I could hear only my own count again.

Above, through the narrow path I'd just crawled, I heard one last drag, a dull thud, and then a sound like someone let go of a rope. I didn't know what that meant. I didn't want to. I stared at the door in front of me instead, because that was the choice on the table: keep moving, or let the house decide for me.

I kept moving.

I crossed the rug and touched the knob. It was warm, human warm, like a hand that expected me. I could feel my own pulse in my fingers. I turned it and stepped through into light that had waited for me for a very long time.

"Riley," a woman's voice said from a couch across a low table, warm and pleased and sharp as a needle hidden in wool. "Finally."

I knew that voice. I hadn't heard it in years. I didn't look yet. I made myself breathe in for two, out for six, that old trick I've used since the crash to ignore the panic and hear the truth. The truth was simple. I was not alone in this room, and the thing I'd left behind me had not given up.

I closed the door softly, like a guest with manners, and looked up.

"Hi, Gran," I said. "I can't stay."

The chain behind the wall tapped again, one last small bell, like a reminder that none of this was over.

THE ROOM LOOKED LIKE a magazine spread from the year my grandmother decided color TV was vulgar. Low couch with crochet throws. China hutch winking with plates no one ate off. Yellow lamp shades that made everything warm and heavy. A dish of ribbon candy sat on the coffee table in front of a neat stack of crossword books. The air carried rose soap, dust, and that old-lady sugar that never quite leaves your sweater.

"Finally," Gran said, hands folded on her skirt like she was about to say grace. Great-gran perched beside her, all bones and purse and eyes that weighed people like produce. Three other old women filled the rest of the furniture, knitting in perfect time, needles flashing silver, yarn vanishing into their laps like it came straight from the air.

"Hi, Gran," I said again, because my mouth needed work to do. "I can't stay."

"You always say that," she answered, kind as pie and just as binding. "Sit. Five minutes. We'll fix your color. You look washed."

Great-gran clicked her tongue. "She looks empty. Wind goes through. No husband. No children. She lives in paper rooms and eats cereal like a boy."

The woman nearest the lamp didn't look up from her needles. "She brought a draft with her. Shut that door tight, dear."

I kept my hand off the knob. I stayed standing.

Gran patted the cushion beside her the way you call a skittish dog. "Riley. Be a good girl."

"I'm thirty," I said. "And I'm leaving."

Great-gran's mouth made a small line. It used to freeze entire Sundays. "Do not argue with the dead," she said. "We won."

The nans' needles made a sound like rain on a tin roof. Their yarn was funeral black. I couldn't see a skein anywhere. It just spooled out of their laps, endless as bad habits.

"You're in danger," I said. "Something followed me."

Gran's smile didn't move but her eyes cooled a shade. "Consequences follow. Not everything is a wolf. Sit. We'll talk about habits. About presentation. You used to be pretty when you tried."

"I'm pretty now," I said, because some days you have to be your own mother. "I'm just tired."

"You're wrong," Great-gran said, soft and final. "You've been wrong since the day you left the church and didn't help your mother see people."

"We did it alone," Gran added, still pleasant. "You left us with the flowers and the casseroles. You left your brother on the road."

The room shifted, a gentle sway under the carpet. My throat tried to close. I kept my breath long. "The drunk driver killed him," I said. "I lived. I'm sorry every day. That won't make me sit."

The middle nan finally looked up. Her eyes were bright and flat, marble that learned how to judge. "We'll make tea," she said, like it settled things. "Sugar helps with shock."

"No tea," I said. "I know what happens when I drink things in this house."

Gran's smile lost its corners. "Riley." She put my name down like a plate she didn't want chipped. "Five minutes."

"No," I said.

The room took that personally.

The three knitters stood at the same time. The needles were longer than they should have been, bright and clean. The one by the lamp moved faster than her hips allowed and was on me in a blink, the needle a silver quickness in her hand. I jerked back. The point kissed my forearm and then bit. Heat flashed, followed by the sting. Blood slid fast, bright as candy against the room's butter light.

"Hey," I snapped, automatic and old. "No."

Great-gran didn't flinch. "Hold still."

The second nan came in low, needle for my thigh. I pivoted and she grazed me, shallow but mean. It burned like a paper cut from God. The third moved straighter than her back should have allowed, shoulder flat, face gone soft and hungry. Her needle flashed for my eye. I got my forearm up and she skated the cheekbone instead, a quick white-hot slice that filled with warmth.

"Riley," Gran said, disappointed. "Stop acting feral."

I backed toward the archway. The room tilted again, as if the house were breathing and this parlor was the lung. The wallpaper's tiny flowers seemed to turn their faces toward me, small polite witnesses.

"I'm not sitting," I said, and the shakiness in my voice made me mad enough to steady it. "I'm not letting you fix me. I'm leaving."

"Then we'll help you leave in pieces," Great-gran said, so gently it took a second to hear it. She stood without effort, purse still on her arm like she might go collect tithes after.

The knitters fanned to block the obvious door. The arch to my left had been a hallway when I glanced earlier. Now it was a shallow recess with a framed sampler: Home is where the heart is, red thread on yellow cloth. The H was bigger than the rest, a little crooked. The air leaned toward that frame. I did not.

"Window," I said to myself, because sometimes you have to narrate the solution. The curtains hung fat and heavy, lace underneath, floral over top. I grabbed the side and yanked. The rod popped free at one bracket with a tired squeal. Light behind the lace wasn't daylight. It was the same old-lady gold pressed up against dirty glass.

The nan nearest me darted, needle low for my ribs. I slammed the metal curtain rod down onto her knuckles. She hissed, more offended than hurt. The second came in for my calf. I jumped back, heel catching the braided rug. My knee buckled and I took the hit on the meat of my shin instead. Fire climbed my leg.

A laugh bubbled out of me, sharp and wrong. "Ow. Okay. We're stabbing now. That's where we are."

Gran stood. She didn't pick up a needle. She didn't need to. She had the room. "Riley," she said, and under the name was a weight I remembered from childhood, the one that made you hand over the thing you loved because it was time to be reasonable. "Enough."

"No," I said. "Not anymore."

I hauled the curtain aside. The window didn't give me street or yard. It gave me a panel that opened onto a shallow shaft, boards on boards, a wooden lip where a dumbwaiter used to live. Somewhere down there, air moved. Cool and mean, but it moved.

"Do not," Great-gran said, not loud, and my body almost obeyed out of long practice.

"Watch me," I said, because it has become my favorite prayer.

I slung the curtain rod through the handles of the nearest end table and jammed it between the table and the hutch, a quick little barricade that would slow exactly one person for exactly one heartbeat. It bought me that heartbeat. The first nan hit the table and stuttered. I grabbed the dumbwaiter frame, swung my legs through, and dropped.

My hands burned on old wood. Splinters drove into my palms like the room wanted a souvenir. The shaft sides were close enough to brace. I slid fast. A ledge broke under my boot with a rotten crack. I fell the rest of the way and hit hard on a floor that answered back like a drum.

Above, needles ticked the frame with angry little dings. Gran's voice drifted down, no longer sweet. "Riley, be sensible." The last word clipped off like a scissor cut.

"Not a great recruiter pitch," I muttered to the dark.

I stood. My cheek leaked warmth in a lazy line down my neck. My forearm throbbed in time with the house. The room I'd landed in breathed around me, soft pressure pushing and easing. The heartbeat room. Of course it was.

I turned in a slow circle, keeping my light down so it couldn't play tricks in the corners. The tea table sat where it always sits, ring of old stain shining in the flashlight like a target. The wallpaper hung in patient strips. Nails winked along the baseboard where someone had done a quick job and promised to make it neat later.

The floor under my boots lifted a hair and settled. Above, the needles tapped one more time, then stopped as if a signal had passed between them and the beating in the walls. Farther off, through wood and plaster, a weight moved the way a person takes a step when they are sure of the stair. The chain in my head tapped once against bone.

I wiped my cheek with the heel of my hand. It came away red and normal. The sting grounded me more than anything else tonight. I pressed my palm to the wall and felt for the pulse without letting my heart match it.

"Okay," I breathed. "Okay. You wanted a polite visit. You got me instead."

The house answered with a small, pleased thump, like laughter under a floor.

"Not funny," I said.

I kept my hand on the wall and walked it slow, the way you follow a fence line at night. The beat pressed back steady and smug. Somewhere inside the bones of the place, something else drew closer. Heavy, dragging. Patient. I could feel it in the screws, in the studs, the way you feel a train before you hear it.

"Gran?" I said to the ceiling, and my voice didn't shake. "You should lock your doors."

A low crack ran through the plaster over the arch, one line finding another like two strangers recognizing each other in a crowd. Dust came down in a soft veil.

Right. No more parlor voice. No more lessons. I wasn't the kid at the family reunion in a dress that itched. I wasn't the girl who left the church hall because the casseroles couldn't bear to watch her cry. I was a woman in a bad house that thought it knew me and I had a cut cheek and a working set of lungs.

I set my feet. I kept my breath long. And when the wall gave its second, deeper laugh, I laughed back.

THE ROOM BREATHED LIKE a chest with a fever. Not loud, not dramatic, just that steady push against my skin, then the easing back, a rhythm that wanted me to join it. I kept my hand flat on the wallpaper and counted the beat the way you count ceiling fan blades when you are trying not to cry. Two in. Six out. My breath, not the house's. The paper felt warm, almost damp, like it had learned skin from someone.

"Stay with me," I told myself. "My count."

Memory slid in sideways, the way pain does when you think you have it handled. Night wet as ink. Wipers crossing the glass like a metronome with a bad idea. My brother slouched in the passenger seat, making a case for the louder song. Construction cones spinning by like drunk fireflies. Headlights where they should not be. That cheap sick feeling when a person's future gets smaller inside your chest and you cannot make it stop.

"Not now," I said, and I did not close my eyes. If I closed them the house would hang pictures there.

The wall pulsed under my palm. A little stronger. The room pleased with me for paying attention. I stepped along the baseboard, shoulder to the paper, flashlight low. The beam bowed at the edges. Dust drifted and made slices in the light like old film. Nails winked in the trim where someone promised to come back and make it neat. They never did.

Above me, plaster cracked in a slow Y, then found another line and shook a dust veil loose. Farther off, through wood and air and intention, something heavy moved with patience. The way a person climbs stairs when they are not worried about time. That weight spoke to the studs. The studs told the rail. The rail told my bones.

"Mom," my mother said in a memory that did not belong to this room, a phone call inside a quiet library. You cannot keep living like this. I walked between Tall Grass and Teen Romance so I could cry in a section that would not judge me. I said I am doing the best I can. She said then do better.

The door I had shut a minute ago bulged inward. The latch tore free like a decision. The wood bent and snapped back, a stubborn rib. Once. Twice. The third hit brought a crack that ran straight down the stile. The fourth took the frame with it. The fifth made the hinges tired of their whole job.

I did not look. Looking is the invitation. I kept my fingers on the warm paper and found the seam I had felt before, that soft place where the heartbeat shifted under the wall like a fish turning in a pond. The house wanted me to match it. I refused. I pushed at the seam without giving it my count.

The door gave up. It did not swing open like a normal door. It scooped inward and stayed crooked in its sad shape. The thing that had been using it as a drum came through sideways.

I turned, because I am a person, because even smart animals look when the brush moves. The first shape through the gap was his shoulder. It caught on a hinge and tore skin in a long quiet peel. The color under the peel was wrong. Lake gray. Freezer white. The chain knocked the wood and made a small bell of sound that I felt in my teeth.

He was close enough now for detail. Hair stuck to his forehead in flattened cords. Lips parted, then forgot what to do. The charm at his throat took a slow swing and tapped the broken pane in the door, a merciful little cling that did not belong to any of this. I tasted metal before the chain touched me, the way your mouth knows blood is coming.

"I am sorry," I said, not smart, not useful. I said it anyway because I have carried the sentence in my mouth for years and it is heavy.

The first lunge was clumsy. He led with a shoulder the way boys do, like the world has always been the right size for them. I rolled right. His hand slapped wall where my face had been and left a print like a pressed leaf. A black shape bloomed under it and spread through the paper like oil in a napkin.

The second lunge had memory in it. He grabbed for my calf and got skin. Heat and cold at once. I kicked and saw stars and kicked again and the grip let go. The room rocked. The heartbeat shoved. The pulse tried to pull the shape of my breathing into itself. I shook my head hard enough to make the bruise at my hairline flare. The ordinary pain found me and held me down.

"Riley," my father said in a voice from a church hall full of casseroles. Stand up straight. Smile for the people who came. Do not make it harder than it is. I walked outside and let the rain wash my face so I did not have to make it do anything.

He swung a dead arm the way a living boy would. The hand missed my jaw by an inch and hit the wall. The sound went through the studs, through the floor, through whatever kept this room pretending to be a room. Something behind the boards flinched.

A plank popped near the baseboard. It came free like a bad tooth, loud for a second and then all at once. I smelled wet meat and old pennies. I saw red that was not paint. Not pretty. Wet, working red. Slick and shifting with veins that tightened and let go in slow, sure time. The wall was not a wall. The room was a rib cage wearing wood like a suit. The heart pressed itself against the opening, white film nursing a shine back to red.

"Got you." It came out like someone else said it. Mean as prayer. True as it needed to be.

My flashlight clattered under a chair. The beam went sideways and found the corner where dust had been saving itself for an event. I did not chase it. The broken plank lay half free, jagged point like a spear, three nails along one edge like teeth. I grabbed the wood with both hands. Splinters went in and my skin woke all the way up. Blood made my grip tacky and strong.

He reached for my throat. Fingers cold and thick, skin too smooth, pressure wrong. The charm at his throat knocked my lip and I tasted the quarter machine from the day he begged for it. He had been so alive that afternoon. Annoying and loud and brave. He had been real enough to take up space, and I loved that about him even when I said I did not.

"Enough," I told the house. I told the thing with my brother's shape. I told the part of me that wanted to hand the decision over to anyone who would take it.

I shoved the plank through the opening. The point hit slick red and skated. It squealed like glass under a shoe. I pushed harder and the point caught. The house made a noise that did not come through ears. My teeth grabbed it. My eyes watered. My hands tried to let go and I told them no.

The heart jumped. The whole room clenched and tried to spit the plank back out. I leaned on the wood with everything I had, shoulder to the board, hips braced, feet sliding on a rug that never did anything to anybody. The nails along the edge bit my knuckles and left little crescents. The smell got bigger, hot and salt and chemical, like a clean hospital and a dirty river at the same time.

He shuddered. Not a human shiver. Full body, wire gone slack. He grabbed me again out of habit and found nothing to hold. His mouth opened and shut. A sound came out that did not belong in a room. It belonged in a lake at night with a flashlight that never works.

"Please," I said without knowing who I meant it for. Maybe me. Maybe him. Maybe the part of this place that learned to eat from people.

I drove the plank deeper. I felt the point push past something that wanted to be a wall around a secret. The heart under the paper hammered once, twice, then lost count. It stumbled. It raced. It tried to climb a stair that did not exist. The pressure waves hit my chest in a run and then went thin. The house's hum slipped out of tune. The studs stopped passing messages and started complaining.

He sagged in sections. Knee, hip, shoulder, head. The chain at his throat swung and stopped. He folded down into the rug with that awful heavy surrender you see in empty coats. He was quiet in a way that did not belong to boys who argue about songs. The quiet made me sick and grateful in the same breath.

I held the plank until my arms shook. I held it until the pulse under my palm got smaller than my own. I held it until I realized I was crying and that the wet on my face felt normal. Salt and skin and the copper edge of a split lip. Nothing clever. Nothing haunted.

The wall flexed once around the wood, like a hand trying to keep a knife out after it is already in. The plaster above my head sighed. A thin line of water ran along the baseboard and turned pink and then went clear again, like the house was making an effort at dignity.

I eased the plank a half inch to see if the room would take the bait and spit it. It did not. It held. The beat stayed small. My own breath filled the space the house had been using, and that felt like a miracle you only notice because it has bad lighting.

I let the plank go. My palms were full of splinters. The skin at my knuckles looked like someone had practiced sewing there. I sat down hard because my legs told me the truth. They were done with my nonsense.

I looked at what the house had animated for me and hated it and loved it. It was not him. It had used him to get to me. The boy in the hall had held the door and bought me a minute. This thing had tried to spend that minute to make me give up.

"Thank you," I said, to the kid who had his ears red from the cold, to the girl I had been who wanted to run and did, to the stupid, stubborn woman on this rug who just put a board where it mattered.

Above, somewhere back in the parlor, needles clicked twice and then went quiet. The house breathed again, smaller now, like the fever had broken and left it tired. It would still try. That is what hunger does. But I had my count back, and the door I needed next would show itself because rooms make mistakes when they bleed.

I stood, slow so the room could not steal it and pretend it was mercy. I kept my eyes open. I kept my breath long. I kept my hands ready, even if they shook. The wall did not talk. The floor did not argue. The heartbeat did not set the pace anymore, and that was something I could call a win without lying to myself.

"Okay," I said, voice rough and mine. "You wanted me to join the rhythm. I will pass."

I touched the plank once, like a superstition, like a thank you, then I went to find the door that would hate that I had learned how to open it.

Chapter 14
DEATH OF A HOUSE

THE PLANK WAS BURIED in the wall up to the bruised heel of my hand. The wood around it had stopped trying to spit it out, like a throat that finally realized it had lost the argument. The heartbeat was smaller now, a dry flutter in a chest that used to be proud. The room breathed once like a tired dog and then settled into a shallow rhythm. I put my weight on the plank, felt the last stubborn twitch, and pried it free. The wet sound that followed shook the studs and rode the grain of the floor into my knees. The point glistened, then dulled. I did not look too closely at what clung there. I wiped it on the rag rug because that was what the house had used me for and it could have the stain.

When the plank came away, the wall flexed inward and then drew itself together with a shudder. The paper lifted in a ripple and lay back down. A seam opened in the corner where there had not been one before, a tidy doorframe hidden under two coats of paint. The latch learned itself into metal. The knob found a shape my hand knew. The house was dying and still remembered how to be polite. That might have been the meanest thing about it.

I pushed the door and stepped into a corridor that had decided to rot all at once. The plaster sagged in long soft folds and peeled in sheets that clung to my boots. Nails showed their teeth through paint and lifted like a dog that had heard footsteps on the walk. The floorboards cupped and opened their seams so that light from somewhere below sketched thin lines between boards. Frames on the wall had turned themselves around to show their gray backs to the room. A few had fallen. The glass had given up in place and sat as a slick lake of shards that had not worked up the energy to spread.

Movement shifted to my left where a bedroom had been. Mara stood in the doorway with her shoulder on the frame like she had been there for years and expected me to be late. Her hair hung to her shoulders in that nursing home way, too clean and flat from inexpensive shampoo. Her face had the waterweight look of a person pulled out of the wrong place. Her eyes cut through it. They were bright and resigned in a way that made my jaw ache. Behind her, other shapes stepped out of the architecture. An older man with carpenter shoulders and a plaid shirt that had worked a thousand mornings. A woman in a church dress with a corsage smashed flat against her collar like she had hugged too hard. A kid in a varsity jacket with numbers in a font that belonged to a high school four decades ago. A nurse. A man in coveralls. A woman with curler dents pressed into her hair like the day had caught her before she wanted it.

They did not run. They did not lunge. They advanced the way water moves up a beach when the angle is right. My skin tried to come off my body and leave without me. I moved because every animal knows to run from tides that come indoors.

The corridor stretched in that trick the house loved, like chewing gum pulled by a bored kid. The farther I ran the more hallway I bought. Doors drifted past, new ones, wrong ones, doors that should have been outside, doors that belonged in schools and hotels and church basements. The house smelled like wet paper and hot wiring. The air tasted like nails and sugar dream dust. Dust skated up from the floor in little eddies and tried to choke me sweetly.

I hit a double door with my shoulder. It opened inward on a dining room that had been dressed for a holiday the family never made it to. Three long tables ran the length of the space with lace runners and plates that threw back my light. The cloth had yellowed to the color of old piano keys. I could feel the dear expense of it all sitting on top of the rot, the way people save their best for moments and miss the moment in the saving. The chairs were high backed and looked both fragile and smug. Above, two chandeliers hung with crystals that trembled when the house breathed wrong. They clicked against each other and made a sound like ice cubes in a glass.

Place cards waited in tidy angles. I glanced at the nearest one while my hands were still deciding where to go next. Riley, written in a precise hand. The next one read the same. Every plate had my name. The house had set a table I would never sit at. The petty cruelty took my breath for a half second. That was all it got from me.

The corpses filled the door behind me like a school of fish turning a corner. The group from the hall had become a crowd. Different decades had joined them and brought their regrets like casseroles. I saw a hairnet. I saw an apron. I saw a man in a suit with wet shoulders and mud spatters at the knee. I saw a little boy with a toy car clenched in one hand like a weapon. Mara stood at the front of them. She did not move her feet. She did not need to. Her presence leaned in the room like a person with perfect timing.

I ran down the right side of the nearest table and the table shifted under me. I had forgotten how old wood cheats under linen. The leg at the far end gave a tired surrender and the whole length tilted. Plates slid and kissed and shattered in edits. Glass rained from the chandelier when the tilt pulled the wires in the ceiling. I ducked and put my forearms over my head as the first crystals came down in sheets. They struck the table and bounced and skittered. One broke and the edges were fine as hair. Another hit my coat and stayed. I felt the weight and wanted to laugh because it was showy and wrong. Of course the house would cut me with decorations.

I climbed across the collapsing table like it was a surfboard going out from under me. The tablecloth took that as encouragement and rode with me. A runner wrapped itself around my boot. I kicked free and felt the lace tear in a way that made some mean corner of me cheer. The table groaned and dropped another inch and then gave up pretending to be furniture entirely. I slid off the far side as it went. I landed on my hip and rolled a half roll that had learned itself in junior high when gym teachers still believed in mats.

The doors at the far end were shut with chair backs leaned against the handles. I yanked one chair and the joints protested in a small animal voice. It came away and tried to fold. I shoved the door with my shoulder and it did not give. A hand closed on the wood above my head. Another hand balled a fist and prepared to knock. The hands were not in the same place. They were on different doors. The room did not need me to choose. It wanted to keep me while it made the decision on my behalf.

I dropped to my knees and reached for the gap under the doors. Cold air breathed there like a subway coming in. I shoved my fingers under and felt clean wood, then grit, then a wedge somebody had kicked in decades ago and never removed. I pulled. The wedge did not move. I swore and reached for the other door. My knuckles met old gum and a sticky bit of tape. I dug with my nails until the tape gave and a second wedge loosened. The door shook and took pity. It opened a mean two inches and stopped. I shoved my shoulder into it again and felt a bar on the other side give up with a shrug. I thought of all the stupid toys I had broken as a kid because I did not know how to be gentle. I felt grateful for once that I had learned to be a bully at the right time. The gap went to six inches. I pushed through sideways, reached back and pulled my bag after me by the strap.

Behind me the crowd reached the edge of the tables. The boy with the car put it down for a second as if he had found the exact right place to play. The little wheels spun on linen full of glass dust. Mara stepped onto a chair seat without looking down. She moved the way you move when you have lived through a hundred clumsy rooms and do not consent to fall for them.

The corridor beyond the dining room had learned to be a spine. It ran straight, too straight for a house this size. Doors opened into it at precise intervals like the ribs of a whale. Light bulbed and dimmed in the ceiling. Wiring buzzed behind cracked plaster with a fast burr that made my teeth crawl. The air felt moist like a mouth and cold like an old fridge that never learned how to seal. My footsteps sounded wrong in the space, too thin, like the floor had become a bridge over a long nothing and was tired of the job.

A portrait on the wall tried to face me. The canvas had been turned to show the gray back like the others. The nails had worked loose from the plaster and the frame twisted on one screw and learned an angle that felt like a neck. I did not give it my light. I did not give it my eyes. I had no more time for the house's small art.

I ran. The corridor learned to be longer with each step and then gave up on tricks and threw me out into a utility space that should not have fit inside a house that used to hold leftover women and arguing families. It had the narrow concentration of a service hallway, lined with enamel sinks and metal racks and two machines that belonged in a laundromat. Steam coughed up from a pipe near the ceiling and condensed on the tile in a film that made every edge shine like a trap. The air smelled like bleach and the river we had picnicked beside when we were kids. The combination punched me in the head in a way that teetered between old summer and hospital panic.

Laundry baskets sat on wire shelves with masking tape labels that ran across decades. Jean. M. Doyle. Mrs. Herz. Mara. Someone had written that last one in black marker on a sock that had been pinned to the line with a wooden clip. The sag of the sock put a face in the knit. That was my brain, not the house. I forced my eyes to the machines instead.

A wringer sat in the corner, the old crank kind with rollers that should have belonged to a movie about women with kerchiefs and cigarettes. It turned by itself, a slow rotation that wanted to be hypnotic. The mouth of it yawned wider than it should have, like a smile. I hugged the wall wide of it. The rollers reached like they were trying to meet me halfway and grazed the cuff of my sleeve. The pull on the fabric was small and deep and ugly. I yanked free and left a crescent of denim in the rubber. The wringer got a souvenir. I got my arm back.

The washers thumped like heart chambers. One of the lids shuddered, then popped on its hinge, and hot gray water sloshed over the rim. It ran to the floor grate and then chose not to go down. It gathered along the low spots in the tile and turned pink under my light. I refused that hint on principle. If the house wanted to color my fear it could find a new box of crayons. I focused on the far door where a small wire window gave me a square of a pale refrigerator glow.

The corridor behind me filled with sound. Feet shuffled and rubber tires squealed in that sharp, small protest wheelchair wheels make in hallways. A laugh arrived, too high for an adult and too steady for a child. The sound did not bounce around the tile like it should have.

It came straight, like a wire under floor that carried things you did not want to hear.

I threaded between machines, shoulder brushing enamel, the heat of a motor breathing into my coat. The wringer mouth followed me on its slow axis and found my sleeve again. I twisted away and my backpack strap got friendly instead. The rollers tasted the nylon and then bit. The pull was sudden and greedy. It yanked my shoulder sideways and spun me in place. I jammed my hand into the rollers, palm flat on rubber, and shoved like I was feeding the house a piece of me it would not know what to do with. The motor ground. The belt squealed. The teeth on my spine sent up a flare to remind me that I was not an appliance.

"Let go," I told the machine, which is not how machines work. The motor burned my palm through the rubber. The wrinkle in the strap gave. The roller coughed the nylon back in a wet little spit. I stumbled and caught myself on the slop sink. The water in it was gray and thick and did not slosh right when my hand hit the edge. I pulled away and wiped my palm on my jeans because a person always goes back to what has saved her a hundred times. The denim took my fear. It did not care.

A man in coveralls stepped out from behind a dryer. Half his face had collapsed into itself sometime after he lost the ability to care. The other eye watched me with the steady blue you see in a person who learned to stare everything down by keeping his jaw shut. He reached for my ankle as I passed. His hand closed on my boot with the kind of familiar grip that felt like a bad memory of a boyfriend I should never have let drive. I kicked the wrist. The bone gave under the leather like an old chair when you put a suitcase on it and lie to yourself about the weight. He held on anyway because sometimes stubborn is the last thing left. I kicked again and felt something shift. The hand fell away and the body tipped like a dented soda can.

Pipes banged overhead. A valve blew with a whistling hiss and a ribbon of steam cut the air in front of me. It laced my face, hot and thin and mean. I lifted my forearm to take it and hissed because I am alive and skin remembers. We formed a little triangle of pain, me and the steam and the tile that wanted me to slip. I stayed upright through luck and rage. The others reached the door to the laundry and hesitated because they were learning the room and the room had too many rules to learn quickly. I took the second it bought me and broke the only rule that still mattered to me.

I killed the lights.

I slapped my hand to the switch and snapped it down. The fluorescents cut. The room fell into a slow, oven hot dark. My flashlight took over. The beam wrote a path for me across tile the color of old gum. In the dark the bodies forgot the room for one beat, which was all I needed. The wringer mouth did not forget. It reached for my light instead and I let it because I am done being tricked by small hunger pretending to be big.

I used the wringer belt as a handhold and slung myself past, pain singing in my palms where the rubber and heat had already burned me. The far door waited with a wire window that shivered under my light and showed a slice of a countertop that looked almost mine. The doorknob was cheap steel gone slick with humidity. I twisted and it held because the house will always try to teach even while it dies, and sometimes it picks the most boring lesson.

I kicked the door right at the latch like my brother used to kick the bottom of the vending machine when his Snickers stuck. The cheap latch popped. The door shuddered open six inches and tried to slam back. I slammed first. The hinge screamed. I pushed through into a kitchen that was not my kitchen, but wore the costume well enough to pass in bad light.

Behind me, somewhere in the laundry, a wheelchair squealed again, then stopped in a way that made the hair between my shoulders stand up. Water ticked along the floor into the grate and went down with a wet reluctance. Someone laughed, smaller now, as if I had walked farther away from what made the laugh sound like a person.

HUMIDITY HITS LIKE A wet towel to the face. The tile is the color of old gum and shines from a film that never dries. Steam coughs from a pipe that someone patched with a clamp and a prayer. The air tastes metallic with a top note of bleach that sits at the back of my tongue and refuses to leave. I keep my light low and move in a line between enamel sinks and machines that look like they were stolen from a laundromat in 1979 and taught to hate.

A wringer sits crooked on a steel cart by the slop sink. It turns by itself, slow and patient, like it has all night to pull something through. The rollers shine with a coat of rubber that looks soft until you think about how many knuckles it has met. The mouth of it is too wide, a little grin that makes me keep my shoulder tucked as I pass. I smell hot motor windings and the sour of old suds settling in a trap. Somewhere behind the wall a pump kicks on and off in a rhythm that tries to talk my heart into keeping time. I put my breath back on my count and refuse the invitation.

Feet begin to drag in the corridor behind me, rubber soles squealing when they forget the angle. There is a smaller squeal that rides on top, that high wheel sound you only hear on tile in schools and hospitals. It hits my spine and crawls down. The urge to sprint is loud and stupid. Sprinting is how you skid into a grab. I stay fast without losing traction, hands up where I can use them, flashlight painting me a clean line to the door with the wire window at the far end. The glass glows with the pale square of a refrigerator light. It should comfort me. It just makes me aware of how far that door is.

The wringer's mouth finds my sleeve. The pull is so deep and sudden it feels personal. My arm yanks sideways and spins me a quarter turn. The cart wobbles. The motor hums harder like it is pleased to be useful. My brain serves up a memory of my grandmother telling me not to play with things that do not love me back. I jam my free palm against the top roller and shove into the spin. Heat comes through the rubber and bites the heel of my hand. The belt under the casing squeals like it has been asked to do something outside its job description. The cuff of my sleeve stretches, gives a thread, then another, and finally rips free with a soft, mean sound. The roller burps a scrap of denim like a souvenir and goes back to its lazy turn.

I move again, faster now because the room is awake, across a checkerboard of cracked tile and low puddles where the floor does not drain right. The first industrial washer clunks and shudders, lid trembling against the latch. Gray water sloshes over the enamel rim, hits the floor in a flat sheet, and makes a run for the grate. The second machine thumps like a heart chamber and then bangs hard enough to walk an inch. I give both a wide berth. A pipe above me knocks, then explodes at a corroded elbow. A thread of steam stitches the air from ceiling to shoulder. It hits my forearm and writes a fast line of pain along the skin, the kind that makes your breath stop just to count it. I take two steps sideways, out of the plume, and feel the water on the floor turn warm around my ankles. The puddle picks up a pink tint like someone dropped food coloring in and forgot to stir. I do not chase that thought. I do not give the room my imagination for free.

A shape rises from behind the dryer with the small grunt of a man who always stood that way. Coveralls, zipper buckled at the throat. Half his face drifts toward collapse, the skin settling in ways it never planned. The other eye is the steady blue of someone who fixed things for a living without a lot of noise about it. He steps out with a rhythm that used to belong to union floors and reaches for my ankle like it is the next job on the clipboard. His fingers find the top of my boot and clamp. The grip is strong and greedy with that lost-human persistence that has nothing to do with anger. I kick his wrist twice. The first kick makes his hand tighten. The second finds the thin bone along the thumb and makes a small shift that feels like permission to leave. His hand falls. He goes to one knee like a man checking a leak and stays there, patient and wrong.

The corridor behind me fills with bodies that have learned enough to care about angles. The wheelchair squeal comes again, closer now, paired with the rubber scuff of someone pushing a little too fast. A laugh floats under the machine noise, small and delighted, the sound a kid makes when his toy finally does the thing. I do not turn. The lights are a grid of humming tubes and they make the steam look like curtains. I reach the switch at the end of the rack and snap it down.

Dark changes the rules. The fluorescents cut and the room drops into the thin cone of my flashlight and the glowing rectangle of the far door. In the dark the dead forget the floor for one beat. They pause like birds in a gust. The wringer keeps turning because machines do not notice theater. I keep moving. I slide along the wringer cart and, because I am done letting the room set the moves, I grab the return belt with both hands and use it to sling myself forward. The friction heats my palms again and scrapes new skin. The belt lurches and drags me half a step farther than my legs planned. My shoulder clips the edge of the slop sink. The stainless rim punches a new planet into my upper arm. I swallow the noise and keep going because pain is information and I have learned to sort.

Water sheets over the tile, finds my tread, and tries to make me choose the floor. I set my weight flatter and ride it. The far door waits with that stubborn cheap knob and the wire glass that makes everything look like a memory. The glow on the other side is steady and domestic in a way that feels like a trick but still moves me faster. I hear the cart wheels behind me now, the squeal and chatter as they cross puddles and find resistance. Someone's shoe squeaks the way kids learn to make it squeak in gym to get attention. It all hits my back like a crowd at a parade starting to lean.

The door is locked. Of course it is. The latch has the same cheap rattle as every interior door in this house. I put my hand on the knob and it slips under my wet palm. I wipe my hand on my jeans and try again. The metal squeals but does not give. I can feel the cheap screws flexing in the strike plate, a tiny complaint that suggests it has never been asked to do real work. The wheelchair bumps a machine behind me and the wringer cart rolls a few inches over my shoe. I plant my feet. I kick the door right at the latch the way my brother used to kick the vending machine when his candy hung up. The metal shim inside shifts and snaps with a noise that makes me feel ten years younger in a single mean rush. I shoulder the door. The gap opens. The house tries to close it. I put my hip into it and push until my legs shake.

I get six inches, then eight. The hinge cries out. The frame whispers. The door wants to come back out of habit. I keep it open because I am in no mood to be polite. The rectangle of the wire window slides past my shoulder and shows me a countertop I know too well and a cheap fluorescent that buzzes with a pitch I could hum in my sleep.

The fridge light bleeds along the base of the door in that tired lemon glow. The air that leaks through is colder by a clean degree. It smells like my house when I forget to turn the heat up before bed.

The floor behind me slicks again as more gray water finds its way to my shoes. A soft, rubbery thump tells me someone tried to step fast and found the wrong lesson. The wheelchair squeal stops dead and then begins again with an angry little hop. The laugh returns, smaller now that I am leaving, like a radio turned down in a room I no longer rent. I do not look back. I put my shoulder to the door and carve another inch.

The wringer nips my backpack strap one last time like a bitter aunt calling you by the wrong name at Christmas. I let it have a thread and take the rest with me. The knob bites my forearm as the door flexes, then gives me my own skin back. The opening is wide enough now to let a person through without losing a shoulder. I step into it sideways with the bag high and the flashlight low. The cold from the other side curls around my shins and promises me linoleum that does not shift. I take it.

For one second I hang there, weight split, one boot on slick tile and one toe on the threshold, listening to the room behind me breathe through the machines. I hear water hitting water. I hear a belt complain. I hear a wheel learn it cannot turn where it wants to turn. I hear the air conditioner hum on the other side of the door and feel stupid relief flood my chest because a normal noise is the only prayer I have left. I pull the door wider, put my heel into the kitchen, and step through into light that is wrong in all the right ways.

THE DOOR GIVES AND I spill into a kitchen that looks like mine put on wrong. The hum is a hair low. The light burns a tired white that makes the corners feel farther away than they should be. The linoleum has the same fake stone pattern, but the seams wander like a drunk signature. The pencil mark on the baseboard sits two inches too high, a lie told with confidence. The chair that should brace the pantry is there, but it leans at a sulky angle that says it was thrown instead of placed. The air carries a cold clean edge that rides under something sweet and stale, like a bakery closed on a hot day.

I keep the flashlight low so it cannot paint ghosts on the oven glass. I move along the counter with my left shoulder to the room and my right hand on the bag strap. The drawer pulls are the same cheap brushed steel I keep meaning to swap out, but they feel heavier here, as if someone added grief when they were not looking. The stove chip at the front corner is larger and the enamel around it has a wet shine like the wound refuses to scab. The cabinet doors sit a touch proud of the frames. Someone slammed them and never learned how to be gentle. It feels like a joke meant for me.

I see her in the oven's reflection before I turn. The glass throws back a narrower version of me with a split across the brow and sugar clinging to my coat, then folds that image around Mara standing three feet behind me. Her hair lies flat and obedient. Skin rides soft over bone the way water does after too long in a bed. Her mouth looks trained for company smiles. The eyes are wrong for all that. They are bright like a hidden match and they look straight at me.

"You got farther than I did," she says. The voice is the one from the notebooks, consonants clipped a little tight, vowels practical, a person who writes lists and then eats the lists when she runs out of paper.

"You're Mara," I say, and hearing it out loud makes the room feel smaller but more honest.

She looks past my shoulder to the pantry door without moving her head, like the thought itself has a weight. "I tried to map it. The house reads. It turns pages. It liked that I thought I could leave notes for anyone but it."

The dead fill the doorway behind her in a slow, neat fan. The man in coveralls comes first with his wrist at a crooked angle that does not trouble him. The church lady with the crushed corsage follows with her hands folded like she is waiting for the blessing. The boy in the varsity jacket shifts his weight with a bored patience that makes me want to throw him into adulthood just to wipe the look off his face.

The little boy with the toy car holds it against his chest. Others I do not know crowd behind them in a gray arrangement of decades and bad endings. They do not reach. They make a shape around Mara like a halo you would never invite into your house.

The fluorescent strip above the sink buzzes hard enough to set my teeth on edge. The kitchen timer on the stove wakes up and starts counting backward with a cheerful click that does not care about context. The cutlery drawer shivers against closed wood. The cabinet above the sink yawns and shows me the bottoms of clean plates stacked by a person who needed order.

"I need the door," I say. There is no please left in me.

"It is a door," Mara answers. She takes a step that is almost a sway. "It is also a mouth."

I keep the pantry in my peripheral because the house loves nothing more than a last second from the wrong angle. "Did you ever get it open?"

"I reached it." Her fingers flex and I see raw places on her palms where skin tried to leave. "It stuck. It liked the sound I made when I thought it would move and it did not."

The timer ticks down through a number that belonged to a birth-day I hated. My stomach flips for no good reason. I set the bag on the counter within reach because I started the day as a practical person and have had trouble letting that part go. The dead in the doorway shift their weight in a tiny wave. It is the same motion you see in a line when people realize the cashier is about to switch lanes. I can feel the room waiting to see if I am going to perform the part.

"You wrote things in those journals that felt like an instruction manual," I say, and I know I am stalling, but the mouth of the room wants more than my legs and I am not handing it over. "Half of it made no sense. The half that did saved me twice."

"The rules rearrange." She looks at the oven glass again like she can see the picture that held her last time. "I wrote anyway. I thought that would count for something."

"It did," I say. "It does."

Something is learning to run in the laundry behind the door. The small wheel squeal jumps, then stops, then starts again with a bad angle. The sound pulls my jaw tight. I try the pantry latch without looking at it, thumb on cheap metal, a little push, a little twist. It stays a joke. Of course it does. I leave it before it can tell me a lie I want to hear.

"You want to talk me out of this," I say. "Or you want to help me."

Mara steps close enough that the sugar dust on my coat catches on her dress. She smells like roses that forgot how to be fresh. "I want you to say my name," she says. "They said I was sick. They called me a vandal. They put my things by the street and I watched people stop and stare and decide they needed my lamps. If you leave, tell them what it is. Tell them I was not wrong."

"I will," I say, because it is the only honest thing available. "I will say your name. I will say this house read your life and learned how to eat. I will put it in a place people cannot ignore. I will make them mad enough to ask questions."

The line of dead ripples again in a way that has nothing to do with wind. A small relief passes like birds lifting on a streetlight. The timer ticks into a number that means nothing and stops for one second, then continues like it is embarrassed to have been caught. The chair that leans against the pantry shivers on the tile.

Mara's face changes in that small way you only notice if you have been watching someone for too long. The show face slides a little and the fury under it shows through. She looks like a person who has been asked to smile while being devoured. She reaches for my shirt and hauls me backward from the pantry. It is a fast, competent move, the kind your big sister would use to stop you from stepping into traffic. Her nails bite through cotton. My shoulder hits the fridge and a magnet pops off and skates under my boot. The room tips hard and settles. The dead lean forward without meaning to.

I punch without grace because there is no time left to be decent. My fist hits her shoulder and meets meat and nothing else. She does not react with sound. She reacts by tightening her grip and dragging me two more steps. The counter takes my hip. The utensil crock tips and spits a wooden spoon across the floor. The drawer below the counter rattles and slides open a finger's width. The knives clack together like teeth. I do not want to learn what that means in practice.

I throw what I can reach because I am a creature of habit and chaos. The can opener arcs and hits her collarbone and bounces. The skillet catches her upper arm and changes the line of her pull. I get the width of my shoulders back. The sugar bag splits under my hand and sends up a white storm that coats the floor and her dress and turns the air into a snow globe. The jar of pickles is heavy and cold and the brine inside has the hospital smell that kitchens get when no one is cooking. I pitch it. It explodes at her feet and floods between us. Glass slides and chatters under my boots. Pickle rounds scatter like green coins. The room smells like a deli cut with formaldehyde. It would be funny anywhere else.

The dead behind her move in the way a crowd moves when someone takes the first step. The boy in the jacket squeaks his shoe on brine and grins like a joke landed. The church lady lifts her hands the width of a prayer. The man in coveralls puts his weight forward and almost forgets the glass until it reminds him with a small skid. The little boy keeps the car locked to his chest. Their bodies angle without haste but without confusion. They are going to make a decision for me if I cannot make one for myself.

I plant my feet in sugar and brine and glass. The sting comes through my soles and climbs my calves. The pain sharpens me to a point I can use. I set my voice in my throat so it cannot get taken and I talk to Mara like I would talk to a woman on the curb who needs to hear herself out loud.

"I will tell it," I say. "I will say your name. I will write it. I will put it where it cannot be misfiled. I will make the library give it a case if I have to build the case myself from scrap. I will say the dates and the rooms and the pantry that eats and I will say you were right. Let me go."

The kitchen listens. It is the strangest thing, to feel a room give you one breath of attention that does not come from hate. The light flickers once, not in the spooky way, in the electrical way. The timer clicks backward to zero and shows me a blank face, then starts again like it is trying to be brave. The chair at the pantry stills. The hum under the fridge swings toward my heart and misses it on purpose for the first time all night.

Mara's fingers loosen on my shirt. She looks past me at the pantry door and her mouth learns a strange line that is not a smile. It is closer to relief than anything the house has allowed, and it makes my throat feel dangerous. She turns to the man in coveralls without looking away from me and clamps his wrist hard enough to lift him to his toes. He stares at her, then at me, then forgets to look at anything. The dead in the doorway make the sound you hear when a crowd remembers where the exits are.

"Then go," she says, and the words are not ceremony. They are a mechanic's instruction.

I do not waste the second. I step into the brine and sugar and the floor tries to write my footnotes in blood. I keep moving. The pantry latch is stubborn and cheap and familiar. My palm slips on the metal. I wipe my hand on my thigh and try again. The latch turns and sticks. It likes this part where it gets to be the problem I can name. I take a breath that belongs to me and turn harder. The cheap screw inside shifts. The latch coughs itself loose. The door gives me an inch and asks me to earn the rest.

The chair that was leaning against the pantry is not here to help. I put my shoulder to the wood and my hip to the jamb and haul. The strip along the edge kisses free with a soft peel that turns my stomach. Cold rides across my shins in a clean ribbon. The gap grows a hand's width. The kitchen doubles its tantrum and bangs its drawers and rattles the oven like the world is going to end if I leave. The dead crowd in a last-second swell that speaks to every mistake I have ever made. Mara holds the line with both hands and her mouth set. The boy in the jacket shakes his head like he cannot believe this is how it goes.

I pull and the door opens enough to show me my linoleum with the seam in the right place. I smell my house on the other side, the tired heat, the lemon of dish soap, the late afternoon dust that settles whether you own it or not. I reach for the notebooks on the counter because a promise is a practical thing, not a verse. My fingers close on cardboard and a scramble of Polaroids that try to run. I shove both into the bag hard enough to bend the corners. The strap bites my shoulder and keeps me real.

I look at Mara because I am stubborn and human and the house does not get to dictate my last glance. She looks like a woman who has watched too many people fail and is tired of attending this performance. The fury is still in her face. So is the relief. So is the part that had room for a joke once. It nearly kills me to turn away, but it will not kill me today.

"Thank you," I say. My voice is sanded down to something useful. "I will say it."

"Go," she says again, and her hands tighten on the man in coveralls when he remembers who he used to be and tries to reach for me.

I slip through the gap sideways with the bag high. The pantry's cold slicks my arms to gooseflesh. The door moves on its hinges like a body with a pulled muscle, working despite itself. I pull it another inch to buy myself space for my hips. The sugar on the floor turns to paste on my boots and holds me one second longer than I want it to. I wrench free and step over the threshold into air that has a normal temperature and a normal taste. The door begins to swing back on habit and I let it go because sometimes you need to let a thing have the last movement just to get out alive.

The seam narrows. The last slice of the wrong kitchen holds Mara in profile with her hands full of a dead man's wrist and her chin up like a person who chose to stand at a bad door and keep it closed with her body. Her eyes meet mine for one more heartbeat that belongs to neither of us. The latch kisses home. The sound is ugly. It is perfect.

Chapter 15
COLLAPSE OF HOME

THE KITCHEN BREATHES LIKE a tired animal. The ceiling has started to bubble in slow blisters that show the lath below. Paint lifts in curls that move when the room exhales. The hum is wrong in that way I can feel in my teeth. I sling the bag high and pull the top two notebooks from the counter with a fist of Polaroids that try to skate out from under my palm. The photos flash me back a dozen wrong kitchens and one real one. I do not look. I shove everything into the bag and fix the buckle. The strap bites a new bruise into my shoulder and keeps me honest.

The hall is a mess, an exploded diagram of a house that used to pretend it had nothing to hide. Frames have given up and lay face down as if someone called a drill and forgot to dismiss them. The narrow runner has buckled into ridges that want to catch my toes. A fresh vertical crack runs from the ceiling to the baseboard and widens as I watch. The sound that comes out of it is a dry whisper, like paper being pulled too slowly from a box. I put my breath back on my count and keep moving. Two in. Six out. My heart tries to argue with the wrong rhythm in the walls. I ignore it and choose mine.

I detour through my room because I am still a person who wants a bag with clothes and a toothbrush when the day ends. The closet rod has collapsed in a gentle surrender and the coats look like they decided to take a nap. I grab the backpack I packed on the second night here, the one I told myself was not superstition. Jeans, shirts, socks, chargers. The library lanyard and keys. I take the photo of my brother and me from the little frame. The glass stays behind because I am tired of giving the house something to break for free. The window looks

205

normal, which is its own trick. I do not touch it. Door. Stairs. Street. Keep it simple.

The stairs feel the way an old knee feels the day before rain. The banister shifts under my palm and then decides to hold because it recognizes a person who means to come away from this intact. The runner on the treads has bubbled into gentle waves. My heel finds one and slides. My knee bangs a riser and wakes up a bruise that has been waiting for an excuse. Plaster dust falls from the ceiling at the landing and turns the part in my hair gray. The newel post cracks with a dry pop and lists like it has chosen a side in a fight. I do not slow. Slowing makes space for reconsidering, and I am done reconsidering.

The foyer has become an autopsy. The transom over the door has let its panes sag in the putty like tired eyelids. One pane has slipped and hangs by a corner that will not last. The rug looks chewed. The air tastes like drywall and the sweet rot I used to call old house smell because I wanted to believe in charm. The front door is still the same heavy wood with too many coats of paint and a latch that never lined up with the strike. It sticks at the top. It sticks at the bottom. I brace my feet and pull on the knob and get an inch that the house tries to take back. I push. I pull. I find the small rhythm inside the metal. Push. Pull. Push. Pull. The latch tooth whispers across the strike and then spits itself clear like a stubborn kernel.

Cold air slides over my face and hits the back of my throat with a taste of wet dirt and truck exhaust. I put my shoulder into the door and open it far enough to think about a person with a bag. The top hinge screams. The bottom hinge groans like a tired animal. The jamb complains and then decides to be obliging because it has lost the vote. The door yawns the width of my shoulders. I go through sideways with my palms on the cold outside and my boot heel catching on the threshold like a child who wants to stay in the pool five more minutes. The nail that has been working out of the trim for a decade finds my coat pocket and unthreads it like a little thief. I jerk free and step onto the porch.

The porch leans more than it did an hour ago. The balusters shed paint in long curls that lift in the wind and stick to my jeans. The rail flexes under my hand and then remembers its job. The first tread of the steps sinks a half inch and tilts. I shift my weight forward and keep going. The second tread holds. The third has a crack big enough to trap a heel. I plant my foot to the left and feel my ankle roll just enough to keep me upright. The bag thumps my ribs because it wants me to remember it is there. The house mutters behind me in the way of large pieces deciding where to fall.

The yard meets me with grass to the knees and shrubs that grab sleeves like rude hands. Dandelion clocks explode against my legs and turn to fluff that clings to the sugar dust on my coat. The maple at the curb smears a puddle of shade on the lawn even though the sky is a flat winter white that cannot commit. The street smells like the mill and someone's compost and a little bit of gasoline. It smells like town. I want to cry because it is so ordinary.

I make it three steps into the yard before something deep in the hallway goes. The sound is not loud at first. It is the shift of weight when a big man decides to sit down. The porch floor lifts and rolls under my feet like a wave and then folds inward with a long wooden howl that climbs my spine and rattles my teeth. The front door swings wide and smacks the wall, then swings back half as far with the disoriented grace of the dazed. A column of brown dust pushes out of the foyer and across the stoop like tired smoke. The pressure hits the back of my neck and shoves. I go to my knees in the wet grass with my hands out and my bag thumping the ground.

I crawl backward three yards because my body still belongs to an animal that learned to survive by not standing up and giving the world a bigger target. The crack that ran up the front of the house widens and runs through a window frame to the roofline. Glass slumps in the front parlor window and then slides down in a slow sheet that breaks in expensive sighs. The sound is gentle. It is wrong. I stand because I refuse to be the woman collapsed on the curb while the house gets the last word.

A neighbor in a robe appears at the sidewalk and freezes with her hands at her mouth. A car slows at the far end of the block and then keeps going because the driver does not want to be the first person to decide this is their business. Sirens rise from two directions. The blue and red wash begins to paint the trunks of the maples in soft waves.

I walk toward the broken line of the walkway like I own it. The mailbox leans with its flag snapped off and its door catching on a burr. There is a flyer inside from a pizza place that does not deliver to this street. For a second I want to laugh because the world is full of stupid grace notes and I am still paying attention. I lift my hand to wave at the neighbor so she can stop holding her breath. She lowers her hands and cries in a quiet way that does not ask for attention.

The first cruiser slides up and stops half in the street, half in the mouth of my driveway. The officer behind the wheel leans over the steering wheel to get a look. He climbs out before the car is fully in park and calls to me from the walk.

"Anyone else inside," he asks, and he does not raise his voice because he has already decided I am not the kind of person who needs to be shouted at.

"Just me," I say. The words scrape a little because the dust has lined my throat.

He glances past me at the gap where the foyer used to be and then back at my face. I watch his eyes trace the cut along my eyebrow, the sugar on my coat, the burn along my forearm that is starting to blister at the edges. He lifts his shoulder to key the radio there without looking away.

The ambulance pulls up and parks against the curb in a wash of blue and red. The paramedics swing out with that focused calm I love because it makes people remember how to breathe. One is my age and has her hair buzzed down and eyes that have learned the trick of being soft without letting anything in. The other is older with a mustache and the kind of broad hands that can lift a couch and set it back down without making it feel ashamed. The younger one comes straight for me with her hands open where I can see them.

"I'm Luci," she says. "Can I touch you, Riley?"

"Yes," I say, and it is the easiest agreement I have made in years.

She shines a small light in my eyes and makes a face like she is deciding how many stitches my pride can handle. She checks the cut on my brow and the burn on my forearm. Her thumb presses the edge of the blister and I hiss because I am alive and skin still knows its job. She lets go immediately like we are partners who have been at this a long time. The older paramedic walks to the porch and looks at it the way a carpenter looks at a problem he cannot fix tonight. He whistles once under his breath and keeps his opinions to himself.

"Fire is on the way," he calls without turning. "Keep her off the line of the posts. If that header goes she is in the bite."

Luci guides me two steps back into the yard with her hand a respectful inch from my elbow. The grass soaks the cuffs of my coat and wicks cold up my sleeve. Another cruiser arrives. A younger officer gets out and tries to look bigger than he is. He fails at it in a human way that makes me feel tender toward him.

The house complains again and then changes shape. The porch posts slide in slow motion and then speed up as the load shifts. The header goes with a sound that traveled through forests and learned new words on the way. The porch drops into the crawl space with a shrug. Dust lifts in a thick brown column and rolls over the yard like fog from a bad machine. People down the block make small sounds and then fall quiet because there is nothing useful to say.

The engine noses in behind the ambulance and takes half the street with it. Firefighters hop down and do their walk, that businesslike march that keeps neighbors from getting clever with cigarettes. One peels off and comes straight to us with a helmet under his arm. He looks at the house, then at me.

"Anyone else inside," he asks.

"No," I say. "Just me."

"Gas on," he asks.

"Bank cut it when the place went vacant," I say. "Old boiler, diesel, dead as long as I have been here."

He nods and goes back to his crew. They lay hose in neat loops and do not charge it because there is nothing left that water can save. The officer with the clipboard asks my name again and writes it. He asks for a number. He asks if I have family to call. I give him the number of a co-worker who owes me a shift trade and says yes when anyone asks for help. My phone vibrates with a text from an unknown number that might be the bank or a bored kid. I ignore it because I have finally learned which problems can wait.

Luci wipes the blood from my face with a pad that smells like the inside of a first aid kit and a high school theater. She tapes the cut and wraps my forearm with a bandage that has a cool square in the center. It feels like someone pressed forgiveness into gauze. The older paramedic returns to us and nods once toward the house.

"Hall floor dropped," he says to Luci so I do not have to carry it. "Stairs went with it."

The roofline settles one slow breath at a time. The chimney decides to lean away from the house and lets go of a few bricks like a gentleman leaving a tip. One brick hits the porch rail that is no longer a porch rail and goes straight through with a small, wrong sound. The air from the front room carries the sugar smell that has become my private word for death. I gag once and pretend it is the dust.

People gather at the edges of their lawns and hold their phones at their hips without lifting them. I love them for that. Someone's kid cries once and is hushed with a hand on his back. The mill horn blows the top of the hour and makes the whole moment feel like it belongs to a town that will keep going when this street remembers how to be quiet.

"Medical transport or a ride with the officer," Luci asks. She meets my eyes like she wants me to choose the thing that keeps me safest.

"I can ride with him," I say. "I just want a place to sit that is not about to change shape."

"We can do that," the officer says, and he opens the cruiser door like he is inviting me into a diner.

My knees argue. Luci helps me sit on the grass first and drapes a space blanket over my shoulders. It crackles and smells like new plastic and the back hallway of a theater. It does not warm me much, but it tells my skin what to do next. I put my hand on the bag and feel the edges of the notebooks through the canvas. The promise I made sits in my mouth like a coin.

Luci crouches and keeps her voice in the small space we have built between us. "Do you want information for trauma counseling," she asks. "We keep a list."

"Yes," I say. "I will probably pretend I do not need it tomorrow."

"That is why I am giving it to you today," she says, and for a second I feel okay.

We watch the house finish dying. It does not go all at once. It settles into a shape that is not a house. Steam rises from the ruin in thin threads and disappears. The blue and red lights wash everything into slow color. The night here is going to smell like dust for a week.

I stand with help I do not pretend to refuse. The blanket slides and makes that crisp sound again. The officer asks if I can give a statement at the hospital. The fire captain says the working theory is gas and a void in the soil under the foundation. A neighbor offers a coat I do not need and kindness I take anyway. The street feels like a set waiting for the next shot.

I look at the ruin and then at the bag. I touch the notebooks through the canvas so I can feel something that made it through. The words sit there like a new tool, heavy and plain. I lift my head and speak them because the promise was not poetry.

"I will tell it," I say. The wind carries my voice into the cold yard and across the broken porch and into the soft roar of the engine. No one answers. That is fine. It was for me.

THE ER SMELLS LIKE lemon cleaner trying to arm wrestle old coffee. Fluorescents flatten the world to a clean white that keeps trying to make my eyes water. A nurse with a braid down her back clips a wristband around my arm and takes my temperature with a thermometer that whistles when it is done. My name prints in tiny black letters, neat and official, the kind of font that does not care what your life looks like.

They park me in a curtain bay where the wall clock ticks a second faster than my heart. My bag sits on the chair within reach. I keep a hand on the canvas the way people keep a palm on a sleeping dog. The top edge of a composition book presses back like a spine.

Luci, the paramedic, appears at the foot of the bed with a smile that uses only her eyes. Her hair is buzzed close and sits under a beanie that says County EMS in letters that have seen a lot of washer cycles. She asks if I am still okay to be touched. I say yes. She checks my pupils again and shines her little light. She cleans the burn on my forearm with something that smells like a swimming pool and lays down a square of cool gel. The bandage pulls snug. It feels like the first orderly thing that has happened today.

"Lucky," she says, but not like a Hallmark card. "You will be sore. You will swear someone hit you with a truck tomorrow. Hydrate. Eat something with salt. Sleep where a person can wake you if they need to."

"I have alarms," I say. "I will make too much tea and line the mugs up like soldiers."

"Good," she says. She tucks a little card under the band of my watch. It lists trauma counselors who work on sliding scale and two local groups that meet in church basements. "You do not have to be tough every hour. Take the easy hours when they show up."

A curtain whispers and a uniform presses through. The officer from the house, hat tucked under one arm, edge of his hairline damp from the cold. He glances at Luci and waits until she nods before he steps in.

"Riley Cross? I can do this quick," he says. "You can tell me to go."

"I am here," I say. "Go ahead."

He thanks me, then clicks his pen and runs through the things the form requires. Name, address, time I called, if I smelled gas, if I heard anything unusual. I laugh once and he smiles because he knows what passed my lips before I caught it. He writes anyway. When the boxes are full he gives the speech I did not know I was waiting for.

"Fire is calling it accidental pending full report," he says. "Looks like a gas issue that dated from before the bank took the property. There is a void under the foundation, probably an old shelf collapse in the basement. When the joists let go, everything followed. Code will condemn what is left. The bank will tear it down and fill the hole."

His voice is even and careful like he has said this kind of sentence before. The words sit on my chest and do not match the shape underneath, but they do not feel like lies. They feel like the town's language for things that should not be explained any other way.

"I did not smell gas," I say. "But I believe you about the rest."

"That is enough," he says. He asks if I have a place to go. He offers a motel voucher for two nights. It comes from a drawer that looks like it used to hold coloring books. I take it because it is a door I can lock that belongs to the living.

Luci steps out and returns with a Styrofoam cup that calls itself coffee. It tastes like late nights and old paper. She sets a granola bar on the tray. My stomach has opinions I did not ask for until it smells the oats. I eat half and realize how long it has been since a normal thing held still for me.

The curtain pulls aside again and a rectangle of blond hair and anxiety steps through. It is **Jess from the library board** in her brown cardigan with the elbow holes and the tote bag that says Read Local. She has a hoodie slung over one arm and eyes already watering from the overhead light.

"I saw the lights on Weaver and I kept refreshing the scanner page," she says without preamble, then stops because a hospital curtain is not a place to cry on someone you do not know well enough. She takes a breath and corrects. "Are you okay. That is the actual question."

"I will be," I say, and I mean it for the first time tonight. "I need a shower and something salty and cruel. Also a hug."

She leans in and gives me a hug that remembers my bandage and avoids it. The hoodie goes over my shoulders like a blanket that knows my shape. On the way out of the curtain she tells me quietly that the mill's third shift supervisor already called the mayor and asked about helping the bank clear the lot. Towns work like that when they are small enough to know each other's voicemail tones.

A nurse runs through discharge instructions in a voice made of competence. Concussion precautions. Burn care. No heavy lifting. Hydrate. The words feel like someone has laid a plank walkway over mud and told me to stay on it until my shoes dry. I sign the line with a pen that squeaks.

Luci walks me to the sliding doors because she has decided she is invested in how this movie ends. Cold air hits my face and puts my brain back in my skull the way winter can. The parking lot lights make sweatshirts look like armor. She hesitates like she has one more line and does not want to burn it.

"Riley," she says. "If you wake up and the story will not stop running, call one of the numbers. You told me you write. Put some of it there too. Just do not let it live in your body alone."

"I will not," I say. "Thank you."

She lifts a hand and goes back inside where the lights never turn off. I stand there with the motel voucher and the hoodie and the shape of the night in my mouth. The town air smells like wet asphalt and distant cigarettes. Main Street runs left from here and ends at the square where the library lights glow behind frosted glass. I turn my head and choose that direction to walk toward tomorrow in my mind. For tonight, I accept the bed with the hard pillows and the loud ice machine. I text **Jess from the board** a thank you and a promise to open the stacks on time next week if my head cooperates. She fires back a thumbs up and a sandwich emoji that makes me smile.

I pull the bag tight under my arm and step out into the lot with the easy ache of someone who plans to be sore and safe at the same time.

THREE WEEKS LATER THE town has put itself back into the order it likes best, which is a little crooked in the corners and solid in the middle. I live above a shop that sells candles and postcards and the kind of soaps that smell like ideas. My stairs are narrow and honest. The studio has windows that look over Main and a floor that leans gently toward the radiator. The pipes in the wall ping a few minutes after the heat clicks on. I have learned to love that sound because it tells me exactly what it is and nothing more.

Insurance did what insurance does, slow at first and then all at once. The settlement is not generous and not unfair. It covered the deposit and the first months here, a secondhand couch with clean lines, and a desk from the thrift store that still smells a little like someone else's polish. I keep the Polaroids in sleeves now, each labeled with a name or a question mark, and the notebooks sit in a neat stack that does not leave my sight.

The walk to the library takes six minutes if I do not stop at the bakery. I stop at the bakery most mornings because Mrs. Doyle has decided I am too thin for winter and because she made a punch card with my name on it and taped it to the register. I open the library a quarter hour early so the regulars can stand in the warm vestibule and pretend they are not waiting. I run the returns cart like a parade float. The spider plant on the reference desk has stopped sulking and started throwing new shoots. **Jess from the library board** wears her brown cardigan with the elbows patched and tells me the board approved ten new picture books and a replacement for the printer that eats quarters.

The kids whisper in the stacks with the wild confidence of people who have not learned to measure their voices. They ask if the house on Weaver had a witch and if I saw bones. I tell them the same line every time and it has turned into a ritual now. I tell them I saw a hungry building and that the hungry building is gone. I tell them stories are safer than rumors because stories have a job to do. They nod as if I have said something wise and then ask if we have any new dinosaur books. I make a show of checking. They giggle because they know I was waiting for the question.

Evenings, the shop downstairs clicks its bell and shuts its lights. I climb the stairs with a bag of groceries and a stubborn loaf of bread that will be soup tomorrow. The studio warms fast. I work at the thrifted desk with a cheap lamp that throws a cone of gold across the page. I put the title block at the top because naming a thing matters. The Dead House sits there like it has been waiting. Under it I write a second line that will change twelve times and still mean the same thing. A testimony, a record, a warning. The first paragraph starts with Mara's name. I build out from that like a person putting a fence around a garden for the first time.

On Tuesdays I meet with the **library board** in the side room that smells like old carpet and coffee. I pitch a local history display that is really a memorial without using the word. We talk about humidity control and light exposure and whether the case can be locked without making everyone feel accused. A small grant exists. I offer to write the placards. I print a test card on the office machine and set it in a spare frame and the tiny serif font looks braver than it has any right to.

On Sundays the neighbor upstairs practices guitar. He is not good yet and that is a comfort. He misses high and corrects and then misses low and laughs like he is alone. The sound finds its way down the stairwell and into my kitchen with the chipped mug and the kettle that complains before it boils. I wash dishes in water that runs clear. I lock my door at night and press my palm to the wood for one second, not out of fear, but because gratitude deserves a ritual.

Sometimes I walk to the lot on Weaver after work. The bank hired a crew to knock down what was left and fill the hole with a kind of careful dirt. There is orange fencing and a sign with a phone number for questions. Boys throw rocks at the sign and pretend they are not doing it when someone looks. The maple at the curb still throws an hour of shade in a shape my body remembers. I stand across the street on the safe side and breathe the smell of raw soil. It smells like clay and rain and a little bit of old nail. That is all.

I go home and sit at the desk and write until the cheap lamp heats the base and the tea goes cold. Sometimes the story runs ahead of my hands and I let it. Sometimes I stall on a sentence and open a Polaroid sleeve and hold someone else's moment against the light until I can see what corner of the room they were standing in when they took it. I put a name down when I have one. When I do not, I write the word witness and circle it to remind myself who I am trying to be.

Jess from the board reads pages in batches and leaves me sticky notes that say things like, Condense here, and, You are allowed one swear per page if it helps. Luci stops by with a takeout coffee when her shift brings her near Main and never mentions the house directly. She taps the side of my bag once when it is sitting by the chair and says, You still carrying the heavy things, and I tell her that is the job.

On the night I finish the first draft, I carry the last paragraph to the window and read it aloud to Main Street because the windows here like to prove the soundproofing is honest. I do not expect an answer and I do not get one. It is not that kind of story. I close the laptop and set my hand on the notebooks one more time. The room is quiet except for the radiator ticking its small metal language. The door is just a door. The walls are just walls. The night is just the town's breath moving along the bricks.

I turn off the lamp and let the dark be the good kind.

EPILOGUE

Morning begins the way it always does here, with the bakery bell
downstairs and the radiator knocking a short argument with itself.
Light comes in pale and square across the floorboards that lean toward
the window. I lie there for a minute with the kind of slow, lazy comfort
you get when life has given you a couple of quiet years in a row. The
kettle on the kitchenette counter clicks in the corner of my eye like it
knows I will want tea. Somewhere up the stairs my neighbor mis-hits
a chord and laughs at himself, which is how I know it is Sunday.

I get up with the heavy socks and the sweater that still smells faintly
like apple soap from the shop below. The apartment is the same honest
box it has always been, with the thrifted desk at the back wall and
the manuscripts stacked by the lamp that throws a small gold cone
when the sun gives up. The shelves hold more than they used to. My
sticky notes have turned into tidy binders with tabs that say things
like interviews and deed records and speculation I will regret. Mara's
notebooks are in a case I built with Jess and the board, under museum
glass that hums with a little fan to keep the humidity right. I have not
opened those books without gloves in a long time. I still say her name
sometimes when I pass the case and it always feels like the right ritual.

I walk toward the kitchenette and stop because the door that should
not be there is there. It sits where a blank wall has lived since the first
day I moved in, in the narrow stretch between the coat hook and the
calendar where I keep a pen to cross off days. Same cheap white paint
as the rest. Same hardware as the bathroom door and the hall closet,
brushed nickel that never looks clean no matter how you wipe it. The
trim matches the other frames exactly, mitered a little sloppy at the top

right corner, which is how I know a local did the finish work. If you did not live here, you would tell me it had always been there. If you did, you would see the wrongness like a note out of tune.

There is no draft and no cold lick under the sill. The air on this side is the kind that settled with me, warm and dry and lightly spiced with tea and old paper. I set my palm flat against the panel to prove to myself that I am not dreaming and I feel it at once, the soft push and pull behind the wood that my skin still knows like a scar. The heartbeat is gentle at first and then finds me where my own pulse lives, the hollow at the base of my throat and the thin skin at my wrist. It tries to talk me into time the way a metronome talks a child into playing the song slow. The breath goes out of me in a long, honest shiver and I stay there with my hand on the paint until I am sure my knees will not do anything stupid.

I try all the sensible tricks even though I already believe the result. I look for seam lines in the plaster where there were none yesterday. I crouch and run my fingers along the baseboard for the little nails I know the landlord uses. I press my ear to the panel and hear only the quiet insistence of that other rhythm, the one I learned to refuse by counting to six on the way out of a dying house. The knob is cool but not cold. The plate has no scratches, which means no one else has tried it yet. For a second I hate that I notice these things, then I forgive myself because noticing is how I lived.

My phone sits on the counter in a line with the kettle and the chipped mug. Luci's card is still rubber-banded to the back even though her number is in my contacts and she has come by with coffee enough times to stop being a stranger. Jess would answer a text with three offers and a mild scold about calling before breakfast. I do not reach for the phone. I look at the case by the desk, at the spines of the composition books under glass, at the Polaroids that still make my stomach flip even as they yellow. It would be easy to dress, to go downstairs and knock on the shop door and ask Mrs. Doyle to tell me that walls cannot grow doors. It would be easy to walk to the library, unlock the vestibule early, and sit in the warm light that smells like lemon cleaner until the feeling passes. I stand barefoot on the floor I pay for and know the truth that will not move. None of that is what this morning is for.

The room holds its breath with me. The radiator settles into a quiet tick. The bakery bell does not ring for the longest ten seconds on record. On the street, someone walks a dog with little nails that click on the sidewalk in a rhythm that should be cheerful and is suddenly only far away. The heart behind the door thickens, slow, patient, attentive. It is not the wild thud of panic. It is the sound you hear when someone is waiting and has time.

I think of the lot on Weaver and the orange fencing that went up and came down. I think of the little marker the board put by the library case, the one with Mara's name in a font that makes her look like she belongs to the town now. I think of the nights I read out loud to the empty apartment, stubborn and grateful, telling the walls how it ended. I think of how endings are only true until the next morning asks a question. The kettle clicks again as if it wants the last word and that makes me laugh once in a dry, sharp way that puts my lungs back where they belong.

I put my hand around the knob and breathe on my count because the body learns what you teach it. Two in. Six out. The metal warms under my palm like it always does, furniture pretending to be a choice. The heartbeat does not speed up or slow down in response. It holds steady, polite and hungry and wrong. I look at the desk where the second book sits under its working title and at the case where the old notebooks sit like a pair of spent hearts. I say Mara's name because some rituals are for armor. I say my own name after it because I am still the person in this room.

The knob turns the way cheap hardware turns, with a little grit at the start and a slick give once you commit. The latch pulls back from the strike with a sound that is not dramatic at all. It is an ugly, ordinary click that belongs in any apartment in any small town. For a breath I let myself love how unimportant the sound is, how it could mean a closet full of brooms, how it could mean nothing at all. The heartbeat reminds me where I am, and the memory folds itself over the hope, neat and patient.

I put my weight into the door and feel the paint stick to the frame where humidity got there first. The seal peels with a soft sigh I hear more than feel. The crack appears between jamb and edge, thin as a held breath, and widens to the width of my thumb. I smell nothing at first, just my apartment and the tea I have not yet made. The cold rides out across my toes one inch at a time, then rises to my shins in a ribbon that knows me. I look into the sliver of dark and think of all the sensible lives I could have had if I were built for them. I am not, and I have been honest about that for years now.

I open the door the rest of the way and let the morning go where it was always going to go.